Sally Piper's debut novel *Grace's Table* (UQP, 2014) was shortlisted for the Queensland Premier's Literary Award – Emerging Queensland Author category and she was awarded a Varuna Publishing Fellowship for her manuscript. Her second novel, *The Geography of Friendship* (UQP, 2018), was shortlisted for the Australian Book Industry Awards – Small Publishers' Adult Book of the Year category. She has had short fiction and non-fiction published in various online and print publications in Australia and the UK, including *Griffith Review*, *The Saturday Paper*, *The Sydney Morning Herald*, *The Weekend Australian* and other literary magazines and journals. Sally holds a Master of Arts (Research) in Creative Writing from Queensland University of Technology. She is an active member of the Queensland writing community, where she presents workshops and seminars, leads in-conversations and mentors other writers.

www.sallypiper.com
Bookclub notes are available at www.uqp.com.au

Also by Sally Piper

Grace's Table
The Geography of Friendship

SALLY PIPER

BONE
MEMORIES

UQP

First published 2022 by University of Queensland Press
PO Box 6042, St Lucia, Queensland 4067 Australia

University of Queensland Press (UQP) acknowledges the Traditional Owners and their custodianship of the lands on which UQP operates. We pay our respects to their Ancestors and their descendants, who continue cultural and spiritual connections to Country. We recognise their valuable contributions to Australian and global society.

uqp.com.au
reception@uqp.com.au

Cover design by Sandy Cull, gogoGingko
Cover artwork by Tiel Seivl-Keevers // www.tsktsk.com.au
Author photograph by Fiona Muirhead
Typeset in Bembo 12/16 pt by Post Pre-press Group, Brisbane
Printed in Australia by McPherson's Printing Group

 University of Queensland Press is supported by the Queensland Government through Arts Queensland.

 University of Queensland Press is assisted by the Australian Government through the Australia Council, its arts funding and advisory body.

A catalogue record for this book is available from the National Library of Australia.

ISBN 978 0 7022 6557 0 (pbk)
ISBN 978 0 7022 6688 1 (epdf)
ISBN 978 0 7022 6689 8 (epub)
ISBN 978 0 7022 6690 4 (kindle)

University of Queensland Press uses papers that are natural, renewable and recyclable products made from wood grown in well-managed forests and other controlled sources. The logging and manufacturing processes conform to the environmental regulations of the country of origin.

For Aaron and Liam,
sons of my bones.

This novel was written on the unceded, sovereign lands of the Turrbal and Jagera people, and I would like to pay my respects to their Elders past and present. I acknowledge their continuing connection to Country and recognise that sites in this fictional story are ones that carry deep spiritual and cultural significance for First Nations peoples and are places of real life dispossession and trauma.

1

TUESDAY AGAIN. TIME TO CLEAR the litter of the living from the path to the dead. The gate in the back fence opened noiselessly. Billie kept it well oiled, liked that her comings and goings went mostly undetected. She glanced back towards the main house, its windows mirroring the sun's early glow, brightening its otherwise plain facade. All seemed quiet inside. She took the narrow cut-through she'd forced through the scrub over the years. Passed the large staghorn fern that had attached itself to an Ash tree a long time ago, and thrived. An ancient species. Resilient. Maybe she could learn something from it.

Once on the main trail, she moved slowly, the contents of her backpack tapping gently against her spine. The garbage bag she carried in her hand scratched against dry branches as she stooped to pick up discarded cigarette butts, muesli bar wrappers, tissues and plastic water bottles. Organic waste – apple cores, banana skins, orange peel – she threw into the scrub to rot. She picked the items up without judgement or anger. It was a task – a purpose – that she'd set herself long ago.

Six women walking two-by-two came down the trail towards

her, each slick as seals in Lycra. Their arms pumped like pistons, their feet stamped in sync; all were talking, none listening. They blazed past and Billie had to put the garbage bag behind her and squeeze to the side of the track to let them through. She watched them march off, moving without lightness. There was a kind of violence to the way their feet struck the trail. They saw nothing, were merely commuters.

Alone again, she resumed her careful search for things that didn't belong. The bag was half full by the time the picnic area came into view. Billie eased out of her pack, removed the cleaning equipment she'd brought with her, and carefully laid it out on a picnic table, the items obscuring hearts, initials and obscenities gouged into the timber. If it were Jess doing this task, she'd have tipped the daypack upside down, everything emptying out with a clatter. Not because she didn't care; Jess cared more than anyone Billie knew. It was because her daughter believed she had so much living to do that she was in a hurry to fit it all in.

Her daughter had been in a rush to be born, too. Billie had birthed her alone. Just three big pushes and her harried little body tore free, squalling, onto the bathroom floor. Billie had trembled for a time, more shocked than cold. She'd wrapped the baby in a towel and held her against her chest till the ambulance came.

Perhaps her quick entry into the world was a sign of things to come, as later Jess seemed able to pack four days into one. Maybe she was meant to live for only twenty-five years? Not a long time, only a fast time. Would she ever have learnt to slow down? Calm and steady Angus was her daughter's best hope for that. But they'd not been married long enough for him to influence a change. What would this steadier, less impulsive version of her daughter look like now if he had? Another thought to add to the list of things she'd never know.

Today, Billie started with the memorial plaque. *Loved then taken,* it read, with her daughter's name and the date she was killed. Sixteen years it was now.

The plaque's wording was something Billie had wrestled with. Nothing seemed to adequately express the love or the loss. She'd considered plenty of options. Mostly angry and bitter words: *Murdered here* or *Mercilessly taken*. But they lacked grace. Jess would have been ashamed. For Billie, though, the bitterness remained as ripe as split fruit.

She took up a square of old flannelette sheet. Put a smudge of stainless-steel cleaner onto the soft cloth and set to work. She scratched at something on the plaque – bat or bird shit, it was difficult to tell – with her fingernail. Took care to run the cloth all along its narrow edges. She stepped back once she'd finished and studied her handiwork.

Who was this glinting piece of metal for? she wondered. Who did it benefit? What was its purpose? Was it just for Billie, or did others – strangers – take something away from it, too? Did anyone even pause to consider the name and the words or was it passed off as just another blemish on the tree's trunk, a kind of gratuitous graffiti? It probably prompted conversations at times, especially during family picnics.

Some girl murdered here apparently.

Heard someone say her kid was with her. Witnessed the whole thing. Imagine.

And because Billie could, she pictured one of the mothers indicating towards the children, mouthing, *Not now*, and they'd all go back to shooing flies from warming salads, taking sips from sweaty bottles of beer.

For Billie, the plaque brought a story to the tree, gave it a heart. She swore there were times she could hear it beating.

★

Her grandson had taken out an act of rage or frustration on the tree once – Billie had never been sure of the motivation. Had come upon him thrusting the blade of a pocketknife into the tree's trunk.

'Daniel?' she'd called softly.

He was thirteen or fourteen at the time. A difficult enough age. But how to explain this cruel gouging to her, his grandmother?

Without acknowledging her, Daniel had folded the blade away and slipped it and his hands into the pockets of his grey school trousers. He stared at her then, face neutral, no trace of guilt or surprise at being caught; not even a chin lifted as a dare for her to challenge him.

'Help me tidy the place instead,' she said.

'What's the point? It's not like it's a house.'

'Brings calm. Purpose.'

He hadn't look convinced.

'Honours her memory, too,' Billie added.

He jammed his hands deeper into his pockets, lowered his gaze so his untidy brown hair obscured his face. 'What memory?' he replied, and kicked at the ground, not so parched back then, with a scuffed black school shoe.

Billie resisted the urge to say, *The memories are there. They're all there.*

'Come on,' she'd said instead, passing him a short-handled rake, one she'd cut intentionally to length to fit inside her backpack. Held it out to the boy. 'You can help.'

When he wouldn't take it, she tossed it on the ground near his feet for him to pick up when he was ready.

'If you like, I can give you a memory,' she said, and stooped to pick up a chip packet.

He didn't respond but neither did he walk away. She took it to mean he wanted her to continue.

She searched her mind for something small, innocuous. Anything too direct and she knew she'd scare him off.

'Your mother had a way of scratching your scalp,' Billie started. 'She had long nails, perfectly rounded at the ends and always painted … soft, pale colours mostly.' Billie looked to the ground as she spoke, hand dipping like an ibis's beak to pick up sweet wrappers, pieces of broken glass, beer bottle tops.

'She'd hold her hand like one of those things that clutches for soft toys in a fun parlour machine. She'd press quite firmly. Never cruelly though.'

Daniel put his foot on the rusted metal tines of the rake so that the shortened handle stood upright.

'She did it right from when you were born. Scratch, scratch,' Billie mimicked the action in the air. 'Scratch, scratch. And you'd push your head into her fingertips like a cat.'

Daniel rubbed the rake up and down his shin as Billie spoke. She wondered if he even noticed he was doing it.

She paused to look at him. 'This wasn't just some fleeting touch by your mother, Daniel,' she said. 'Some token gesture. She wanted you to *feel* her in a way that you'd remember. *Do* you remember it?'

Daniel looked up sharply. 'I only remember you doing it.'

Billie had tried to mimic the action after Jess had gone, but felt her pressure was never quite enough, her nails never quite the right shape or length.

'Shame,' she said, struggling to hide her disappointment.

'Don't, Nan,' he cautioned.

'It can't hurt to try and remember.'

She heard the rake drop to the ground and soon after the sound of him fleeing.

'They're all there,' she called after him. But it was too late. He was already gone.

★

5

She added juice boxes to the garbage bag, the plastic wrap from a tray of cheap supermarket sausages and squares of grease-stained paper towel. As she raked through the leaf litter that had blown into the recesses between the trunk's massive flanges she tossed in a faded and tatty hair band, two halves of a bald tennis ball, the broken plastic arm of a doll. Some spaces stunk of piss, another of vomit. She scouted around for ring pulls from soft drink cans. Found two five-cent coins, left them on the picnic table for someone to pocket. She carried the garbage bag, slung over one shoulder, to the green council bin, felt the usual frustration at how little the lid opened as she forced the bag into the gap.

The area looked tidier once she'd finished. But Daniel was right, it wasn't a house, although Billie wished it was and this area a room within it. One where she could switch off the light and close the door, leaving a capsule of care and order restored. And her daughter's spirit living there in peace.

Turnover at the garden centre was unseasonably fast. The drought added to the pace of it, with plants dying and leaving gaps in private gardens that needed refilling. There were a few enduring native old-timers though – Quandongs, Coolamons, Melaleucas. Billie liked these plants best; liked who bought them. They knew what was good for their gardens, went straight to a particular specimen confident it would survive. Others were caught up with short-lived, flamboyant blooms or plants with large glossy leaves. But a garden centre, Billie had learnt over the years of working in one, was as much a showroom for human personalities as it was for plants.

To avoid the heat of the day she'd positioned herself with the hose near the potted bamboo along the back fence. She didn't care that Russell or the other staff would struggle to find her. Instead, she skewed her focus through the tall straight canes and hunched down like a cartoon thief, easily able to imagine that the small girl on the other side, with her wild brown hair and a grin that looked up for a trick, was Jess. But Jess from a long time ago. Back when it was just the two of them: mother and daughter. A happier time.

Jess would have played the game, too, just as this girl was now, her small frame hunched like Billie's on the other side of the long stalks. Billie stopped, stood tall and jumped to the left. The girl copied her, grin widening. With one hand teapot-handled on her hip, Billie held the hose up like the spout so that water rained down on the plants and lightly sprayed the girl's freckled cheeks. The way she held her face up to the spray nearly undid Billie. It was exactly how Jess greeted the rain as a child, eyes closed, mouth open, as though receiving a blessing. She dropped the still-running hose onto the concrete path and parted the canes with both hands to better see the girl. For a fleeting moment, she hoped to make Jess real again.

'Billie! Drought. Remember?'

The boss's voice startled the girl and she ran off. Billie felt the joy of the game empty from her, just as the water had emptied from most of Brisbane's backyard tanks. The future was an uncertain thing. What would this child's be?

Russell turned off the tap and came up to her. He picked up the hose head and held it up like an accusation. 'Water costs me a fortune. Don't waste it.'

Billie shrugged. 'I was distracted.'

'I can't afford distractions. This stuff's the difference between having a business and not.' He shook the hose, drips flying.

Billie ignored him, looked across to the girl who was following her mother out of the garden centre, watched as she turned and waved coyly. Billie smiled and waved back, noticing how her springy hair bounced up and down on her shoulders as she skipped out.

The similarities were unnerving. It was like time had been concertinaed and the past brought close so that Billie might examine it. Memories were all she had of Jess now and, even though some hurt, she'd take them when presented to her. She held up her hand again, but the girl had her back to Billie now, time stretching out long between them.

'Billie, you hear me?'

She watched the girl's final skips out the front entrance, unsettled by the likeness but not wanting to lose its effect either.

'Why do I bother?' Russell shook his head and walked back in the direction of the office without waiting for her reply.

Shaded by a row of golden cane, its papery leaves whispering in the humid air, Billie started pulling weeds instead, edging along the fence line to the car park that nobody seemed to care about but her. She couldn't answer why Russell bothered – not in his work, life, any of it. But she could for herself. She bothered for Daniel. Always had.

From her hiding place she heard Russell exalting the drought hardiness of a plant to a customer.

'Liar,' she muttered.

Russell had a thing to prove. The greater of them being that he could navigate a plant nursery through dry times. He wasn't always scrupulous in the endeavour. If he'd cut back on the water-needy exotics – like the bamboo – and stocked more natives, those already adapted to the dry as Billie had suggested, then maybe he'd stand a better chance. But he, like the customers he catered to, wanted to believe that plants would comply with the ambitions people had for them: a tidy profit for Russell; a front yard that impractically and unsustainably resembled something from *Better Homes and Gardens* for the customers. Billie knew better. Was yet to comply with Russell's ambitions for her: that she lend an air of authority to the place because of her age; a woman who'd grown a thing or two. During the drought, she wouldn't plant half of what he currently stocked. Refused to press others to, as Russell would have her do.

At sixty-three she was old stock here. Odd stock too, some of her young colleagues probably thought. She was like a plant that had been tucked away in a back corner of the place for so long that it had become difficult to extract, overlooked but still a feature. A harmless, but non-conforming specimen. One that hadn't grown in a pleasing way. Some might even say pitiable for its differences.

She gripped another weed and pulled. *I'm a lone tree, Jess.* Billie smiled, knowing her daughter would reproach her for being maudlin.

Better a lone tree than a conforming hedge. That's what Jess would say, because that's what – who – Billie had taught her to be.

Billie thought about what this lone tree might be.

A Wollemi pine. *A survivor.*

The fence line weeded, Billie rested back on her heels. She scooped up a handful of dry earth and sifted it between the fingers of one hand into the other until nothing remained except a film of brown dust over her palms. She wondered about its composition; what tiny grains it might contain. It wasn't the minerals or sand or clay she thought about when she held soil in her hands. She thought about holding the cells of a thousand – a million – different people. Bones and teeth and nails and hair, all those things that remained long after the features people were recognised by had gone. She loved the feel of the earth between her fingers, the give of its minute connections, knowing how they'd rebuild again. Renewal was the imperative of soil. From it all life grew. She witnessed it every day in the plants all around her. Was one of the reasons she loved working where she did. She massaged the fine particles over the backs of her hands, balm and anointment.

'There you are—' Hayley paused, but quickly checked herself. 'I've been looking for you.'

Billie wiped her hands down the front of her trousers then hauled herself up. Rubbed out the creases that had pressed into the skin of her knees. She was glad it was Hayley who'd witnessed her doing that. She was a good kid. Didn't judge.

'You're the only one who bothers keeping this area nice.'

Billie shrugged. Expected her young colleague was the only one who noticed. 'All part of the job.'

'Russ wants us to do a stocktake of the succulents and place an order. They're flying out the door.'

'People are finally getting it.'

'No thanks to Russell. He'd pot those if he thought he could sell them.' Hayley indicated the line of pulled weeds behind Billie.

'At least they'd survive.'

Hayley laughed. 'C'mon, I'll help you clear up here then we'll do the order.'

Billie was the last to leave that afternoon. She'd shooed Hayley out the door fifteen minutes earlier, promising to finish the order. Being Saturday, she figured the girl had somewhere she'd rather be and pointless they both be held back because of a glitch in the ordering system.

Russell came into the small office where Billie was finishing up. 'You still here?'

'Not by choice.'

'Wouldn't be my choice either.'

She eyed him over her glasses, trying to figure out his meaning. He'd been the owner of the garden centre for the last two of Billie's eight years there and still she couldn't work him out. All she knew was that she didn't trust him to do the best by people. 'There was a problem with the system … some order error,' she said.

'Leave it and try again tomorrow. I need to lock up.' He didn't look at Billie, only at his mobile phone. It *pinged* with a message.

'It's gone through now. I was just shutting down the computer.'

She took her backpack from the cupboard, eased a strap over one shoulder. 'See you tomorrow.' If he responded she didn't hear. All she heard was the *ping* of another message.

It was five-thirty but the hottest part of the day remained trapped inside her small car. Billie opened all the windows, turned the air-con on full and waited for the heat to dissipate. The car park had been a dust bowl for months and a utility hauling a trailer stirred it up now as it drove in. Billie tried to think what could be getting delivered at this hour on a Saturday. The driver pulled up in front of the main entrance. Russell came out and waved him round the back. The driver put the vehicle in gear and moved off to the delivery area.

'So much for wanting to lock up,' Billie muttered as she reversed out of her space. In the rear-view mirror she glimpsed the spikey crown of a grass tree just visible above the trailer's high, enclosed sides. *That's a tall one.* Taller than any of the other grass trees they had in stock. Which meant it was old given how slowly they grew. *What's he up to?*

Billie pulled the parking brake on, got out of her car and walked around to where the trailer was parked. She could hear Russell and the driver talking behind the nursery fence. She put one foot up on the trailer's wheel and hauled herself up to look over the top. Inside were about a dozen crudely potted grass trees of varying height; the one she'd spied was the largest. Some were branched with several glorious crowns. Others had single trunks that bent in elegant ways. Each plant was exquisite for its uniqueness. A highly prized feature for any garden. And none, from what she could see, carried an official tag to indicate they'd been harvested legally.

When Russell and the driver came out of the nursery, Billie stepped down from the trailer and confronted them. 'Where have these come from?'

The driver looked to Russell. 'A special delivery I ordered a while back,' he said.

'None of these plants are tagged.'

The driver found his tongue. 'Haven't received them yet. When I do, I'll be droppin' them round to Russ.'

'But protected plants have to be tagged before they're taken anywhere for sale.'

The man dismissed Billie's remark with a laugh. 'You know these government departments—'

'I know their rules.'

'Give us a break, Billie.' Russell pushed past her and began unlashing the rope that held the blue covering around the sides of the trailer. 'Now, outta the way so we can get this lot unloaded.'

Once the grass trees were fully revealed, Billie could better see the wild beauty of them. She also saw their potential for profit. What stood before her would easily retail for several thousand dollars.

Not knowing their provenance made Billie uneasy as she walked back to her car. Uprooted from their origins where many of them had likely held their place in the earth for more than a century. Commodities now, squeezed onto a trailer.

Distracted, she almost failed to give way as she exited the car park, her grip on the steering wheel tight with the certainty she'd witnessed something illegal. The driver of a four-wheel-drive sounded his horn. Billie sounded hers back; an unnecessary retort that offered no release for her anger.

2

Daniel bombed down the trail in attack position, arse out of the bike saddle, hips well back over the rear wheel. The wind was hot against his face, even this early. Did little to cool his skin, despite his sweat-soaked t-shirt. He feathered the brake lever as he approached the turn, worried he'd overcooked it, but a quick release and dab to the ground with his left foot and he was round. He accelerated again, caught air on a couple of dirt jumps on a straight stretch, then slowed as he pedalled uphill, butt back in the saddle now. At the top of the rise, the bike trail joined several others. There Daniel stopped to catch his breath, removing his helmet and ruffling his hair to let the air through. The sun was still low in the sky, not yet reached the time of day when the heat of being out here would suck the joy from what he was doing.

Enoggera Reservoir reflected some of that early light as mica-like sequins glinting through the trees. Once a large creek, now a dammed body of water. Not Brisbane's largest reservoir anymore though, and diminishing all the time with the drought. Daniel wondered what might emerge if the water level kept dropping. Ghost trees. Ghost bones too, his grandmother would say. But he shut that thought down. Didn't want her in his head this early in the morning. Thought instead about how ancient pathways might resurface. He liked that idea, liked to think about where these paths might have led. He could be on a remnant of an original path now, maybe the start of the long walk to Bunya Mountains. Many of Brisbane's roads were, so why not this one?

He rocked back and forth on his bike, the gravel of this maybe-old trail crunching under his tyres. He felt good today. Better than a lot of other days, when he felt burdened by expectations he didn't know how to fulfil. Because a kid's memory could only stretch back so far and his was never going to go back far enough for his grandmother, no matter how much she tried to coax it.

Thankfully, at nineteen, his grandmother had pretty much given up on the hope he'd remember anything useful and concentrated instead on putting memories in. He remained wary though, because any old trigger could set her off. Like the four-year-old kid who'd gone missing. Disappeared two days ago from a campground in the national park at Binna Burra. All it took was some human catastrophe like that and she'd look at him in that way again: face all anguished and frowning like he was a combination lock she'd forgotten or lost the code to.

Right now, though, he didn't want to think about his grandmother or a missing boy. And he knew how to prevent it: don't stop long enough to think. Better to ride like he had no skin in the game. Like he was invincible. Flout the reality that anyone's time could come early, as his mother's had.

Daniel pushed off and clipped in. Aimed for a fast but clean ride home, all the corners and obstacles flowing together perfectly as he floated along the trail. Over this, he had some control. And for those times when he didn't, the stakes weren't too high: a bruise here, a bit of skin off there, a broken derailleur or chain off his bike. Events that didn't make his grandmother look at him with the determination that he'd eventually give her what she wanted: justice.

Daniel dismounted as he came down the path at the side of his father's workshop. Wheeled his bike across the browned-off grass, past his grandmother's raised herb garden, the purple flowers of the lavender bush alive with native bees. Past her small granny flat and onto the back patio of the main house, at which point he heard his name called. He turned to see Billie standing on her small front veranda. He rested his bike against the wall of the house and took off his helmet.

'Hey Nan. How was your weekend?'

'Awful.'

'Why? Work busy?' As he made his way across the lawn, he could see she was angry. Lips thinned, body held tighter than usual, arms fixed like splints across her chest. He hadn't seen her like this for a while. Mostly, she held it in. Only released the occasional firecracker of anger in brief but startling ways. Like the time he saw the silver cross.

The cross had come to him in a kaleidoscopic image during a migraine; those debilitating events he sometimes had to get through. He'd come to think of them as Picasso portraits into the past. During them he glimpsed angles and shapes of possibility, which he'd try to give form to, his mind working like a dreamcatcher. But the fragments remained frustratingly disordered and before long they disappeared again. Except for the silver cross. It had swung before him from an earlobe. Some place in his young boy's mind had known it was important, so he'd told Billie about seeing it.

'He had a god?' she had demanded, and there was the sound of something breaking in the sink. Everything she did for a while after that, she did loudly.

He knew now that she hadn't expected an answer from him. But at the time he believed she did, and he'd cried because then, as now, he couldn't give her one.

No opportunity was lost to try and mine his memories back then. She'd gone to extra lengths that day to lay out as many new images of men's faces as she could fit across the kitchen table; wouldn't let him up from his chair until he'd studied them all. But despite her years of effort, her scrapbooks held few faces that might bear any resemblance to his mother's killer. And many of the men whose images were glued to the pages had earnt their place there for no other reason than that Daniel – unable to stand looking for evil anymore that day – had offered up any old face as sacrifice. Just to appease her.

But this anger seemed different and Daniel was relieved. Maybe he could talk her down.

'The place is run by a crook,' she said.

'Who? Where?'

'Russell. At work. You should see them, Dan. Beautiful big, old things. And I just know that man won't be licensed … that he's taken them illegally.'

'Slow down, Nan. I'm struggling to keep up.' He guided her to the top step of her veranda where they sat side by side.

'Protected for good reason,' she said.

'What are?'

'Grass trees. You hear rumours about this sort of thing going on, but to actually witness it …' She shook her head, like she didn't – couldn't – comprehend the audacity of it.

'And your boss has something to do with it?'

'*Everything* to do with it!'

'What makes you think they were taken illegally?'

'No tags or labels on them like there should be, that's why. Nothing to say where they were taken from. No licence or exemption number. Nothing. The bloke who delivered them said he was waiting on them to be sent through. That he'd drop them round when he got them.'

'Maybe he will.'

'I doubt it,' she said bitterly. 'Russell has already started selling them. Just the one, so far. Snuck it out the back entrance yesterday afternoon to a customer, like the criminal he is.'

Every blow against nature was a blow against his grandmother. He'd learnt that. He'd also learnt that such attacks made the black centres of her blue eyes larger, wilder. Made her unpredictable.

He put his arm around her shoulders. She was as rigid as a bike frame.

'They belong in the wild, Dan.' He felt her shoulders sag. A battle, then the war, lost. 'The worst bit is, most of them will die. They hate being disturbed … don't transplant well at all, not even when they're harvested properly. What chance do they have when a cowboy does it?'

Daniel pressed her in closer. Her short white hair tickled him under his chin.

'It hurts me, Dan … *here.*' She pressed a fist into her breastbone.

Not for the first time, he thought about how it should be his mother consoling Billie now, not him. How she would be better equipped to help. Would know exactly what to say. How was he supposed to know what his grandmother needed? All he could offer was his ear. It had worked well enough so far. But there were times, too, when he wished someone else could step up to fill the gap in the generations, take the place of the one lost. Sometimes he wished he was a backpacker, like the ones he served drinks to four nights out of seven, that he could flee with everything he needed in a pack on his back. Reinvent himself in another country. Leave this whole other sorry life behind. His past kicked into the gutter, no longer snapping at his heels.

For a moment he resented the bony shoulders under his arm, the annoying tickle of her hair, this misplaced empathy for plants while all around them any number of crises could be playing out. But guilt crashed through and he pressed her more firmly against him.

'I know they're only plants,' Billie said into his chest, as if reading his thoughts, 'but they've already seen more sunsets than I'm ever likely to. That kind of endurance deserves respect.'

For all her quirks and obsessions, many of which he failed to understand, his grandmother remained the closest witness to Daniel's childhood, closer even than his father. She could tell him about the day he was born, right down to the time and the weather. The day he first crawled, walked, clapped. She knew the origins of his toddler scars; the words he mangled as he learnt to speak: flingo-flamingo; poon-spoon; dumple-dimple. All the things a mother would know.

As the guardian of his earliest memories, Daniel would always be connected to his grandmother in unassailable ways. That was the inescapable truth of their closeness. But also his burden.

'Nan was pretty upset this morning.' They were in his father's workshop.

Angus glanced at him now over the timber he was working on, quickly hid the look of *What now?* 'Was she? What about?'

'Says her boss is illegally selling protected plants.'

'That would upset her.'

'I haven't seen her so angry for a long time.'

'Did she say what she's planning to do about it?'

'No, she didn't. By the end of the conversation she sounded pretty defeated, to be honest.'

'That's not like her.'

'I know.'

'Well, we both know whatever she does will be driven by what she thinks is best, and there's nothing you or I can do to influence it.'

Daniel nodded, knowing his father was right.

'Try not to worry about it, son. I expect it'll blow over soon enough.'

Neither spoke for a time. Daniel watched his father work a cloth across the timber. This piece was one of five slabs, each about two metres long. They once formed the trunk of a large blue gum. The wood was honey-coloured at its once bark-clad perimeter, darkening to Hereford red at its heartwood. The grain was a river delta of whorls, swirls and lines. The other four slabs were rough sawn and stored flat down one end of the workshop. This slab, the one his father was working on, was over a metre across. It was the widest of the five, a long, central slice taken lengthwise from the centre of the tree trunk. Each would become a dining table, its form and finish decided by the tree as it had grown, but its surface now made smooth and lustrous by his father over many hours. This final polish was the last stage before it was handed over to the people who'd commissioned him to make it.

There was a box of clean rags in the corner. Daniel took an old t-shirt from it now and went to the opposite end of the table from his father. He started to buff the timber, too.

'It looks good,' he said, working the cloth in circular motions. 'Nice grain.'

'It's not bad.' His father leant down to view the table's surface at eye level before straightening again and moving his cloth to a new area.

A farmer friend from out west knew his father was always on the lookout for furniture timber. He'd called to tell him the tree had come down in a violent storm, its roots weakened by the drought and soil erosion. Angus had hooked the trailer onto his work ute, loaded the portable sawmill in the tray. When he returned with the wood he called it a rare but sad haul. That the tree was likely over two hundred years old.

'Do you ever have trouble giving up a piece?' Daniel asked.

What he really wanted to know was whether particular pieces of wood spoke to him – like this one. Had there been a keening under the saw, a resistance to being cut, a sense of it holding on?

His father laughed. 'Not if we wanna eat.'

Daniel didn't laugh, and his father knew why. 'It'll talk to its owners for a while,' he said. 'They'll hear it make cracking sounds from time to time as the wood settles on its base. Almost like it's still alive. Who knows? Maybe it is for a time, eh … keeps a sense of its whole self.'

This is how Daniel liked to hear his father speak about the wood he worked with, and Angus knew it. It justified how his grandmother felt about the fig tree in the park: that it was alive, had witnessed things, maybe even held memories. Justified the trips she forced him to make there with her when he was younger.

The workshop, once a two-car garage, was a cramped space, which probably explained why his father kept it so tidy. Timber off-cuts stood on their ends in three old tea chests in one corner. Kiln-dried hardwood was stacked neatly along the back wall. Every tool had its place and every shelf a purpose, but still space was limited.

When he was a boy, his father would lift him onto the workbench where he'd sit, legs swinging, and watch his father work. He'd take in the smells of beeswax polish and oils, glues and varnishes, along with the saw-cut scents of different timbers: the spicy smell of camphor laurel, the cool, minty tones of pine, the sweet caramel of coachwood. Over time, his father let him handle a small pocketknife, which he used to whittle pine off-cuts. He enjoyed the rhythm of this activity. Finding the orientation of the grain. Working with it.

The whisper of the cloth was broken by the start of the ABC News bulletin. Angus reached over and turned up the volume. The headline had not changed in two days: a four-year-old boy holidaying in Australia from Italy with his family, had gone missing. It still wasn't known if he'd wandered off and got lost in the national park, or if he'd been taken.

'What d'you reckon the chances are of finding him alive?' Daniel asked.

Angus stopped buffing the table's surface to look along it towards Daniel. 'It's only been forty-eight hours,' he said, 'so I should think fairly good.'

Daniel hated it when his father tried to bullshit him. 'I'm not ten anymore, Dad. You can have an opinion now that doesn't have a happy ending.' His father looked hurt, but Daniel figured the truth could do that.

'Just being optimistic,' Angus said.

'I reckon he's already dead.'

His father looked at him as though about to speak, but then thought better of it.

'It's been so hot, even in the rainforest of Binna Burra, so two days in that … and if he was taken, well …' Daniel shrugged, left the possibilities to speak for themselves.

'Hope isn't something I'm prepared to give up on so easily,' Angus said. 'My guess is his parents and the emergency workers won't either.'

Daniel wondered if you had to be a parent to be this hopeful. That having brought a kid into the world you then had to hold on to the belief that you'd done the right thing. And not that you'd delivered another person into a life of hardship or disappointment.

The boy's disappearance had made Daniel wonder how parents did it – parent, that is – without actually going mad. And not just your regular feel-a-bit-anxious kind of mad, but a paranoid sweaty-palmed heart-attack kind of bat-shit crazy, just from the worry of a moment's inattention in which something awful might happen. Daniel didn't think he ever wanted to be a parent. Because if – *when* – it went wrong, when that vigilance lapsed for even a few seconds and the thing that gave you the sweaty palms and the racing heart actually happened – when optimism *failed* – and your kid was hurt or worse, disappeared like this one, how the hell did you live with yourself?

He thinks his father had struggled to live with himself for a while. So maybe finding optimism – *hopefulness* – was the only way he'd known how to keep going. *I should've been there* was something Daniel had heard his father say over the years. Not to Daniel so much as the room they both happened to be in at the time.

If his grandmother was in the room too, she'd say, 'You weren't though, Angus, so what's the point of torturing yourself?'

Angus would look at Billie, and sometimes Daniel saw gratitude on his father's face. At other times he saw an accused man.

His father had slept in the day his mother was murdered. It was assumed she'd not wanted to wake him, had slipped quietly from the house with Daniel. Not that he'd walked with them that often, according to Billie, but in Angus's reimagining he would have on this particular day. So yes, Daniel supposed his grandmother was right, it was a kind of torture his father put himself through, working back from that day, shifting its actors to more favourable positions, despite the end already being written.

When news of the missing boy broke, Daniel had been at Billie's. The TV camera zoomed in on the boy's parents. They were clinging to one another, along with a younger child, as though a single organism. They were a dishevelled trio, out of place among the order and uniforms of the emergency workers.

Daniel had wondered how many times these people would ask themselves what they should have done differently.

The image of the family together like that had brought a memory of his three-year-old self being held by his father. He couldn't be sure if this memory was real or imposed from the pictures he'd seen in the vast archive of newspaper cuttings that his grandmother kept. Regardless, Daniel had taken this memory as his, made it so real he could still feel the shelf of his father's arm under his buttocks, the other up high on his back, pressing him against his chest. He had the sense of being held like that for weeks. He couldn't be sure now if his father had been trying to make him feel safe or if it was some of the crazy coming through.

His grandmother had stopped what she was doing in the kitchen to come and watch the news, tea towel in hand. Daniel saw how her eyes darted round the television screen. He knew she would be studying the faces of individuals, the way she used to make Daniel study them. She was like a bloodhound when it came to looking for signs of guilt.

'They'll never be the same again,' she said.

'Even if they find him alive?'

'Grief starts with imagining the loss, even before it's confirmed,' she said. 'It's hard to un-imagine something like that once you've let it into your head.' His grandmother had sounded so certain that Daniel was inclined to believe her.

Sometimes he wondered at the value of strong human connections. They only set you up for pain, which no amount of optimism or hopefulness could protect you from. Maybe the best thing to do was to learn to live away from the heart?

'Awful things happen to hopeful people too, Dad,' he said to his father now, as they stood at either end of the finished table.

There was silence for a time, long enough for Daniel to think about his choice of words.

'I know that, son.'

3

CARLA HEARD WHAT COULD ONLY be Angus crashing through the back door.

'Carla!' he bellowed. 'Can you fix this up, love?'

She came into the kitchen to find him with a bloodied rag around his shin. 'What have you done?' She almost added *now*, but that would be unfair. As a man trying to make a go of a furniture-making business from a barely adequate backyard workshop, he had fewer nicks and scrapes than he probably should have.

'Just a flesh wound,' he joked.

Carla shook her head. 'Spare me the Monty Python.' She guided him to a chair, knelt to inspect the wound. The rag he'd covered it with was at least clean. Beneath it was a four-centimetre void of skin as though he'd run a plane down his shinbone. She wasn't squeamish, but the sight of it turned her stomach as she imagined how the wound would have first blanched white like pork fat before the blood came. 'Jesus, Angus, you've nearly taken this down to the bone. How did you do it?'

'Tripped and caught it on the edge of a metal trolley.'

She imagined the shaved skin still hanging off the edge like a snakeskin.

'Tripped on what?'

'Not much more than my own feet as it happens.'

Which meant he was struggling to find space just to walk round the piece he was working on.

'And what's that tell you?' She could answer that for herself. That it was time to be smart and safe. Get a proper industrial space for his work. Room enough for the apprentice he wanted and needed. That it was time to sell. Time to move on. But she needed him to make that decision. It couldn't come from her.

He leant forward, kissed the top of her head. 'That I've got big feet.'

She smiled despite herself. 'I think you've got a bigger fear of change.'

At the sink, she turned on the tap, fingers in the stream waiting the interminable amount of time it always took for the water to come through warm. When it did, she dampened an old, clean tea towel. She returned to Angus with it, knelt before him again and cleaned the skin around the wound with the soft fabric. When she glanced at him, he looked pale.

'You alright?'

'Just seeing it properly for the first time.'

'It's not pretty.'

'Lucky the rest of me is.'

'There's not much I can do with it,' she said, 'except clean it and keep it covered till it heals. You're going to have a hell of a scab.'

'Just as well I'm not Scout then. We all know what she'd do with it.'

So calm. So easygoing. So able to place himself just outside the harsh reality of any difficulty; not make it the focus. This optimism, despite everything, was one of the things she'd come to love about him. She squeezed his knee. 'I'll go and get the first-aid kit so I can dress it properly.'

She made her way up the hallway, past the rooms that opened off it – three bedrooms, a fourth now a home office, the children's bathroom, a laundry – to the linen cupboard at the end. Were it not for the skylight, she'd be fumbling in the dark. She took the first-aid box from a shelf and returned to the kitchen.

Angus rested his hand on her shoulder as she tended the wound. She felt his thumb press a little more firmly into her collarbone at times, before quickly easing the pressure off again.

'Send me the bill,' he said, looking from the freshly covered wound to her face. He smiled, but she didn't return it.

'You can settle the debt by looking seriously at what you're trying to achieve in that cramped space.'

'That new timber's made it tight is all. I'll get by.'

'It's not the new timber, Angus. You're always just getting by.'

He wouldn't look at her now. She knew why. They'd been here before. Both knew an admission would require action.

She placed her hands on either side of his head, fingers pressed into thick, greying hair. 'There *is* an alternative. Consider it. Please.'

He took her hands in his, kissed the palm of each then rose gingerly. 'Look, in perfect working order again.' He jiggled his leg about. 'Back to it then.'

Except nothing was perfect. Not where Angus worked, nor where they lived. And neither was Carla. Because there were times she'd tried to force things. Times she forgot and failed to read or understand the shared air in these rooms. Didn't notice how sometimes the oxygen seemed to be sucked from it, like everyone was holding their breath, wouldn't pick up on it in time to help them breathe out. Forgot that the three people she'd married – Angus, Daniel and Billie – shared something she never could. Forgot they were victims of something that only a victim truly understood. That theirs was a nucleus of experience she couldn't enter. The best she could hope for was to steady the static it generated. And there were times when she'd felt its sting, just as Angus had felt it in his wound just now.

If Carla had recognised the craftsmanship of Angus's gift, the generosity of it, then she might have guessed at the inevitable: that he saw her as someone he could trust to hold his past as well as hold him.

'I bet you make these for all the girls,' she'd teased, when he gave her the large bowl meticulously crafted from a eucalyptus burl. She knew now it was worth quite a bit of money if he were to sell it.

He smiled shyly, which she also now knew was because she'd been the first woman for a long time.

'They're not easy to make,' he said. 'The wood's hard and can warp when you start turning it, so it needs regular resting and reworking. This one took six months, on and off.'

Red mallee, he told her. The bowl's edge was framed with blond sapwood. The polished knotted grain of its red heart looked liquid, like bubbling lava. She turned it over, easily pictured its shape and texture as a bulbous protrusion on the trunk of a tree.

'Hard to believe something like that comes from disease, isn't it?' he said.

She'd laughed. 'They say what doesn't kill you makes you stronger.' Tilting the bowl in her hands, she marvelled at how the shifting aspect revealed something new each time, some beguiling pattern or marking. She hadn't known it then, but it was as complex as the relationship she was about to enter.

'It's beautiful,' she said. 'Thank you.'

Over time, she learnt that Angus had a skill for finding beauty hidden in wood. He saw it beneath bark, in the rough-sawn face of milled timber. In contours and grains, imperfections and anomalies. He made features of flaws. Was charmed by simplicity. A carpenter once concerned with functional utility who had learnt to let art in.

He worked with a quiet patience, reverence even. No job was rushed. Allowed his designs to honour the way the wood had grown, let it show him what it could be. He made most things by hand. There was no computer-assisted design or manufacture in his workshop. No standing back while a machine churned out templates for him to assemble.

'Putting my mind to making saved me from putting it elsewhere.' He told her this after he'd given her the history of his widowerhood, delivered abbreviated and factual a couple of months after they'd met. 'It was that or booze,' he said, and laughed. She wasn't sure if he was joking.

His history hadn't made her want to run. But it had made her realise that life with him would be different from her other relationships. Because she couldn't see how people moved on from that kind of violence. How it had to move with them. Like the permanent markers in the blood studies she saw at work that told a person they'd had chickenpox or measles: it was always there.

But she also sensed theirs wasn't a relationship that would fail like her others had. The difference was in his hands. She'd come to think they could define a person. Angus's were steady and sure. To watch them was to observe a study in efficiency, but also grace. It was hard to know if these qualities had led his hands to a hobby, then a career as a furniture maker, or if the craft had shaped the action of the hands. They were roughened by his work, but he was mindful of it. He touched her using the smooth tips of his fingers, their less blemished backs. Other men hadn't been so considerate. One insisted on wearing his wristwatch to bed that would graze her bare skin when he reached for her. Another had used his angrily, gesticulating denials or challenges. She'd had to step well back from them near the end.

Her relationships with these other men were brought down by their confident assumption that she'd always be there. Angus knew otherwise. He never took a moment, let alone her, for granted. And for her part, love, not pity – *never* pity – had its own mind about what she was capable of taking on, and it had told her Angus was special and that she ought to hold on to him. And she had. For eight years now.

She knew she'd married more than a man with a love for timber. She'd also married his son, who'd seemed older than his eleven years at the time. While father and son looked little alike, they were similar in height – Daniel was longer in the leg, Angus in the waist. Angus had pale skin, an Irish heritage; Daniel's swarthier, more European. And where Angus's hands were large, broad and purposeful, Daniel's were finer, less sure.

Photographs of Jess showed that she had left the greater mark on her son. Each had light brown wavy hair – Jess's long, Daniel's to the collar – that fell about their faces untamed and untameable. Carla thought it suited her stepson's disregard of the trivial. He had his mother's piercing gaze, too. The one she'd given the camera in the photographs Carla had seen of her anyway, like she was returning the scrutiny of its lens. Eyes that said *I see you*. No wonder these images had unnerved Carla so much early on.

The photographs had been moved now, some into Dan's bedroom, others to Billie's granny flat. Carla had never asked for this to happen. Never would have. Gradually they'd been eased out of rooms, one by one, till those penetrating eyes no longer looked back at her.

It wasn't just the photographs that were relocated when Carla moved in. Billie had been, too. It was a shift of only thirty paces – that's how far it was from the main house to the granny flat in the backyard where Billie lived now. But it had also been a shift of a life: Billie's.

Later, from the kitchen window, Carla watched as Billie came through the gate in the back fence. A route she used in preference to the front drive. Carla wished Angus would get rid of the gate, had hinted that he should return the timber palings he'd removed to install it – at Billie's insistence, apparently – and stop an entry and exit that had always felt dishonest, creeping even. She watched as Daniel came out of Angus's workshop and greeted his nan. Watched as he cleared the two steps to her front door in one lunge, and after their warm greeting they sat side by side on Billie's front step. It was early evening, still warm after what had been a hot day. Even in the declining light, Billie's white hair, cropped short like Judi Dench's, shone like a beacon. Her face was deeply tanned and lined. She looked older than sixty-three.

They were alike in many ways these two, Daniel and Billie. Each beholden to things most others disregarded or failed to notice. For Billie it was things in nature, the soil and trees; for Daniel it was the randomness of events that sculpted and re-sculpted the Earth's surface: volcanoes, earthquakes, sinkholes. She thought it an unusual preoccupation for such a young man. Expected his grandmother had encouraged it. It was as though they lived in a different universe from everyone else, one concerned with what the ground was capable of as much as the people who lived upon it. She'd always put it down to their trauma; that it had tilted the axis of their world so they saw it at an angle. Other times she wondered if they had some otherworldly knowing, human but also something else. Something numinous. Whatever it was, Carla felt shallow in its presence, a thing *on* the world, not *of* it. Maybe it was this that had kept her and Billie at arm's length, their ideologies as divergent as religions.

She wished they were closer, she and Billie. That they embraced. She didn't remember now who'd failed to step into the gap. Had it been Billie, still raw with her loss when Carla met Angus, even though eight years had passed? Or was it Carla, subconsciously afraid of never being as good as a dead woman? Deep down, Carla felt the failing was in her. That it had been her responsibility to step in. Not with the hope of filling the space left by Jess – she was nobody's fool – but she could at least have tried harder to give Billie something to hold that was uniquely Carla-shaped.

'Raargh!'

Carla jumped now at the roar behind her. She turned to see her daughter with a lion mask covering her face.

'Gotcha!' Scout giggled behind the mask.

'You shouldn't creep up on people like that.'

Scout lifted the mask onto the top of her head, light brown hair pushed out either side of it like the lion's mane. 'Should've seen your face, Mum. Woo-hoo.' She mimicked a ghostly figure with her arms.

Carla flicked the mask back down over her daughter's face.

'When's dinner?' she asked from behind it. 'I'm starving.'

'Sooner if you'd help. You can set the table.'

Ignoring her, Scout gripped the kitchen bench and pressed up onto her toes to look out the kitchen window. 'Ye-es!' she said and headed for the back door, mask discarded behind her.

'Hey! Table!'

'Later,' she bellowed, and the screen door slapped shut as Scout ran across the lawn.

Billie's face lit up and she held out her arms on seeing Scout, who fell into them.

And then there were three on the step and Carla didn't doubt her daughter, at just seven, was being coached in Billie's language of soil, rocks and trees, too.

4

THE GLOSSY CERAMIC FINISH OF the Talavera pots and planters on display at the counter showed the dust in a way that the terracotta and matte-glazed pots didn't. Still, Billie thought them fun – a taste of Mexico in Australia that suited the succulents so popular now – and didn't mind that they needed regular cleaning. She picked up a donkey-shaped planter, ran her cloth over its head, its two side baskets empty and each ready to hold a plant.

It was a mundane task that left too much space to think; a void she filled with thoughts of the missing Italian boy, Marco. He'd not been seen for six days now. In her heart, Billie hoped he was still wandering in the bush, sustained by sips of creek water, and would soon be found, thin and weak but still alive. In her gut, though, she believed him already dead. It was what precipitated his death that most preoccupied her. She hoped nature was responsible. A boy hopelessly lost, succumbing to dehydration or exposure, a calamitous fall, a fatal snakebite. Tragic as these fates were, they were ones she could understand, even accept. The alternative – that someone had taken the child – chilled her, even on this blisteringly hot day.

'Please let it have been the bush,' she said softly. 'Not some bastard.'

'Huh?'

Her back to Hayley, polishing pots, too, but at the other end of the counter, Billie had forgotten the girl was there.

'This one's silly,' Billie said, holding up a pelican-shaped planter for Hayley to see. 'All beak and not much of a body for a plant.'

'It's that turtle I don't like.' Hayley pointed to a pot further along. 'It's got a mean face.'

Billie put the pelican down, picked up the one Hayley indicated and inspected it. 'You're right. It does look mean.' She glowered at it, the same way it seemed to glower at her. 'Grrr,' she said.

Hayley laughed. 'You're funny, Billie.' She lifted up a pig-shaped pot, aimed it at Billie. 'Oink.'

Billie selected a cow. 'Moo.'

Hayley a frog. 'Croak.'

They both laughed.

Hayley was a sweet girl, and these were the girls Billie feared for most. Like children, they trusted easily, saw the good in people. Weren't afraid of eye contact or to pause and say hello, to give directions, provide the time. It led a girl to lower her guard, ignore the protective force they held within: their instinct. That wise old woman embedded in the psyche who divined the hidden, and without whose guidance these unsuspecting girls risked stepping inside the dangerous perimeter of another.

Jess was a sweet girl. Trusting, too. Was she first asked directions? The time? Was the missing boy? Lured over a line from which she – he – couldn't quickly escape. Had her daughter's wise woman rallied too late? Billie would never know.

'Learn to be mean, too,' she said to Hayley now.

Hayley looked at her, confused.

Billie wanted to say: *It might save your life.* Instead, she said, 'It can be a superpower.'

Hayley balled her small hands into fists, jabbed at the air. 'Already got one,' she said, grinning. 'Boxercise.'

Billie placed a hand over each of her young colleague's tight little fists, felt the childlike vulnerability of them. Wanted to tell her they were unlikely to be enough, but instead she told her to keep up the good work and released them.

Russell approached the counter, wheeling a trolley for a woman. On it were several plants, among them one of the grass trees: medium-sized with a branched trunk and two full crowns.

Apart from the one she'd seen Russell slyly wheel out the back entrance last Sunday, the grass trees had remained in the stock area. Now, back from her days off, there were few left and those that remained were out on display for sale. The others, she assumed, had already been sold. None of them had been tagged, only priced. She'd tried to raise it with Russell earlier, but he'd brushed her off. Told her he was too busy to talk.

'Survive anything, you say?' the woman asked him.

'Uh-huh. Drought. Fire. Pestilence. You name it.' Russell laughed and the woman beamed at him.

'I've lost a few plants with the drought. This'll fill the hole left in one of the gardens nicely. And good to buy natives, as you say.'

'Can one of you put these through for me please?' Russell asked, ushering the woman to the front counter.

'I'll put everything through but the grass tree,' Billie said.

Hayley took a quick intake of breath. Russell glared at Billie.

Billie turned to the woman. 'If I sell you that plant, I'll be breaking the law.'

The woman looked from Russell to Billie smiling, probably wondering if she'd missed a joke. But it was no joke and Billie told her so.

'It's a protected plant. Without an official government label indicating it's been harvested legally, I have to assume it's been taken illegally and I can't sell it to you.'

'Oh. But it's *perfect* for the place I've got planned for it. And look, here it is,' the woman indicated to the trolley, 'already potted and ready to go, so what's the harm?'

'The harm is it shouldn't have been taken from the wild in the first place.'

'Ignore her. She doesn't know what she's talking about.' Russell came round to Billie's side of the counter, forcing her out of the way. 'Hard to get good help these days,' he joked and flashed his best smile at the woman. 'I'll put it through. Card?'

'I'll treat it like family,' the woman said to Billie, voice smarmy. 'Pinkie promise.'

Billie wasn't a child and neither was she a pushover.

'I wouldn't get too attached to it,' she said. 'It'll be dead inside two years.'

'That's rubbish.' Russell turned his back to Billie.

'Even those harvested properly from the wild don't transplant well and you know it, Russell. And you can bet your mate who delivered them wouldn't have known what the hell he was doing.'

The woman hesitated for a moment, long enough, Billie assumed, for her to picture this prize somewhere in her garden, because she still reached for her wallet. Billie looked on as Russell depleted her card of hundreds of dollars.

'Two years,' she called after the woman.

In her heart she hoped she was wrong. But her instincts – her wise woman – told her differently.

Billie expected there would be consequences. An icy look for the rest of the weekend, or he'd ignore her altogether. A dressing-down perhaps in Russell's office, door closed. It eventually came at close of business that Sunday in the form of a letter stating her employment was terminated. Immediately. Notice period paid out as gardening leave.

'Work's slowed down a lot with the drought, Billie. I've had to rethink things … do a bit of belt-tightening.' That's how he justified it anyway. 'Sorry to do it to you.'

She knew he wasn't.

'Figured the younger ones are at the start of their working lives. You must be close to getting the pension, eh?'

'We both know why you're sacking me Russell, and it's not because there's not enough work.' He'd put off two young casuals a few months ago. Those of them left behind had picked up their workload. Most days they were too busy. 'You're doing it because you're a crook, and I called you out for it.'

'Maybe I'm doing it because you lack respect.'

'You earn it,' she snapped, 'like everyone else.'

'I'm the boss. I *have* earnt it.' He held the office door open, swept his arm in front of him, indicated that she should leave.

Would she still have done it, knowing the outcome? She expected so. It was part of the *mean* she'd spoken of to Hayley. To say nothing placed her on the wrong side of the line. Made her complicit.

It hurt, though, to find herself crossing the dusty car park for the last time. Apart from the handful of years she'd spent at home with Jess, then those with Daniel, Billie had always worked. Retail mostly. When she landed the job in the garden centre eight years ago it was like a homecoming. Plants – unlike humanity – were benign and generous all at once. She would miss giving them her attention. She would miss their calming influence. And prospects for a new job – in a garden centre or anywhere – weren't good, not at her age. Which left time stretching out before her. A frightening thought, one she wasn't ready for.

'Billie! Billie!' Hayley rushed up to her. 'Russell just told me he's had to let you go.'

'Sacked, more like.'

'I think he was warning me.'

That sounded about right.

'I don't know what to do.'

'You do whatever feels right for you, Hayley.'

'Paying my rent at the moment.' The poor girl couldn't look at her.

Billie placed a hand on her shoulder. 'And that can be the right thing to do, too.'

The drive home was drenched in heat. She'd hoped to make Russell feel guilty, put a stop to the corrupt activity before it became a too-easy source of income. Without the thought of her watching him now, she feared more and more illegally harvested plants would arrive at the nursery; that the national parks and state forests would become just another wholesaler. And not only of grass trees. She imagined elkhorns and staghorns delivered out of hours; cycads and tree ferns; king and snake orchids. Plants ripped from the wild, their unique individuality not seen, the ecosystems they helped sustain of no consequence, the threats to their survival not considered. Profit and possession the only imperative. So trying to challenge Russell's – or that woman's – conscience equated to a fraction of a cent's worth of moralising. Practically worthless.

Billie had never felt like company more, but no one was home when she arrived. Daniel was at work. Angus, Carla and Scout were at a barbecue with friends. Instead of going inside she sat on the bottom step of her veranda, the timber still warm from the day. She slipped off her shoes and pressed her bare feet into the earth. Rested her head against the stair post, breathed in the familiar frangipani-scented air.

In that twilight time that marked day's end, fingers of memory touched Billie in welcome ways. Those fingers tapped a tune for Jess to dance to, which her daughter obliged. She twirled before her, bare-footed on the dry earth, the full skirt of her colourful dress flaring at her knees. Her daughter had always danced as though alone, arms aloft and awash like soft coral, even in a crowded room.

As the light faded, Billie went inside to the pine wardrobe in her bedroom. In the weeks after her daughter's death, she'd taken it upon herself to clear Jess's clothes from her wardrobe. Took them, unwashed, from the washing basket, too. The task had required a diamond-hard strength. Something she didn't believe Angus had at the time. He didn't thank her. Billie noticed he filled the empty space soon after by spreading his clothes out along the rail. She expected Carla had bunched them up again now, as Jess once had.

Jess loved colour. Would put coral with red, purple with aqua, green with magenta. There were no rules. Billie ran her fingers along Jess's clothes now, feeling the colourful linen, cotton and silk till they touched upon a favourite dress. She pressed her face into the fabric and breathed. After all this time, it still carried a hint of her daughter's scent.

There were so many memories attached to these items, memories built on the narrative of when and where they'd been worn. Celebrations. Holidays. Every days. The dress Jess had worn to her school formal. The boy who had taken her in his ill-fitting jacket. There were silky evening dresses and lacy tops, pretty party frocks, jeans, sarongs, a turquoise bridesmaid dress from a girlfriend's wedding. What was the girl's name? Billie tried to remember, chastised herself for not being able to.

She slipped the dress off its hanger, draped it over one arm and went into the kitchen. There she lay it across the table, took her sharpest scissors from a kitchen drawer and snipped a strip of cloth from its hem. With small, perfect stitches she started to craft by hand a small pouch. As she sewed, she felt her sadness ease. Inside the pouch, she placed a pinch of ash and several threads of Jess's hair taken from her hairbrush, which she kept in a box at the bottom of the wardrobe. The box held other items that belonged to her daughter, too: hair ties, clips and costume jewellery; lipsticks, loofahs and a nailfile.

That night in bed, Billie massaged the fabric, soft as a lamb's ear, between thumb and fingers. She felt the hair roll under her touch as she drifted off to sleep, a young woman of heartbreaking grace luminous in her mind.

5

THE IMAGE WAS POCKED WITH holes. There were corresponding puncture marks in the back of Daniel's bedroom door, too. A reminder of a once angry boy throwing darts at a face that might or might not bear any resemblance to his mother's killer.

He peered again at the computer-generated headshot. It could be any man with a composite of short brown hair, brown eyes, nose shaped no different from his father's, lips, chin and cheeks all unremarkable in their structure or size. And the one unique identifier – a silver cross in the right ear – was something the killer could make disappear in seconds. Daniel had no memory of giving the police details that allowed this image to be created. But he must have, as the only witness.

With half-closed eyes he shifted the page away from his face then brought it in close again. He did it several times more. Nothing. Not even a soft, unbiased gaze helped. All Daniel registered was the first telltale sparkle of lights flickering before his eyes that came before a migraine, which he ignored.

It was difficult to grasp that there were people out there who knew this man, probably even cared for him – as father, son, brother, lover, uncle, friend – but to the person whose life he'd changed the most, he was a total stranger.

When he was much younger, his grandmother had made him sit beside her at the kitchen table, the killer's headshot to one side, her scrapbook of faces to the other, encouraging him to shuffle different features in his mind, like a game of true crime *Guess Who?*

Deflated, and perhaps finally recognising the futility of it, she'd slumped back in her chair one day and said, 'If only the earth could tell us.'

This remark might have been the one that started his trips to the fig tree for a time as a boy. There, he'd press his ear to the ground where he and his mother had been found. But all his eavesdropping ever brought him was the tick and scratch of creatures in the soil. That same young boy had asked his father if he thought it possible that the earth could speak.

'Yeah, the earth tells us all sorts of things,' Angus said and Daniel grew excited.

'Really? It's true then.' But he'd then received a science lesson.

'Uh-huh. Through fossils and the work of geologists and archaeologists. They can tell us about past civilisations, extinctions, climate change, natural disasters. You name it.'

He still recalled his disappointment.

Now, Daniel recognised Billie's hopeful earth-listening as a desperate act of longing. Sometimes, though, he still held on to that childhood fantasy that the earth could talk and he imagined the perfect Identikit it would allow the police to construct. Or, better still, how it would lead them right to the killer, whispering – *Him, there* – as it guided them across the land.

He sometimes studied the headshot with hopes the blurred fragments that flickered through his mind would suddenly slow down, come together and find focus, allow him to fill in the gaps and create the exact likeness of the man. Maybe there was a scar he'd suddenly recall, or a hooked nose, a gold tooth or a blackened one; features that could have remained with the killer for the past sixteen years. Anything that might set him apart.

There was a price Daniel sometimes paid for his scrutiny of this image, and the sparkle of lights before his eyes was just the beginning of it. The lights manifested as small white explosions, as if he'd looked at the sun. They were three-dimensional. Each white burst in sharp focus. Daniel reached out with his hand and tried to pluck one from the air, it was like swiping through a hologram.

Now was the time he should take the medication that would stop the migraine, but he resisted. In half an hour a strip of blackness would fall down the centre of his visual field, slicing his bedroom in two, erasing a section of it altogether.

Daniel put the image of the man on his desk, went across to the window and closed the curtains. Not just because the light would hurt his eyes soon, but to provide the dark backdrop for the mosaic of visual hallucinations that were to come. He lay on his bed then and waited.

It was a kind of perversion, he supposed, to submit to the discomfort and pain, especially when there was a ready solution in the top drawer of his bedside table. But while the earth might not speak to him, maybe, just maybe, his unconscious would. So he let the migraine arrive and hoped it would bring something more than a sickening pain behind his eyes and the loss of half his bedroom.

A psychologist told him once that his migraines were more than a collection of symptoms. They had meaning, even if obliquely. Daniel thought of them as storms. Memory storms. In them, fragments of the past were tossed about like leaves in a gale. And when the gale calmed, and light was restored, those fragments were left scattered about in new and confusing ways. His memories had been jumbled so many times in this way that he no longer knew which ones to trust. Which were real? Which were imagined? Which were plagiarised, given to him by his grandmother and claimed as his own? And what about those blacked-out spaces? What was hidden there?

There was a knock on his bedroom door followed by it being flung wide open. Daniel grimaced, sensitive to the light that now streamed into his darkened room from the skylight in the hall.

'I'm gonna ask Dan!' His half-sister's shrill voice hurt almost as much as the light.

'Turn it down, Scout.'

She plonked herself on the edge of his bed. 'Feel here,' she said, and pushed her forehead towards him, fringe pulled off it.

'Do I have to?'

'Ye-es. You do.' Even Scout's vigorous nodding hurt.

Daniel lifted his hand and rested it on her brow. The skin felt cool and dry.

'Hot, isn't it?' Scout winked at him. One side of her face scrunched up. It was a work in progress, this getting a wink right, let alone subtle.

'No,' he said. 'It feels normal.'

'It is so hot. Feel it *properly*.' She took his hand in hers, rubbed the palm briskly, and then pressed it firmly against her forehead again, grinning. 'Feel it now? Hot as, eh?'

'Nup. Cool as.'

'What's the good of having a brother if they won't lie for you,' she grumbled. She got up from his bed and went to the bedroom door, bellowed, 'Mum! Daniel says I'm on fire, so I guess there's no holiday camp tomorrow!'

Carla either ignored his half-sister or she didn't hear, which was harder to believe. Scout shrugged and came back into Daniel's room. She sat in his desk chair and started spinning circles.

'Don't, Scout.' The movement made him nauseous.

She spun round once more and stopped to face his desk.

Daniel put his forearm across his eyes to block out the light. 'Can you leave, please. And shut the door behind you. I've got a headache.'

He could hear her rustling through the things on his desk. 'And keep out of my stuff, will you.'

'Dad says you shouldn't look at this.'

Daniel lifted his forearm to look at Scout. She was holding up the computer-generated image of the killer, his face pixelated by pinholes of light that shone through the back of the page from the open door.

He groaned softly and got up from his bed. He snatched the page from Scout and shoved it in the bottom drawer of his desk. 'Just go you little snoop.'

'Grum-py.'

Carla came to his bedroom door. 'Scout, will you please come and clear your stuff away as I asked.'

'I can't. I'm sick.'

'No, you're not.' Carla looked at Daniel. 'Now *you* look sick. Migraine?'

'Uh-huh.'

'Come on. Leave your brother alone. Can I get you anything?'

Daniel shook his head.

Carla looked at him concerned. 'Are you sure?'

He nodded and got back under the bed covers.

Carla came and rested her cool hand on his brow, gentler than he'd done with Scout. It made him feel like a child again, but he didn't mind. 'I'll look in on you later.'

'It's not fair,' Scout moaned as she walked with Carla from the room. 'There's *always* something wrong with his head and I can't even get a temperature.'

★

He moved quickly from table to table in the courtyard, a tower of empty glasses building against his chest. The migraine hangover from yesterday had gone. Now it was his turn to sell hangovers to others. Manoeuvring through the crowd took patience, which he mostly had, even in the stifling heat of the place. There was a lot of skin on show most nights. Girls glistened with glitter, men with sweat. T-shirts stuck to the guys' backs and their hair to their foreheads. Daniel was glad his t-shirt was black. The sweat didn't show. And neither did the lipstick or lurid spirits from the dirty glasses stacked against it. By the end of a night it was hard to pick the dominant smell on his clothes: alcohol, fragrance or sweat.

He moved among the drinkers mostly unseen. He wasn't recognised by regulars, because there weren't any, not of the solitary, old-timer parked down one end of the bar type, anyway. The Paradise Bar – nicknamed the Para – was a place that attracted backpackers. It was close to hostels and cheap accommodation, so was a united nations' carousel of revellers most nights. Cheap booze and food lured them. Live music as well. Word got around. A crowd attracted a bigger one. For now, this Valley bar was the place to be seen for budget travellers.

He was several hours into his shift now. The noise had escalated as the place filled and glasses emptied. The men's laughs were gunshot loud, explosive and dominant. The girls' shrill, like a whistle. People looked through him or around him. Or they added their glass to his tower like he was just another table. Some people were nice about it, said, *D'you mind, mate?* or *Thanks, pal.*

As he headed back towards the bar he got bumped from behind, was quick to steady the stack against his chest, stopped the lot from toppling forward and crashing to the floor. The bump came from two blokes squaring up to each other.

The steady pulse of the place stuttered like this sometimes, triggered by wrong words or actions, misunderstandings, spilt drinks or refused apologies.

'Settle down, mate. I'll get you another one,' one of the guys volunteered, and Daniel felt the pressure ease around him again.

He made it back to the bar without further incident, started stacking his tower of dirties into a glasswasher rack.

'The place is mad tonight,' Polly remarked over the noise.

Polly was the smallest but strongest woman Daniel knew. Their boss, Malcolm, called her Half-pint Polly, but she could carry six pints of beer on a tray and still keep a smile on her face. Her hair was long, straight and black, and her eyes so blue he wondered if she wore coloured contact lenses. In contrast, her skin was as pale as the head on the beers they poured. He could never figure out how she stayed fair through a Brisbane summer when most people were either tanned or sunburnt.

He'd asked her about it once. 'Because I only come out at night,' she'd said, and bared her neat white teeth at him, then laughed.

Practical and blunt, she was Daniel's best antidote to a life spent too much inside his own head. He could safely say they were mates – workmates anyway. Although sometimes she felt more like an older sister.

'You'd be crushed on the other side of this tonight, Poll.' Daniel indicated the bar top that separated them from the crowd.

'Like a cockroach?'

'I'd never call you a cockroach.'

'Right answer,' she said, and poked him playfully in the side with her elbow. She hauled a rack of clean glasses from the washer, put them on the bench to cool then added the next tray of dirties. 'Don't you wish sometimes you were on that side of the bar having fun and not this one cleaning up everyone else's slops?'

Daniel looked out across the sea of heads. Some were thrown back, mouths wide, laughing. Others nodded, talking. Some swayed, more because they were drunk than in time to the music. If he was out there among them, he'd be nursing a bottle of light beer he had no intention of drinking, probably on the outside of conversations because that was where he'd always placed himself. 'No, not really,' he said to Polly.

She shook her head. This time she tapped him gently on the chest with two fingers. 'I know there's someone else under that skin, Sunbeam.' Polly's nickname for him never felt like a putdown. 'And you're gonna let him out one day, and I hope I'm the first one to shake his hand.' She winked at him before moving further along the bar to serve.

Daniel wouldn't mind shaking this other guy's hand as well. Till then, he was *this* guy, the one in the black t-shirt who worked part-time lubricating the changes in other people.

Not that he always thought he was suited to this side of the bar either. Sometimes it was too much for him, having all of humanity's possibilities and fragilities on display in the one space like this. Playing host to its revellers, its players, its puppets. And perhaps even its killers for all he knew. The way temperaments and egos could pivot on a single sideways glance or a snubbing. How hearts were broken. Self-esteem and reputations, too. How some personalities – good and bad – grew when drunk. How it could be the place of dangerous opportunists, a hunting ground.

Some nights it rooted him, inert, to the spot, while before him the worst of human nature showed its grubby face. How else to explain that he could keep stacking glasses in the washing rack while on the other side of the bar a guy had a girl cornered by a wall against her will?

Daniel had clocked the pair on the way back to the bar. Glancing at them again now, he imagined the man enjoyed the feel of the girl's breasts pressed against his chest; enjoyed the sense of them being moulded to the shape of him as he leant in to kiss her. But the girl was agile and fast. She writhed out of the space between the man and the wall so that his face almost smacked up against the brickwork. As she approached the bar she adjusted her top, pulling it further down over her hips and shaking out her shoulders as though shrugging off a jacket. It brought a cat to mind, one whose fur had been rubbed opposite to its natural lie.

'Vodka, lime and lemonade please,' she said, not looking at him.

Daniel mixed the drink and pushed it across the bar towards her.

She paid but then stayed where she was, scowling into her glass as she took small sips from it.

The man beat an unsteady path towards the bar and pulled up beside the girl. Daniel heard her sigh.

'So where you come from it's okay for girls to tease blokes?'

'What do you mean *tease?*' she asked.

The girl had a European accent – from where, Daniel couldn't tell.

'It means you're in-sin-cere.'

Despite his lofty remark, the guy was a dumb drunk, incapable of reading the situation as one he'd created. From what Daniel had seen, the girl had been tolerant enough of him for a time, smiling benignly the way people do when a dodgy relative makes an out-of-line joke at a barbecue.

'I sin-cerely don't like you,' she said. 'Now, please, leave me alone.'

'Your loss, sweets,' he slurred. The guy was a loose pillar in front of Daniel, tipping a little one way, then over-correcting to the other. 'Give us another tequila shooter, mate.'

The girl looked at Daniel, part imploring, part disgusted, which might have been directed at him as much as it was the drunk.

Daniel took the bottle from the shelf anyway, poured the shot, which the guy downed in one.

The girl starred at Daniel in disbelief. 'Your mother must be proud,' she said, and pushed her unfinished drink aside before turning and walking out of the bar.

The drunk laughed. 'They always reckon takin' a crack at your mum is the worst kind of ball blow.' He pushed his glass towards Daniel again. 'Mine's a bitch, so people can say what they like about her.'

Daniel's boss moved up from the other end of the bar. 'I think you've had enough,' he said to the drunk, removing the shot glass.

'Now *you* know how to wound a bloke,' the guy said, tilting right then left as he melodramatically put his hands over his heart.

Malcolm caught the attention of the bouncer who came over and calmly escorted the man out. Daniel hoped the girl had got far enough away by now.

'I shouldn't be making these decisions for you, Dan. You've done the training.'

His boss was right; he should have called last drinks on the guy.

But the girl's remark? That *had* been a blow. How many battles was he expected to fight?

Polly pressed two fingers to Daniel's chest once more. 'He is in there,' she said. 'Let him breathe.'

She knew a little about his past but how did she know that sometimes it suffocated him?

6

Scout was wrong. Daniel didn't always have headaches. But when he did, they were cruel. So Carla had been surprised yesterday when she got home from work to see Daniel up and ready to head off to work. How had he managed to turn himself round so quickly? They usually wiped him out for at least twenty-four hours.

He looked pale and puffy-eyed but assured her he felt fine.

'Just a bit tired,' he said, and he looked it.

'The noise won't bother you?'

'Nah, not now the pain's gone.'

'You're made of tough stuff, Dan.' She'd squeezed his arm – this son, not-son – and felt the same concern for him as she would if it were Scout.

Angus said Daniel's first migraine had terrified him. At just seven, the same age as Scout now, Daniel was sitting on the sofa and started plucking at the air in front of him, said he could see weird lights. He'd looked at Angus, frantic. 'Dad? Where are you?' Angus scooped him up and rushed him off to the emergency department of the children's hospital.

Doctors' appointments followed, tests soon after – scans, blood tests – extra time with his therapist. It was his therapist, Angus told Carla, who got closest to what lay at the heart of these unpredictable events when she said, 'Maybe, for a brief time he needs to be unwell.' And she'd encouraged Angus to think of Daniel's migraines as an expression of the inexpressible.

Carla glanced over at Daniel now, on the other side of the kitchen table, and wondered what it was he'd needed to express that he felt he couldn't?

Friday lunch had become a thing. It was Carla's day off from the medical centre. Every second Monday she volunteered at the local Vinnies. With Daniel working so many evenings, Angus had complained of hardly ever seeing him. So Carla started to make the three of them a proper lunch on Fridays, nothing too fancy. Today, with fussy Scout away on a play date with a friend, it was salmon. Monday evenings were for Billie. She'd come into the house then, and all five would sit round the table. The ritual of these two meals was Carla's way of making something uniquely hers in this sometimes confused, sometimes awkward household.

Billie's letting go or sacking – who really knew? – from the garden centre last Sunday had made Monday's dinner a subdued affair. There was too much of the sound of cutlery on plates, too much of jaws and throats working. They were all indignant in their own way, except maybe Scout.

'I'll be able to see more of you on weekends now, Nan,' she'd soothed. It was the only time Carla saw Billie smile throughout the whole meal.

Carla had tried for optimism. 'You've earnt retirement, Billie. A chance to pursue other interests, eh?'

But that suggestion fell flat.

'And while I'm doing that, Russell will be pursuing *self-*interests, unchecked.' She went back to stabbing at the lasagne on her plate.

'People like that eventually come unstuck.'

'We both know that isn't true, Angus.' And Billie had held his gaze till he looked away.

Daniel said little. He glanced at Billie from time to time, unsure perhaps of what to say or afraid of what his grandmother might. Once Billie left, Daniel had looked at her and Angus and asked, 'What's she going to do with her time?'

Carla expected that he, like her, had similar concerns: if you give someone with existing fragilities more time to think about them, then what could they become?

'I honestly don't know, son.'

And neither did Carla.

Friday now, and Carla, perhaps selfishly, was pleased it was just the three of them.

'You got through last night okay?' Angus asked Daniel.

'Yeah. Just more knackered than usual by the end of it.'

'And fronting up to do it all again tonight.' Angus shook his head, smiling. 'Oh, to be young again.'

'I expect you're busy with backpackers, being summer?' Carla asked.

'Pretty much always busy with backpackers.'

'The Great Southern Migration,' Angus said.

'Expect it goes both ways … south and north.' Carla offered Daniel more salad. 'Your passport to adulthood … seemed like it when I travelled anyway. And if you hadn't *done* Oktoberfest or *done* Hogmanay, then you hadn't done it properly. Maybe *doing* the Paradise Bar has taken on equal status.'

'Sounds like she drank her way round Europe, mate.' Angus winked at Daniel.

'Hardly. Too cautious. I was more a castle kind of girl.'

'So your ambition for fancy digs started way back?'

The remark stung. 'I don't have ambitions for fancy digs, Angus. *Obviously.*' She cast her hands about to encompass the kitchen: the splits in its pine cupboard doors, the cracked floor tiles, the laminated countertops so old the grey had worn to white in places. She could add the kickboards swollen with water and rotting in the laundry, the wardrobes and doors that stuck, the off-square windows that didn't close properly.

The remark smarted so much she got up to demonstrate, took the face off a kitchen drawer, which had made it unusable months ago, and handed it to Angus. 'You're the carpenter, aren't you?'

Chagrined, Angus put the drawer face on the floor under his chair. 'Point taken. I'll fix it this afternoon.'

'Good.' Carla bit back the litany of other maintenance jobs she could give him.

They ate quietly for a time. Then Daniel suddenly broke the silence. 'I'd like to travel some day.'

'You should!' Carla couldn't think of a better thing for her stepson. Reset his life far from where he lived now so that when he came back to it he might view the place differently. Be his own man, not his grandmother's.

Daniel shrugged. 'I've been putting money away, but I'm not sure.'

'Why not?' Angus asked. 'Don't want to go on your own?'

Had Angus forgotten that his son rarely sought company?

'That wouldn't bother me.'

'You're young. No ties. What's stopping you then?'

'I dunno.' He wouldn't look at them, made a craft instead of separating flakes from his salmon.

Carla knew. 'Your nan would be fine, Dan.' She didn't believe it herself but hoped Daniel would.

Angus, twigging, agreed. 'Carla's right. Don't let Billie stop you.'

'Might be good for both of you,' Carla risked. 'A kind of recalibration.'

Carla noticed Angus's knife pause before he pressed it into the salmon's flesh, like a small gasp that didn't quite cross the lips. One of those moments when the air fleetingly left the room, and she was to blame.

'I'll think about it,' Daniel said, not looking at either of them. 'Don't say anything about it to Nan though.'

'Don't worry, we won't. But make sure you *do* think about it, son. And if you go, Carla can give you a list of her favourite castles to visit, no doubt all drawers still in working order.'

They all breathed normally again.

As Daniel was leaving for work, Carla walked out the front with him. She stopped at the gate. 'I had no idea you were even thinking about travelling, Dan. For what it's worth, I think it's a great idea.'

The more she thought about it, the more she reckoned it was just what he needed. A necessary severance of sorts. No Billie in his ear for a time. Give his endless pursuit of irretrievable memories a rest. And away from home, with no history to account for, maybe he'd make the kinds of friends he'd seemed unwilling or unable to make here. Of acquaintances he had a number. Boys he went to school with. Those he'd had sleepovers with from time to time. Kicked a footy with on weekends. But where was his *best* mate? The guy he mountain biked with, whose car he got lifts in or sat with at their kitchen table, the pair being fed a hangover-curing breakfast after this friend had slept the night on a pull-out mattress on his bedroom floor? Once Daniel finished school, the absence of this kind of friend became starkly obvious.

'Do you really think Nan would be okay about it?'

'She'd obviously miss you … we all would. But I'm sure she'd be excited for you, too.' The lie came easily. But Carla would tell him any number just to see him smile like that, with possibility. Optimism.

She risked taking it further, rested her hand on his arm. 'You don't honour your mother's life by living a lesser one, Dan. She'd hate that.'

'I don't even know who or what I'm meant to be honouring, though.'

She could tell him to take his guidance from her – Carla – and see who, what, she was to Scout, to him. Imagine the life she'd wish – encourage – for either one of them. It was the same. But he turned away before she even had a chance to form the words.

As she watched her stepson walk in the direction of the bus stop, Carla thought about how much alcohol he'd serve that night but how he never touched the stuff himself. She'd always imagined this wasn't because he didn't like the taste of it so much as not liking what it did to people. What it could do to him. Losing control of his emotions: anger or sadness. Risk showing a part of himself that he kept tightly under wraps. She supposed she should be pleased. They'd been spared the worry of a 2 am door knock. But sometimes she thought it might do him good to give in to the stereotype. Get drunk. Loosen up. Rely on a mate to get him safely home. Look sheepish the next morning. Be like other boys his age.

In no rush to head back inside the hot house, Carla lingered out the front, cast her eyes up and down their street. It was really quite lovely, especially at this time of year when the poinciana that grew at intervals along the nature strip were in flower. With other plants struggling to survive in the drought, these flamboyant trees were awash with fiery blooms and feathery green foliage. The trees were protected so the streetscape was unlikely to change. But in other ways it was a rapidly altering neighbourhood; it certainly had been in the eight years Carla had lived there.

This old part of Chapel Hill was quickly becoming new again. Once a street of large suburban blocks with older houses it was increasingly being subdivided, with two new homes filling one old block. These new, large dwellings optimised every scrap of land. The few original homes that remained – squat ones like theirs – were bullied by the shadows of these giants. Their yard overlooked from up high. From what she could tell, theirs was one of the largest blocks remaining in the street, but was also the worst house. A tired, unfashionable old girl, no longer able to hide her blemishes.

They'd played with the idea of selling. Or Carla had anyway. Pillow talk, most of it initiated by her, weighing up the pros and cons. She used to think the prospect of packing up two houses and a workshop was what killed these conversations. A task just too big to contemplate. Now though, she reckoned that was the least of it. Packing up the unseen was the real chore. All those things embedded in the word *home*. Memories and moments. The rhythms of days long past that still resonated in rooms as though a tangible possession. The interplay between a person lost and the place where they once lived. These were the things that couldn't be boxed and taken with them when they left. So to go without them equated to abandonment. Something, or rather *someone*, loved but left behind.

Carla would turn away, frustrated after these conversations with Angus because they always ended with him saying the same thing: *What about Billie?* She was yet to reply: *What about us?*

Castles it seemed, even a humble one, were destined to remain only in her past.

7

THAT SHE WAS EVEN HERE reminded Billie of her new status: unemployed. In the shopping centre – Indro to locals, Hell to Billie – the light was harsh and unrelentingly white. People trapped inside the place didn't – couldn't – possibly know if it was day or night outside, winter or summer. Which was part of the purpose she supposed: forced people to lose their sense of what was real and what wasn't so they might better submit to the impulse of a whim.

The January *Sale* signs were still up, even though it was near the end of the month. Bargain hunters jostled her on the escalators. She had to weave between people as she walked the centre's long corridors or stop suddenly if someone in front of her did. Swarms of chatty, holiday-bedazzled teenagers hurt her ears. The clunk and clomp of hard soles, the slap of thongs. Beeps and buzzes from scanners and EFTPOS machines. Collectively, the place amassed an assault on her senses that made her want to flee.

So disorientating was the place that Billie was no longer sure which level she was on or even why she was there. The need to pay a bill sprang to mind. And was it new underwear she needed?

What could possibly have possessed her to think this was the best place to come for either.

She needed some calm. Sought out a coffee shop. A chatty girl took her order for a pot of English breakfast tea and a slice of lemon tart. Billie took the number the girl pushed across the counter to her and found a seat near the back, less exposed to the thoroughfare of human traffic rushing past its doors. Someone had left a tabloid newspaper on the table. Brisbane's only one. Not one she'd usually bother with, but she picked it up anyway. Any distraction would be good. Or so she thought.

The impoverished, addicted or homeless didn't warrant much ink. That's certainly what Billie had deducted from the murder headlines she'd studied over the years. And neither did sex workers, it seemed. *Deranged knifeman slits throat of sex worker.*

Jess had remained news for weeks after her murder, her slightly crooked front teeth smiling at readers from newspaper pages again and again. Billie knew that she would have hated the attention.

This girl – Susannah, which took Billie three paragraphs to learn – had neat teeth. She had long brown hair like Jess, which she wore loose in the photograph. Jess had worn hers mostly tied back.

Billie scanned the headline again, imagined this murdered girl now labelled by her occupation, no longer the daughter–sister–friend of others, until eventually no one would even remember her name, if they ever learnt it to begin with.

I'll remember you, Susannah.

Disgusted, Billie tossed the paper onto the table beside hers, headline facedown. She hated the word *slit*. It made her think of fish markets and abattoirs and the gore enacted in each. The word's use in this context felt unwarranted. A gratuitous obscenity.

A headline about Jess easily came to mind. Billie had learnt most by heart. *Toddler witnesses mother's stabbing.* Billie was no journalist, but she thought there was a restraint to it, respectability even. Not so the sex worker's. And with Jess's, the crime read as having been committed against two people: a mother and her child. But even her daughter's headline hadn't gone far enough to Billie's mind.

Humanity shamed by mother's stabbing.

That's what it should have said.

A middle-aged woman and what could only be her daughter took their seats at the table beside Billie's. They shared the same blonde bobs, raised eyebrows as though posing a question and each took care with their lip liner. Wisps of blonde hair peeked also from the top edge of a grey baby sling tied across the younger woman's chest. The daughter looked tired but her voice sounded upbeat as she chatted to her mother. They lifted their chairs and pulled them out quietly from the table, something only a new mother would think to do. The younger woman had to sit back from the table's edge to make room for the infant. And once her coffee came – a long black – she drank it with her head turned away from the cocooned child, her free hand pressed to the silent bulge.

'Did she sleep through?'

She. Three generations. A special trinity.

'Till about four.'

'An improvement then.'

'For one night anyway.'

The older woman took a sip from her latte, fingertips of both hands pressed into the white serviette fixed round the glass. When she took it away from her mouth there was a Rorschach smudge of red on its rim. She placed the glass back on its saucer and opened the newspaper.

Billie watched as the woman scanned the print alongside the girl's image.

'What do these girls expect when they play in a snake pit?'

The daughter leant in over her baby's head, coffee held out to one side, to better see the news piece. 'What she got, I suppose.'

She turned to take another sip of her coffee. The two women were silent for a time. Each stared at the newspaper, thinking what, Billie couldn't imagine.

'She's pretty for a prozzie,' the older woman said. She laughed like she knew what she said was wrong-minded. 'Probably not a recent picture.' She folded the paper in half again. The dead girl's image looking up at Billie.

'Would you mind passing that to me?' Billie indicated to the newspaper.

With the front page flat on the table before her, she took a black pen from her bag, set to work. Once she was finished the old headline was blacked out, the new one read: *Daughter murdered by violent man.*

She tossed the newspaper back on their table. 'How does it make you feel now?'

The older woman flinched as it landed. She looked at Billie's handiwork and threw it down the line to the next empty table in the café, without looking up.

Billie imagined the girl's image being shunted from table to table like this until eventually the café closed for the day, whereupon it would end up in a bin, her neat teeth coffee stained, her young skin creased, folded, judged and finally abandoned.

'You shouldn't judge,' Billie said. 'There's no telling what's in your future.' She made a conscious effort not to look at the silky head of the baby.

The older woman glared at Billie, muttered, 'How rude,' then turned back to her daughter.

Billie's tea tasted bitter, the lemon tart even more so. She hacked at the tart's hard crust with her fork. 'Just a girl living the best she could,' she mumbled.

The two women glanced her way from time to time. The older raised her eyebrows even higher at the younger as if to say, *What's her problem?*

Billie's problem was that she was worn out by caring, worn out by other people not. Sometimes, cruelly, unimaginably, she believed every family should be touched by violence. How else to understand the force of it, the way it trickled down and defined your every thought about the world and the people in it?

'She could have been yours.' And this time Billie did look at the baby.

Its young mother reeled back, arms instinctively coming round to protect her child. The baby startled, began to mewl. The older woman stood to confront Billie. 'I really don't think—'

Billie cut her off. 'What? That you should *care*?'

By now the chat in the café had stopped, all eyes on Billie and the other woman as they squared off against each another.

'She's not *mine* to care about.'

'She's everyone's to care about.'

Billie took up her bag. Awkward looks followed her out of the café, whisper muscles working.

Still disorientated, she boarded an escalator, not sure where she was going, only knowing she had to escape that level, if not the whole damn place.

The escalator was crowded. Billie found a welcome distraction in the bulging stomach of the girl behind her. She was tempted to lean gently against the girl, allow the baby's feet to tap at her spine, send out its Morse code message announcing its existence. That would calm her, to feel how life continued.

Billie turned to face the girl, prevented her from walking away, sought to make good her time there. 'I remember being pregnant with my daughter like it was only yesterday,' she said.

The girl smiled politely, but the edges of her mouth were wary. The girl skirted round her and hastened off. Billie admired the swish of her long glossy ponytail, the sway of her broad birthing hips. She couldn't help but reach a hand out after the girl, as though pulled by a magnetic charge.

The lights felt suddenly brighter, the sounds more shrill. She'd never felt more removed from humanity or so abraded by it. She needed to sit, and scouting around she found a bench a little further along. She landed heavily on it; a distinct *plop* sound as her buttocks met wood.

How, Billie wondered, as she pressed her hands into the bench to give herself leverage to stay upright, does a tree hold itself tall for so long? What determination it must require. What perseverance. How easy it would be when times were hard to let the cells dry up, crumble in on themselves, bow out and trust, instead, that the soil will treat you well, give you a new and noble purpose.

To be a whole feeling thing was the greatest challenge about living. To live in fragments would surely be easier. That's what the parents of the missing boy must be feeling now, too. It was disheartening how the news of the boy's disappearance was being reported. Nearly two weeks had passed and they were still showing the same footage as they did on day one. Police, SES workers, volunteers, all scouring the same ground as though there was nowhere else in the national park for them to look. Did they think people wouldn't notice it was a grab played on repeat?

Why not show those co-opted into this tragedy where they were really looking? Billie wanted the reporting to be honest. She wanted to see the ravines and the creek beds. She wanted to see the thick, lacerating scrub. The ankle-turning terrain. Maybe there were crevasses or caves or cliffs. If so, she wanted to see those, too. Because surely there was a pact between reporter and viewer that in reporting the boy's disappearance over and over they hoped to elicit a response of collective national grief. So why not give the nation the truth? Stop this regurgitation of the first day like it was a new day. She, and everyone else, trapped in that moment of when there was still hope, breaths held.

The empty sickness his parents – Susannah's parents, too – must be feeling. The exhaustion. How they'd try to snatch some sleep (but even then, only when persuaded) and when they did, how they'd be suddenly thrust awake by their current reality, hearts racing like they were trying to run from it. She knew something of the long periods of numbness they'd be feeling, too. Body and mind wrapped in wool, something outsiders might think a blessing, a way of dulling the fear or anger or pain that would be eating away at them. But Billie knew this numbness for what it really was: a place where guilt found somewhere soft to rest its spiteful head and lend unreasonable weight to split-second choices. Numbness would open the way for the boy's parents to question their deservedness of having a child. Their culpability in losing one. Too much thought given to those inattentive minutes spent fumbling with a biscuit packet or cleaning their sunglasses or making a coffee. Minutes that would normally account for nothing but were suddenly crucial because during them your child went missing. That was the kind of thinking numbness allowed.

It pained Billie to recall these same feelings now. She'd spent the years since Jess's death trying to quash them, imagining choices that saved people, not killed them; brought people joy not hardship. The kind of choices that brought her Jess.

A memory, there in the twilight of so many others but this one suddenly bright. Throughout her life, there had been strangers with whom she had naturally fallen into step. Not because their pace matched hers or they encouraged or manipulated it so that it would. But because of a shared moment in place or time that allowed people to leap over the often slow and awkward paths of first introductions.

A baby swallow had been the shared moment for Billie and Jess's father. She'd found the poor, weak nestling, yellow beak open and gasping, on the grass under a picnic shelter. It had fallen from a mud nest in the corner of one of the shelter's eaves. The frantic calls from the bird's parents sounded from the structure's roof.

Billie was five foot six, about four inches shorter than she needed to be to return the baby bird to its nest. She tried hard to find those extra inches, stood on her tiptoes on the shelter's seat, bristle-feathered bird cupped carefully in one hand as she tried to reach the nest. She still recalled the tiny piston pulse of its heart against her palm. But it was no good.

She called the young man over when she saw him coming along the path. Fortunately, he had the height Billie lacked and easily deposited the bird back in the nest with its two siblings. It was after this that they fell in step with one another and eventually bed.

Her daughter was the product of a fling, but that had never bothered Billie.

Billie thought *fling* an uncharitable word. *Fling that rubbish in the bin*, people said, or *Fling it over here*, as though the thing flung was of little value.

The word's use in relation to her having sex with a man she barely knew was equally uncharitable. It suggested that something was taken or given without care or kindness.

Jess's father had been kind. Tender as well. But he had also been an unsuitable mate. He was attentive enough, but Billie sensed someone looking for the easy out. A lazy man potentially. Someone who'd be happy to let her carry more than half of life's load.

They only had sex twice; the second time gave her Jess. Then she'd let him go. When she found out she was pregnant she decided if she risked carrying more than her fair share with him, then she might as well carry it all on her own. Never gave him the chance to prove her wrong. Never gave him the chance to know he was a father.

Billie's mother eventually stopped crying and her father started to look her in the eye again, their shame shelved in some place where they no longer had to examine it. The harmless innocence of a newborn proved a great remedy at any rate.

Billie had thought more about this man after Jess's death than she had in the twenty-five years of her life. How he wouldn't have known when he read the headlines that he was reading about his own child. In a way that alone justified her choices. All that heartache she'd saved him.

'Billie. Fancy seeing you here.'

Billie jolted back into the present. 'Namita! What a lovely surprise!' Billie shuffled over on her seat to allow the woman to sit.

Namita was the only one of Jess's friends who still stayed in touch. She and Jess had worked together. Primary school teachers. A confident woman. Not afraid to share a room with the dead. She still visited from time to time, was friends with Angus, and allowed Billie – because it was a kind of permission the grieving sought – to talk about her daughter. Namita's visits were less frequent these days, so maybe they took their toll.

'It's good to see a familiar face ... among all this.' Billie raised both hands to encompass the shopping centre.

Namita laughed. 'I'm only here because I need to pick up some things before school starts back next week.'

'At least you can remember *why* you're here.'

'I thought you'd be at work?'

'Two weeks ago I would have been. Not anymore.'

Billie explained to Namita what had happened at the garden centre. Her sudden unemployment. 'It's going to sound silly, but I miss the plants.'

'That's because you care about *all* things, Billie, not just people.'

'Maybe I care too much.'

'Is that possible?'

Billie didn't know anymore. Maybe if she cared less, she'd still have a job, wouldn't let snooty, self-righteous women bother her. And the missing boy wouldn't be front of mind. She asked Namita if the boy was on hers.

'Expect it's playing on the minds of most people. Every parent's fear made real.' Namita quickly apologised. 'Sorry. That was insensitive. You know that better than anybody.'

Billie dismissed the apology with her hand. 'At least you acknowledge it. So, school starts back next week?'

'Yes … unfortunately.'

'Come on.' Billie gently nudged Namita. 'You know you love it.'

Some people were born to teach. Billie believed Jess was one of those people. Namita too. Something of a naïveté, her daughter didn't dictate what should be learnt. Delivered her lessons as wonder through small moments of shared discovery: a stone turned to its moist underside, the spore-speckled surface of a fern, Fibonacci sequences found in nature, even the content of scat. All of it raw material to fertilise a young, eager mind. Jess approached nothing with preconceptions of what she might find. That was Billie's joy of watching her with her grandson, her daughter teaching him the way Billie had taught her: that they were on the adventure together. And then they weren't. She often wondered: had her daughter not left herself so open to the unexpected, might she have survived?

And what could Daniel be now had he remained under his mother's influence? Certainly not serving alcohol in a bar. Billie had tried to fill her daughter's shoes, as had Angus, but they lacked something. Maybe their own wonder had been robbed from them, made them incapable of producing it in others. Or maybe Jess was unique in this regard. A natural.

'Jess loved teaching, too. Couldn't get enough of those kids.' Billie smiled at the memory. She'd always imagined Jess would have had a large family, that Daniel might be the first of three or four children.

'And she was very good at it,' Namita said. 'More patient than me. Never heard her raise her voice in anger once.'

Maybe she got that from the man Billie hadn't trusted to pull his weight? Because she hadn't got it from Billie. She could raise her voice. Was in part why she'd lost her job.

Jess sometimes asked about this man, as any single-parent child would, Billie expected.

'I can't tell you much,' Billie would tell her.

Not even a surname.

'Light brown hair. Wavy, like yours. Brown eyes.'

'Brown hair and eyes? Is that it?' Jess looked at her like she was holding something back.

Then once, Billie searched her memory for more, came to the truth of why there was so little. 'He didn't take a stand about anything ... not politically or socially. Was neither thinker nor doer. I couldn't imagine loving a man like that.'

'Did you even *want* to sleep with him?'

The subtext of the question suddenly dawned on Billie. 'Oh yes. You weren't born of coercion or violence, Jess.' This had appeased her daughter.

If Billie were honest, her learning so little about this man had probably been intentional. She'd wanted Jess all to herself. The only parent to press their face into her hair. Wipe the tears. Assuage the hurts. Shape and share the patterns of her life. Did this brand her as selfish? She'd asked Jess once. It had taken her daughter a while to answer. Billie remembered feeling nervous, waiting for her response. Fearful of how she would be judged. Because was she enough? Had Jess longed for two parents to shape her life? Had she unfairly denied her daughter this?

'No, not selfish,' Jess eventually said.

Billie remembered the quickening of her relief.

Then how doubt soon followed, when Jess added, 'Resolute maybe.'

Billie looked at Namita now. 'She was the least angry person I've ever known. And the least selfish. Neither quality I think she got from me.'

Which only raised a further question: Could an angrier, more selfish Jess have saved herself?

8

IT WAS A DEFINING MOMENT, one Carla would rather not have had occur, but it proved significant. Mainly for the pattern it presented, one Angus could no longer ignore.

His last injury, the one on his shin, was barely scabbed over enough to raise even Scout's interest if it were on her own leg, before another one occurred.

This time Angus came to Carla at her work. More for the attention of one of the doctors in the practice, than for hers.

'I patched it up myself as best I could.' He held up his right hand to show her a bulky combination of what looked like tissues under a bandage too large for the second and third fingers it was roughly wrapped around. 'Not bad, eh?' He looked pleased but he also looked in pain: pale, sweaty, hands shaking a little.

'Oh, Angus.' Carla came out from behind the reception counter and led him into a treatment room. There, she settled him on the bed, eased a pillow under his head and began unwinding the bandage from his damaged hand. 'How did you get here?'

'Drove.'

She shook her head. 'On adrenalin, not common sense.' Easing the last of the bloodied tissues from round the two fingers, she revealed a middle finger with a macerated tip and blackened nail beds to it and the index finger. 'Jesus, Angus. This is well above my pay scale.'

She left him then with the practice nurse to clean the wound, asked one of the doctors to examine him, and took him next door for the requested X-ray, which fortunately showed there were no fractures.

'No breaks *this* time,' she said to him afterwards.

When she left work early to take him home, his middle finger dressed, the blood drained from both nail beds and a course of antibiotics gripped in his good hand, she started the conversation he must have known was coming. 'Angus—'

'I know what you're going to say.' He looked out the window. 'Not now. Okay? Let's just get home.'

It wouldn't come up again till two days later. They were in their en suite getting ready to go out. Angus had managed a one-handed shower, the injured one held above his head to keep the dressing dry.

'It's driving me nuts not being able to do things.'

'Hasn't kept you out of that shed.'

'Not getting the things done I need to though. I'd hoped to have made a start on the next table by now.'

They were already running late to meet their friends, but a part of her, that place where she knew things could be better if only Angus had the will to make it so, urged her on.

'The inconvenience of these unfortunate *accidents*, eh?'

'It was an accident.'

'No it wasn't. It was a man making do. Taking a calculated risk that didn't work out.'

'The wedge slipped, Carla.'

'A wedge you shouldn't have been using in the first place. You and Daniel can barely lift those slabs of wood, yet you try some half-arsed trick to do it on your own. You needed a bloody forklift, not a wedge!'

Carla stopped messing with her make-up, took the towel from Angus, dried his back where he was struggling. Once done, she placed her hand on his shoulder and gently turned him to face her. 'There *are* other options, Angus.'

He stood before her, naked in body and emotion, looking trapped.

'Yeah, I know.' He took the towel from her, gingerly secured it round his waist.

'So?' She raised her open palms to him.

'So, what?'

'So let's talk about those options.'

'Do we have to do that now?'

'If not now, when? Because now's the time to sell, Angus. The market's strong. Houses round here are going for ridiculous amounts of money.'

Real estate was something of a hobby for her. Angus called it an obsession. She liked predicting the areas she thought were going to take off. Finding worst house–best street scenarios – situations like theirs – and following through with what happened after they'd sold. Her friend Fran, who worked in real estate, fed Carla sales data so she knew how much every house in their street had sold for in the past ten years. She kept it all in a spreadsheet.

'With the money we'd get for this, we could afford a really nice house on a smaller block. New, no maintenance. And you could set up your business in an industrial estate somewhere. Maybe even grow it enough to take on an apprentice like you've always hoped to. Get yourself a forklift.'

'I know, I know.'

'So if you know, why don't you do it?'

'You know why.'

'Billie.'

'Yes. Billie.'

'But what about *you*, Angus? What do *you* need to do?'

Of this there could be no question. He'd been trying to make a living from a backyard shed in an increasingly gentrified suburb. But what to do about Billie choked every conversation they'd ever had about solving the problem. Billie's contribution to the original purchase had been small. Carla had contributed more, money she'd saved to eventually put towards her own place. When she married Angus, she put it towards his mortgage. But it was like the land was Billie's and no one else's. All because her daughter once lived – walked – here. To Billie's mind, Jess's footprints were still impressed into the ground. It was like their backyard was Winton or the Dampier Peninsula, and Jess's memory like dinosaur prints that needed preserving. All Carla saw when she stood in the backyard was dead grass, sinking foundations and a great swathe of bush that made their place a shortcut for snakes.

'You can't do the kind of work you want or need to do in that shed.' Which was to make large, more lucrative, bespoke pieces.

'I can make do a bit longer.'

Carla looked briefly to the black mould spots on the ceiling. 'But for how much longer, Angus?'

Would enough time ever pass for Billie to let go?

'You can't keep making do. Every day you do, you risk another injury. Have you got to lose a whole hand before you do something about it?'

He wouldn't look at her.

'As for the neighbours, I've got no idea why they don't complain about the noise any more than they already do.'

'Because I keep the workshop door closed as much as I can.'

'Well, let's hope I don't miss hearing you scream for help when you need it.' She put her foot on the pedal of the rubbish bin and lifted the lid, tossed a tissue inside, but hadn't meant for the lid to then drop closed quite so loudly.

Angus reached for her. 'Come here,' he said and pulled her in. 'I'm sorry, but—'

'I know. It's complicated.' She eased into him, rested her head on his still damp chest, smelt the *Dove* soap he'd just washed with. Sometimes it was easy to forget his past, to not feel frustrated by the inertia it caused, and she had to check herself.

They stood like that for a while, Angus stroking her back with his good hand. 'Maybe we could look into it,' he said. 'Talk to Fran on the quiet. Get her to come round and do a valuation.'

This was the furthest they'd ever come on the topic.

She looked up at him and smiled. 'I already have.'

'And?'

'Honestly Angus, there's no better time to cash in.'

There was a crash just outside the open bathroom door then Scout appeared sprawled on the bedroom carpet in front of them.

'What are you up to, squirt?'

'I fell off Mum's shoes.'

'And what are you doing in my shoes?'

'Playing dress-up.'

Scout rose, teetering precariously in a pair of black high-heeled sandals Carla was about to put on. She also had her long amber necklace round her neck that hung almost to her knees, and a black handbag slung across one shoulder.

'You know I don't like you playing with my jewellery. You could have hooked your leg in that and broken the string. Take it off.'

Scout, chastened, lifted the necklace from round her neck and placed it carefully on their bed.

'Shoes and bag too, then run along.'

Carla finished the last touches to her make-up, despairing at her daughter's capacity to turn up in places she shouldn't and at the most inopportune times.

*

They arrived at the restaurant twenty-five minutes late. Angus opened the door for Carla to enter first.

'That's not chivalry,' she teased. 'That's leaving me to apologise.'

He winked at her, and with his good arm put a hand to her back and steered her towards the two other couples already sitting at the table.

'Five more minutes and your complimentary bread rolls were history.'

'Sorry. Angus's fault. Can't get him away from the glue.'

They took their places at the table, the three women at one end, the men at the other, ordered drinks, and their lateness was quickly forgiven.

Conversation immediately turned to Angus.

'What have you done to yourself, mate?' Viraj indicated to Angus's hand.

'Pranged it a bit.'

'How'd you do it?' Namita asked.

'Squashed it under a slab of timber.'

'He was lucky. This time.' Carla held Angus's gaze for a time across the table, his earlier commitment sitting in the space between them. He smiled at her and she relaxed.

The wine went down well after that. Carla's mood buoyed by it as much as her sense of hope. A new home might yet be a reality. A place less laden by subsidence and history. Somewhere that was truly hers and not shared with the past.

Fran leant in. 'Spill,' she said.

Carla looked at her friend confused. 'Spill what?'

'Whatever's giving you that gloating look.'

'I'm not gloating.'

'Oh, yes you are.'

Carla glanced at the others around the table; saw they were distracted by their own conversations. She leant in towards Fran. 'I think he's finally coming round,' she said quietly. 'I got past *no* to *maybe* earlier. Then before I knew it he said to get you round for a valuation. That's why we were late. We got caught up talking about it.'

Fran beamed at her. Carla knew it wasn't because her friend thought there was a sale in it for her, but because she knew how much Carla wanted this. They went way back, her and Fran. Pre-Angus. Back when 3 am was an early night and Carla could handle six tequila shooters.

'I can have a *For Sale* sign up by the end of next week.'

'There's still Billie.'

'Ah, yes. The Billie boulder.'

'Fran-ces,' Carla gently scolded, but thanks to the wine she couldn't sustain it.

'What are you two giggling about?' Namita turned to Carla and Fran.

Namita was Angus's friend. Had been Jess's, too. Daniel's godmother. Namita's daughter, the same age as Daniel, no longer had one.

'Angus was a mess,' Namita confided to her once.

Carla and Angus were new to the relationship. She was learning to love him, but was also frightened of doing so.

'We became close,' Namita added.

Aside from the practical support of others – cooking, cleaning, helping care for Daniel – Angus had told Carla that ultimately he had to find the strength in himself to get through it. Not because other people were of no help – they were, he said, in immeasurable ways – but because he alone had to turn up every minute of every day, for months and months, years and years, and face what happened.

'The props had to come down eventually,' he told her. 'I had to trust in myself to stand on my own two feet again, for Daniel's sake as much as anything.'

Ultimately, grief for Angus was a private matter, a passive and enduring void – a going *in* – that no one else could enter or fill, Namita included, despite her best efforts to do so. Billie's grief was outward facing. Every memory a story. Every story worth telling. Still was.

Namita still visited Billie. Billie remarked to Carla once that Namita always knew what to say. Carla supposed this meant she knew how to listen. Their longstanding relationship was enough to remind Carla that the house where she now lived, and those who occupied it, had known different conversations and intimacies. Sometimes she wondered if it was the remnants of these she imagined hearing echo off its walls, lifting from its carpets. Reminding her she'd come *after*.

'They're selling,' Fran said to Namita. 'Isn't that exciting?'

Carla nudged Fran under the table.

'Eventually selling, I mean.'

'Nothing's decided yet.' Carla glanced towards Angus at the other end of the table. He was talking with his hands, even the injured one, which meant he was wholly into something with Viraj and Lewis so hadn't heard Fran. 'Just playing with the idea really.'

'Oh,' Namita said, then quickly rearranged her face into a smile. 'Lovely.'

'Perfect time to play.' Fran laughed and squeezed Carla's arm.

'Yes. Timing's everything.' Namita wouldn't look at them.

Carla felt judged. Someone who'd arrived late to something after all the hard work had been done, there to reap the benefits.

The relaxed glow brought on by the wine dulled after that. Carla felt unsettled. What if Namita called in on Billie and mentioned it? Would she do that? Hadn't she presented herself as someone who helped others through bad news, not delivered it to them? But what if she assumed they'd already spoken to Billie about it and raised it with her in a roundabout way, even if just enough to make Billie think she'd come to the possibility all on her own?

When Namita got up to go to the toilet, Carla made the excuse she needed to go, too. But, once alone with the other woman in the bathroom, she felt awkward.

'That talk earlier about selling,' Carla ventured at the hand basins.

Namita looked at Carla in the mirror. 'Uh-huh.'

'It's not a given yet, so I'd rather you not mention it to anyone, especially Billie.'

'Of course.' Namita pulled two squares of paper towel from the dispenser and started to dry her hands. 'I'll admit though, it took me by surprise.'

'Why?'

Namita shrugged and tossed the paper in the bin. 'I guess because Angus hasn't mentioned it. And ... well ... because of Billie.'

'You think staying frozen in time is good for her?'

'No, but I think going gently on her is. And especially so now, with her losing her job.'

'I've been gentle with her for eight years, Namita. Angus for sixteen ... more ... if you count before ...' Suddenly, it all felt too personal. She didn't owe Namita an explanation. And neither did she need her approval.

The nine-year age difference between the two women seemed vast in that moment, made Carla feel naïve, not up to the complexities of the relationships around her. It was as though Namita believed she knew Angus better than Carla did, knew what was better *for* him, a thought that rose as bitter as bile. Was it possible she was jealous of this woman because she had held her husband when he cried? Carla shook her head, tried to dislodge the shame of such a thought.

'Billie and Jess were more than mother and daughter, Carla. They were like one person born on different timelines. They'd finish each other's sentences. One would get something for the other before they even knew they needed it. Was it telepathy? Symbiosis? I don't know. All I know is it was rare and special and losing Jess has left Billie feeling like half a person. And the half that remains is kept going by the memories carried in the place where Jess lived.'

Namita made to leave but Carla held her gaze in the mirror. 'But while she keeps immortalising her daughter she's never going to move on … find her whole self.'

'Why should she have to do that?'

'So my family can. So *Dan* can.'

That knocked some of the certainty out of Namita, because she looked away.

Emboldened, Carla continued. 'This is where we immortalise the dead, Namita.' She patted her chest with her hand. 'Not here,' she said, tapping her shoe on the tiled floor.

'That's because you're nothing like Billie.' Namita left the bathroom then, leaving Carla to believe she thought her nothing like Jess either.

9

W<small>HEN</small> D<small>ANIEL</small> <small>SAW</small> <small>HIS</small> <small>GRANDMOTHER</small> come through the gate in the back fence, he knew she'd been to the tree. It was the slow and even way she moved that gave it away, as though contentment was a cloud and she was floating on it.

He looked along the bare path pressed into the parched earth that connected the main house to Billie's small one. His grandmother told him once that this path was like a bridge that connected the past and the present. A bridge that Billie believed she literally crossed between her life and Jess's whenever she walked it, barefoot as often as not.

'My feet tingle sometimes, almost like she's tickling them.'

She had looked so pleased with this idea, so *contented*, that Daniel hadn't had the heart to challenge her on how implausible it sounded.

'Look, there's Nan,' Scout said over the Uno cards in her hand.

Daniel's half-sister waved at Billie from the patio where they were playing the game. But Billie didn't notice them as she crossed the yard.

'Na—'

Daniel put a finger to Scout's lips. 'Shh,' he said. 'Leave her.' Her thoughts would be gentle for a time and it was best to allow her the kindness of them.

Scout nodded her understanding so enthusiastically that her purple hair band slipped off her head and onto her nose. Daniel pushed it up onto her head again.

Billie, oblivious to them on the back patio of the main house, walked up the steps to the front door of her home and disappeared inside. Daniel pictured her placing her daypack in a cupboard at the end of the hallway. How the cleaning equipment inside would clatter as she dropped it.

'Your turn,' Scout said, then mumbled something that could have been, 'Uno.'

'Louder you little cheat.'

'*U-no!*'

'Better.'

Scout won the game with her next turn anyway and Daniel re-shuffled the pack. 'Last game,' he said, dealing each a new hand. 'You can go and do something else then till Carla and Dad get home.'

'Not fair!'

'Whinge and I'll put the cards away now.'

'Bully.'

He side-eyed her while he dealt the cards but she wouldn't look at him, exaggerated the organising of her cards in her hand instead. They both looked up when they heard Billie's front screen door slap shut. She held a tray in her hands and looked to one side of it to her bare feet as she negotiated her way down the front steps of her granny flat. Tendons stood out at the backs of her knees and in her feet and ankles from all her walking. They stood out in her elbows and shoulders from all her cleaning. In her neck from always leading with her head, thinking, muttering, remembering. If Daniel's mother were still alive, she might tell him that his grandmother had always been like this. That her strange land-mindedness, was something Jess had witnessed in her mother as a child, but writ large now by the personal. Many things about their lives had been changed, rerouted in unforeseeable ways. Whether or not the grandmother he had now was the one he was always going to have was just another of the many unknowns.

'Hey, Nan! Wanna play cards?'

'Cards *and* cake! How about that?' Billie headed towards them, tray indicating the cake part. 'And cordial,' she added, the dirt under her nails unmissable as she placed the tray on the table.

'You're the best,' Scout said, taking a slice of chocolate cake – the largest – from a plate on the tray.

A third hand was dealt and they settled into a game.

'What did you do in the bush today, Nan?' Scout indicated behind her, to Billie's sanctuary.

'Just wandered,' Billie said. 'Aimfully.'

Was that even possible? For his grandmother it probably was.

'Did you hear any stories?'

To Scout, his grandmother was a nymph, the friend and confidante of fairies and elves. The intermediary between a child's boring reality and the exciting fantasy world they wished for. She'd absorbed Billie's vocabulary into her own as she'd learnt to speak. Nobody corrected her. Daniel figured Carla and his father hadn't wanted to draw attention to it. That way nothing needed to be explained.

'Always, sweetheart.'

Scout beamed at Billie.

Daniel liked that Scout treated his grandmother as though she was her real one. Was pleased she wasn't afraid of, or for, Billie the way Daniel sometimes was. But Scout hadn't witnessed the escalation in her wandering lately. Hadn't seen her on clean-up Tuesdays at the tree, or at the park at all, because Carla wouldn't let Scout go there. She hadn't seen Billie with eyes too bright, too wide, too crazed when tough stories were reported on the news. The way she sometimes licked soil from her hands. Daniel envied his half-sister her immunity.

That wasn't to say Scout didn't know there was a history to their family.

'Sometimes I *hate* being part of a *murder* family,' she declared to Daniel once.

He'd been shocked. She was only six at the time. He was surprised she even understood the meaning of the word.

'Is that how you see us?' he asked.

'*Fact*. That's how *everyone* sees us.'

Scout loved to speak of facts almost as much as she loved to play Uno. But more often than not the facts were those she'd made up herself. This one had felt more reliable than any of her others.

'What makes you say that?'

'People say things … *ask* things.'

The same people who'd let her know she was part of a *murder family* to begin with. Because no one in their household ever had. Their father had forbidden it. Sat Billie and Daniel down not long after Scout was born and said they weren't to speak of it with her. Not until she was much older.

'She doesn't need to grow up knowing her family has that kind of history.'

Daniel, twelve at the time, was jealous because he'd not been given the same option.

'Billie?' His father's tone had been gentle but cautionary. 'Do you understand?'

As far as Daniel could tell, his grandmother had complied.

Only trouble was his father had failed to let the rest of the neighbourhood know. After Scout's first playdate she came home full of questions. Angus phoned the mother. Told her she should be ashamed of herself, exploiting a kid for gossip.

Curious, Daniel had asked Scout, 'What kinds of things do they want to know?'

'If Dad ever talks about it. If *you* do.'

Crash tourists. Still looking for evidence of blood long after it had soaked into the ground.

'What do you tell them?'

Scout had paused, seemed reluctant to answer. 'Nothing much.'

'Much?'

'I don't tell them anything!'

Once it got out among kids at Scout's school – or their parents, more like – Scout became something of a curiosity for a while. Some kids tried to get close to the tragedy, wanted to be its best friend. This had mostly settled down now. Old news. Although sometimes, still, if Scout had friends over to the house he'd overhear one whisper to another: *Is that the brother?* He'd stop what he was doing and go into his bedroom at these times, close the door behind him till they'd left.

'Why are people still so interested,' Daniel had asked his grandmother once.

Her reply had been quick and harsh. 'Because it didn't happen to them.'

People claimed they abhorred violence but then had a perverse fascination with it. *Imagine* is a word he'd heard used around him a lot. Imagine the mother, the boy, the fear, his dreams, the killer still out there. The flashbacks. The memories. (If only there were more.) Strangers inserting themselves into the script of his life from the comfort of a lounge chair or over a coffee or beer. But no matter how wild or colourful their imaginations, no matter how vivid or gory the details they conjured, they didn't have a clue. Only those whose lives had been touched by violence understood the shame and guilt and mistrust. And the periods of blind fucking rage.

'What story did you hear today?' Scout asked Billie now.

'A lovely one involving a dead tree.'

Scout screwed up her nose. 'That doesn't sound very lovely.'

Billie laughed and Daniel thought it sounded like music.

'It had tree hollows,' Billie said. 'So dead, but alive.'

Scout looked at Billie, confused, so she explained. 'When branches break off from a tree, fungi gets in and causes the wood to rot, then termites come along and eat away the wood some more. Over a very long time a hollow forms, like this.' Billie put her cards facedown on the table and cupped her hands to form a tunnel. 'Then creatures move into the hollow and the dead tree becomes their home. So dead, but alive. Like that old tree behind my place.' Billie indicated down the backyard towards a gum tree just outside their fence line. Several branches were broken off close to the main trunk. 'On dusk the other day I saw a sweet little face looking at me from one of its hollows. I think it was a sugar glider.'

'Oh, that *is* a lovely story then.'

'Isn't it. Dead, but alive,' Billie said again, sounding pleased with the idea.

When Daniel was younger, Billie made him go with her to his mother's tree. These expeditions didn't include stories about tree hollows or sugar gliders. But they did include long periods of lying very still on the ground and being told to listen hard because memories were like taproots: dig deep enough and you eventually found what you were hoping for.

Annoyed that his grandmother could disguise what she'd really been doing in a science lesson, Daniel said now, 'I'll tell you both a story'.

Billie and Scout looked up expectantly from their cards.

'If we don't get on with this game, I'm leaving you two to it.'

Scout quickly organised the cards in her hand again and they began to play. But because she wasn't winning, she was easily distracted.

'Come on, Scout. Your turn,' he said for the third time.

Scout pressed her cards to her chest and leant in. 'I haven't got a story, but I've got a *secret*,' she said, teasingly. 'Wanna know?'

'Not if it's gossip from one of your school friends,' Daniel said.

'Nup. I got this one from Mum and Dad. Well, they didn't tell me *exactly*. It kind of accidentally fell into my ears.'

'Accidentally? That means you were snooping again.'

'Wasn't *my* fault. I was trying on Mum's shoes and they didn't know I was in the wardrobe.'

She might only be seven but his half-sister was wily as a fox.

'Anyway, the secret is they're selling the house.'

Daniel immediately stared across at Billie. She looked like she'd been struck. Eventually she found her voice but it seemed to come from a long way away.

'They can't.'

'I don't believe you,' Daniel said.

Scout looked from Daniel to Billie, momentarily uncertain, as if she'd been caught saying or doing something bad. 'They did say it. Honest. Mum was saying Dad needed a bigger shed or he'd lose his hand. And something about how it was time to cash in, whatever that means.'

Billie rested her cards face-up on the table and slumped back in her chair. For her the game was over.

'Don't show me, Nan!' Scout scooped Billie's cards together and turned them facedown.

Daniel kept his eyes on his grandmother. He criticised her otherworldly obsessions, but now he had a sudden image of the soles of his mother's bare feet under the earth, just as Billie had described them to him. But in his imagination Jess was reaching out with her toes, seeking, searching, and not coming up against anything – anyone – she knew. The loneliness of this image caused a physical pain deep in his chest. He couldn't imagine the pain his grandmother must be feeling, but the ropes in her neck had hardened and her face had paled.

'Maybe there'll be a pool at the new house. Wouldn't that be cool?' And his little sister laughed in that joyful, playful, innocent way she had.

Daniel wished he could flee. Get on his bike. Get out of there. Instead, he walked his grandmother back across the parched lawn. Carried the tray for her, the cake plate only one slice down.

'It'll be a rupture, Daniel,' Billie said, 'from everything I know.'

These ruptures from things known made Daniel think of Hiroshima. A documentary he'd once seen. After the atomic bomb had been dropped on Japan, people hadn't been able to find their way home. All the familiar landmarks – buildings, street signs, trees – had been obliterated. As he watched, he remembered thinking about the sense of absolute lost-ness people must have felt. In interviews with survivors – old by then – he'd been amazed by their determination that they find their homes, despite all the evidence around them indicating it unlikely they existed. But still they searched – some people for days – dishevelled and dazed, many with burns and other injuries, trying to locate that one piece of ground that fixed them in place and time despite everything around them being lost. It was as though they hadn't just occupied the place they searched for, they *were* that place and without it they were nothing.

'We don't just vanish when we're gone, Dan.'

Daniel nodded, listening but not knowing what to say to his grandmother. Not knowing how to make it better.

'Traces of us remain. Echoes of conversations … laughter, too.' Billie fixed her piercing blue eyes on him and he felt the force of her expectation that he understand. 'Don't you sense it?'

Daniel wished he could say that he did. But no matter how hard he tried he knew he'd never pick up a sense, force, echo – anything – from the past. All he registered was the hot, humid air that made his t-shirt stick to his back and the sound of his grandmother's angry breathing beside him. And neither could he lie to her, so he shook his head. 'I'm sorry, Nan. I can't feel anything.'

His grandmother looked at him with disbelief, then hurt. 'You think I'm mad, don't you?'

'No I don't.' He said it with force, because it was the truth.

His grandmother had a sense that others didn't. One he didn't know how to cultivate in himself, no matter how much she coached him, but neither did he think it marked her as mad just because she could. It was a gift – or was it a curse? – something she likely discovered through her grief. Or maybe it came before that, was something she was born with, fixed in the very bones of her existence.

'This ground is a raft of different stories, Dan. And they're going to let some bastard dig them up!'

'What about a new story, Nan? Don't you reckon that'd be good for us?' He knew he spoke straight from the Angus and Carla playbook. But part of him wanted to believe it, too. Because he'd happily give up his family's story. Let it be dug up. Built over. Anything to get rid of it. Because living with it didn't feel right. Or normal. *He* didn't feel normal.

'Be better than them, Dan,' Billie snapped and he looked into the distance, chastened. 'Look what's at stake.' His grandmother opened her arms to indicate all that was around them.

But all Daniel could see were sagging structures, scraggly plants and earth as dry as a dog's biscuit. There were no echoes of his mother's voice, or of her laughter. No treasured memories of stories that included her. No sense that she was *here*. The ground was as absent of his mother as Hiroshima had been of the trees and signposts those people had needed to guide them home.

10

BILLIE HAD FOUND IT DIFFICULT to navigate her place in the main house after someone who wasn't really even her daughter-in-law lived there. She supposed Carla was a friend as much as anything else. And a friend's home could never be treated the same as a family member's. Sure, there would have been limits if it were Jess sitting across from Billie now at the kitchen table, Angus beside her, and not Carla. But a mother could take some liberties in a daughter's home; certain boundaries could be tolerably crossed. Truth told, Billie had probably crossed more boundaries than most mothers were allowed. Living on the same block of land as her newly married daughter just one of them.

The main house was classic seventies – low-set, flat-roofed – and it enviably backed onto Mount Coot-tha Forest. This and the big garage, now converted to Angus's workshop, were selling points when Jess and Angus had first inspected the property. With room enough for Billie.

'I can't imagine her not with me, Angus.' Billie had stood away from Jess and Angus during this conversation. Focused on her shoes, quietly pleased.

Angus had used his *not now* voice. 'We'll talk about it later.'

As they left, Jess had put her arm round Billie's shoulder, pulled her in, whispered, 'Don't worry, Mum, you're a shoo-in,' then kissed her temple.

Billie hadn't been in earshot of that later conversation, but clearly it had gone in her favour. For here she was. Not that Angus stood a chance. Her daughter won any number of disagreements if Billie was at the centre of them. But that one was likely made easy given Daniel was all arms and legs inside her belly then. Still, Angus adored Jess, so Billie expected he'd have given her what she asked for anyway.

Billie's small home had been classified as a shed on the title, not a dwelling. But when she'd sold her flat and pitched in for Angus and Jess to buy the property, it soon became the latter. Not that they'd had to do much. The previous owners' son had lived in it, so it was already plumbed with a basic kitchen and bathroom. They modernised each and repainted throughout and while it was nothing fancy, to Billie it was perfect. It was home. And she'd been needed in the early days after Jess's death, had gone and lived in the main house, left her own place empty for a time, so she could care for Daniel while Angus worked. She'd stepped into the role of mother. Then another mother came along when Daniel was eleven. Billie had wondered at the time if eight years was a short or a long time for Angus to wait before taking another partner.

Whenever Billie entered the main house now her mind expected one reality, but her eyes were quickly forced to register another. While structurally nearly everything about the house was as it was when Jess was still alive, the colour scheme and curtains in all the rooms had changed in the intervening years. Most of the furniture had been replaced, too. Jess's belongings were no doubt an emblem of sadness to Carla, a haunting presence. Plus women had nesting instincts just like any animal, Billie supposed. Marked their territory. Made it their own. Now, her daughter was only recognisable in this house when Billie looked at Daniel. You can't rearrange the features of kin.

Some delicacy was required in their exchanges. Carla pulled it off, took care to speak around the past, never to it. Billie didn't trust herself to know or follow the same rules, which is why she kept mostly to herself. On-site but living at its peripheries. An outlier.

She now understood she lived with this family only because of an enduring favour Angus owed his dead wife's mother, which he had no idea how to requite. Except now it seemed he'd found a way.

'You can't sell, Angus.'

'As hard as it is, Billie, I think it's something we need to consider. The business has outgrown the workshop. I need more space, and out of a residential area.'

Angus opened his injured hand to Billie, presented her with his flat palms as if to say the decision was out of his control. All it showed her was that they weren't tied. He had a choice.

'The workshop's not safe, Billie. It's too cramped for the work he's doing. I worry about him.'

Billie ignored Carla. This had nothing to do with her and everything to do with Billie, Angus and a dead girl. She looked right at Angus. 'You'd be selling your own wife.'

'Billie, Carla's my wife.'

'But Jess was, too.'

Angus and Carla were silent for a time, wouldn't look up from their hands. Billie's breathing was the only sound in the room. She wished she could summon Jess now. She wouldn't stand for this. Would remind him that she and Billie had always been together.

'I know it's been a shock.' Angus sounded weary, but she didn't feel sorry for him. 'And I'm sorry you didn't hear it from me first. But I guess it was something that was going to come up eventually anyway. Circumstances change. And tough as it is, the time's come.'

Billie couldn't look at them now. Didn't know what to do with the betrayal.

'A share of the money from the sale would obviously be yours.' Carla sounded too eager, too certain. 'A developer will probably buy it, given the size of the block. So between us we should do quite well.'

Did she think there was a price that tipped grief into something tolerable? 'This ground is my *life*, Carla. But you wouldn't understand that.'

Carla's face hardened. 'Lives can be built anywhere, Billie.'

Angus forged on. 'We'd help set you up somewhere nice, or with us again, similar to the set-up we have here if that's what you want.'

Carla flinched at this, but Angus either failed to register it or chose not to. Did that mean there was still hope? That he was still on her side?

Jess, help me! Talk to him like you used to.

'I don't want to go anywhere else. I *need* to stay here, with Jess!'

She thought of her well-oiled gate. The path she'd worn from it to the park over the years, how it would grow over; evidence of her pilgrimages lost. She thought of Jess. How the ground knew her. Remembered her. *Was* her. Allowed Billie to remember her, too.

'If you force me to leave, I lose Jess all over again.'

Angus put his head in his hands. Carla looked to the ceiling. Billie was encouraged by their divergence.

It took her hours to dig the hole. It needed to be deep, deeper than the excavators that might maul the earth. She wanted this prize to remain buried. She'd chosen an area to one side of the gate in the back fence. A spot not tramped down by foot traffic. Even though the earth was dry and unyielding to begin with, she persevered.

Used the heel of her shoe to rock the cutting edge of the shovel backwards and forwards, made an impact inch by inch.

They might take this ground from her but that didn't mean she couldn't leave something behind. Something of Jess. This thought kept her going and the mound of dirt beside her steadily grew. The moon gradually eased past her right shoulder to her left, remained bright enough to guide her shovel. The depth of the hole slowly increased.

As she dug, Billie thought about all the living things within the rich grains that she excavated. Earth that masqueraded as empty but which she knew was a borderless home to billions. A teeming, breathing, reproducing, co-existing mass of organisms, each interacting with and advantaging another, almost like they formed a whole. It was the closest thing to eternity that Billie could think of. And she would add a piece of her girl to this eternal community; allow her to live on through its function.

When the hole was deep enough, Billie lay on her stomach in front of it, reached down and carefully rested the pouch she'd made from Jess's dress, the ash, the six strands of her daughter's hair stitched inside, at its bottom. She crumbled the loose earth on top of the pouch then, felt the fibrous connections of that life network being broken further, mumbled her apologies for the disturbance. She was confident, though, that soon enough it would be a life restored. Soil was like that; it knew what was good for it. Jess now a part of that goodness, too.

When the hole was filled, Billie lay on her back alongside it and cleaned the soil from under her nails with her teeth as the lava sun poured over the horizon.

11

A REFUSE STATION WITH A conscience. That was how Carla thought of the charity shop where she worked every second Monday morning. A place that allowed people to believe their once treasured items were being given a second chance at love when they deposited them there.

Repurposing was a necessary part of life. Carla believed that. Was one of the reasons she volunteered at Vinnies. Their house – while a very different commodity than anything that passed through the store – would also be repurposed, once sold, to meet another person's ambitions for it, just as the clothing, bric-a-brac and homewares were in the op-shop. And she didn't doubt that it would look a whole lot better for their efforts. Maybe Billie should spend some of her spare time standing where Carla was now, so she could see how things were given new lives, new opportunities. And in the case of where they currently lived, that reinvention could only be a happier one.

'How much do you think I should put on these, Maeve?' Carla held up one of two identical business shirts, still in their plastic packets, for the other woman to see.

Maeve was a Vinnies veteran. Had volunteered there for twenty-two years. Carla figured she'd seen more unsaleable stained shirts and worn heels than most. She was a giver this woman, cheery regardless of weather or circumstance. Why couldn't Billie be more like her? Benevolent. Generous. Progressive.

'Five dollars, love. That colour never sells well.'

Carla priced the items, took them over to the display shelf and arranged them among the other business shirts.

Thrift shopping was a necessity for a lot of people. For others an obsession. Some an abhorrence. For the two girls – uni students, Carla guessed – rifling through the women's clothing racks now, it was a great place to source fancy dress.

'What d'you reckon?' One of the girls held up a tasselled brown faux suede sleeveless vest for the other girl to see. 'Seventies enough?'

'Absolutely,' Maeve called in her faded English accent. 'Used to own one of those myself. Cut a good figure in it too, especially over a Led Zeppelin t-shirt. And don't hold back on the costume jewellery.'

Billie and Maeve were a similar age, yet Carla couldn't picture a younger Billie in a fringed vest or a Led Zeppelin t-shirt.

But how would she know? She'd asked Angus once what kind of person Billie was when he'd first met her. He looked to think hard on the question, whether unsure or trying to remember, so she'd coaxed him. 'Was she … I don't know … a hippy? Eccentric? Shy? Was she ever *funny*?'

'Yeah, she could be funny. But she wasn't any of those other things. I dunno … she was a mother. Like you're a mother. Loving. Protective. Always there. That's the best way to describe her. Jess was her life. Then after Jess, Dan was. Everything she did, she did wholly for him.'

He'd made her sound like she lived solely for the benefit of others. This didn't fit with Carla's image of her. Sometimes she

98

thought Billie selfish. That she placed demands on people. Didn't care that those demands might hurt others, might stop them from growing.

'Did she ever just live for herself?' Carla asked.

But Angus had misunderstood her, assumed she'd meant if Billie had ever lived away from them.

'They came as a package,' he said. 'I learnt that early on. Jess still lived with Billie when we met. I didn't see it at the time, but the granny flat here probably cinched the deal more than the workshop did.'

'So, Billie moved in with you whether you liked it or not?'

And here he was now, prepared to let it happen again. Except Carla was no Jess.

'Yeah, but it was no hardship having her round back then. She was easygoing.' Angus paused, remembering. 'Didn't suffer fools though. Would let you know if she thought you were acting like one, but not in a mean way. Mostly she reasoned a good argument, got you onside.'

Carla didn't suffer fools either, but she was being asked to. And if Billie could reason such a good argument, then how could she think selling equated to a double death?

Eight years Carla had been with Angus and there was still so much she didn't understand about the family she'd married into. What she did know, was that she wouldn't miss living in the shadows of their past life. Increasingly, she felt the need to be free of the place, its hold over everyone. When she moved in, she'd tried to build a parallel life alongside the one that already existed. But there were so many memories, so many reminders, that those parallel lives – hers and Jess's – would always be intertwined, always shared, despite one of them being absent. It wasn't like a divorce or a separation. In those situations, one or both parties were usually eager to be shot of the other. Carla knew the feelings of relief and salvation at finally having someone out of your life.

A brief marriage at just nineteen had been a fleeting flirtation with what she foolishly imagined at the time proved she was an adult. But she'd been naïve. Everything about the union had been selfish – income, workload, intimacy. She'd been in love with a fantasy, not a man. Looking back on it she was little more than a child, playing house.

But the absence in their house was different. It was a big gaping hole of sadness. One that Carla needed to plug at times, skirt around at others, or risk falling into it.

It was a risk she'd been willing to take from the beginning though. Because Angus had made her feel his equal, not his minder. Made her believe she was more capable than she'd ever been made to feel in her life. Carla felt chosen in a way. Trusted. Especially to love his fragile son. She'd never forgotten the honour of this, despite the responsibility that came with it. Daniel had been less forthcoming with her. Initially anyway. He circled her for the first few months after she and Angus got together. Kept his distance. Would step a foot into her zone every now and again, seek her out with a homework question or to tell her brief, abbreviated anecdotes about school. Testing her solidity perhaps. Not yet sure of her permanence.

Carla thought back to when she and Angus first met. Both of them on their knees out the front of Woolworths. Her laughing at her clumsiness, Angus at the speed with which a lime could roll away. And when they'd finally looked at one another – *really* looked – there was a pause in everything, certainly for Carla: movement, breath, even in the air and the rush of people around them.

She tried now to distil what it was that had passed between them that day. Not love, not immediately, that would take a little longer. But she was sure she'd felt its precursor: faith in a person's goodness. Something she'd been denied in past relationships. Had Angus allowed, consciously or not, for the barriers to come down a little that day, for this felt thing to reach out and touch Carla in subterranean ways? And if so, what had he sensed about her that enabled this? Did it still exist? These were questions that hadn't had a bearing on their relationship for a long time. But Carla now found herself examining them again.

If time could be turned back, the actions of one man recast, and the past made good, would Carla let it? Even if it meant her erasure from this family, Scout's too? Could she be that selfless? She'd likely still have a daughter, a version of her anyway, or maybe a son, with a different man. Maybe someone as good and as kind as Angus; Scout might have blue eyes instead of hazel, blonde hair instead of brown, living in a suburb far away or just down the street.

But as was the way with these kinds of jumbled thoughts, imagining lives rerouted by chance, Carla wondered if this life – scarred as it was – had been predetermined for them anyway. That the routes each had taken were destined to drop them exactly where they were now, like a pin on a map. Because there were such a bewildering number of possibilities for people to brush up against on any given day. Those mindless choices to go left or right, to do something now or later, to drive not walk or walk not drive. The broken shopping bag at the supermarket that gave her Angus, just one of those head-spinning flukes. What if she'd taken the bag with the stronger handle from the boot of the car instead that day? What if Angus had gone to Coles and not Woolworths, where he usually shopped, so hadn't ended up helping her chase rolling tins of corn and wayward limes across the footpath? What if it had been raining the day Jess was killed and she and Daniel hadn't gone to the park? What if the killer had slept in that morning, lost his nerve, lost his way?

But this was the kind of thinking that sent a person mad, and for a split second Carla had a sense of what it might be like inside Billie's head. Even though it was impossible to know who, or where, Billie was half the time. She'd barely seen her since that awkward conversation in the kitchen. She'd notice her slip through the gate in the back fence and wouldn't see her again for hours. Where did she go? What did she do there?

Billie was an enigma. But Carla couldn't know if this was by design or circumstance. Did any of the person she was before she had Jess remain – a woman like Maeve, someone who accessorised the shit out of a Led Zeppelin t-shirt – or had what happened to her daughter completely repurposed her life?

She turned to Maeve again now. 'You're a rare bird, Maeve,' Carla said, putting her arm round her colleague's shoulder once the two girls had left the shop. 'We could do with more like you.'

'Takes all sorts, love.'

Later, as she lay on her side next to him in bed, head propped in one hand, Carla realised guilt was messing with Angus and she felt the opportunity to sell slipping from her. It was a bitter pill, one she wasn't prepared to swallow, certainly not after finally having got this far.

More pillow talk. But this time she had momentum on her side. 'We've done the hard part, Angus, in telling her. The rest is time, as she adjusts.'

'I just wish she'd heard it from me first. Dan, too. It might have gone better.'

Carla doubted it.

'That kid … she's gotta learn about boundaries.'

'She's seven, Angus. A child.'

'With big ears and a mouth to match.'

Carla bit back what she wanted to say. That it wasn't Scout's fault. That neither was it Billie's or even theirs. Fault rested with an eggshell past.

'There was never going to be a right time or person to tell her, so stop pretending you could've made a difference.' She could see the admonishment hurt. But he must have recognised the truth of it because he took a deep breath, released it slowly, evenly.

'You're probably right. Guess we got the response I expected from her. But Dan … he didn't say anything.'

'He's a thinker. He'll be trying to work out what it means, especially for his grandmother.' And she didn't doubt Billie would try to have some bearing on that.

'You reckon he understands why we have to sell, don't you? He's helped me in the workshop often enough. Knows how tight it is in there.'

Carla didn't believe he did. Not yet. But when she looked at Angus, she saw the son in the father: their shared need for certainty. She leant in, kissed him on the lips once, twice, three times. 'Trust me, we've made the right decision.'

'Right isn't always easy though is it.'

She wanted to tell him that depended on whose *right* they were aiming to please. Instead, she traced her fingers down his neck to his chest, used the flat of her palm to travel lower, sought to please what came naturally, easily. He reached for her, forgot his injured hand for a moment and winced. She took it gently in hers, placed it back on the mattress beside him. Gave the moment to him. Stilled his worry and pain for a time.

12

DANIEL FLICKED HIS THUMBNAIL ACROSS the edge of the letters, restless to leave. He wished someone else had delivered them to his grandmother.

'The kooks are calling,' Billie said.

She was standing in front of the television screen watching the news. Daniel wished she wouldn't. Wished she'd fill her newfound time with something less grim. It was almost like the course of her life – her CV of loss – demanded her participation in this family's tragedy.

It had been almost four weeks since the boy had disappeared and despite all the searching, there was no trace of him. Not a sandal, not an AC Milan Football Club cap or scrap of fabric from his blue and white whale-patterned shorts. And February had arrived with malice during that time. Temperatures soared, topped thirty-nine degrees for five days straight, then reined itself in again to the low thirties. Some reprieve. Daniel imagined the boy's body desiccating under the scorching sun.

'We don't want to hear about people's dreams or visions,' the investigating inspector said to the reporters. 'What we do want is credible information. If you heard or saw anything out of place the day Marco went missing … no matter how small or insignificant it might seem, then we would ask that you contact police. And we would particularly like to hear from anyone with information about an old-model white Camry seen in the area that day.'

This was something new.

'Some bastard's taken him.' His grandmother rarely swore.

Daniel looked at her, tried to gauge the extent of her anger. Her eyes were fixed on the screen, taking it all in. Consumed. Maybe she wasn't angry at all and it was frustration that made her swear? That sense of *here we go again*. The merry-go-round of cruelty with people intent on making it turn. What drives a stranger to so decisively and cruelly alter the trajectory of other people's lives? How do they choose? Are there trophy features they seek: age, hair colour, gender? Or is it purely random opportunism? What catalyst makes them act on the day that they do? And what do they do afterwards? Crack a joke with a work colleague? Coach a football team? Sell cinema tickets?

'How much longer d'you think they'll look for him?' he asked instead.

'They may as well stop now. He's dead. Probably buried miles from where they're looking.'

'You think so?'

'I *know* so. He comes to me.' Billie side-eyed him; dared him to challenge this. 'While I'm out walking.'

Daniel kept his face neutral, as he'd learnt.

'All the details of his disappearance will end up in cold case boxes, just like Jess. No body for his parents though,' Billie said.

He skirted round this reference to his mother, brought it back to the boy and his family. 'They must want to just get home to Italy.'

Billie shook her head. 'They won't want to leave.'

'Why would they want to stay?'

'Because the ground here owns them now, too.'

Daniel thought about what freedom might look like as he finally pedalled away from home. He pictured it as a pack on his back, everything he needed inside, and striking out across the world. Freedom was foreign villages and cities far away from this one. It was swimming in unfamiliar oceans, road-tripping across vast plains, riding trains through the bellies of great mountains. Freedom was to travel across many lands and not be tied to this one place – feel *owned* by it. Because it did feel like it owned him sometimes; that it had wrapped an invisible root round each of his ankles and held him there. Roots his grandmother summoned.

To travel, to leave, that was the escape he dreamt of. A bigger escape even than the one his father and Carla imagined they'd achieve by selling. Sure, they could pretend their reasons for moving were about a lack of space or about how old the house was or for the chance to make a profit, but Daniel knew that wasn't the whole truth. They wanted to put physical distance between themselves and the past, too. Who could blame them?

For now, his escape was confined to a fast ride beside Brisbane's wide, brown river. Daniel's legs set a rapid cadence. The tyres of his bike made a drone-like thrum along the concrete path, the air hot on his face as he moved faster even than the cars travelling along Coronation Drive. Only the City Cats passed him, brown water churning into twin white wakes behind them. He'd take the sound and movement of this busy part of the city over the still and haunted ground where he lived any day.

The city stood tall ahead of him, the skyline made jagged by great columns of concrete and steel. And because it was his nature to think about what could have been, he obliterated the city's structures from his mind for a moment, wiped it clean from the landscape, pictured instead the swampland with its lily-covered waterholes, its springs and lagoons. The path he rode along now likely once a strip of beach and the water beside him not brown back then, but clear with a sandy pebbled bottom. To the north there would have been open woodlands of blue gum and ironbark, undulating grassy slopes. To the south – across the river to West End – he pictured swathes of rainforest, thick with ferns, palms, vines and many towering figs, not just the one always forefront in his family's mind. A single history lesson had taught him all of this, the advances trumpeted by his old history teacher as a triumph of humankind.

At the Cultural Centre he chained his bike to a rack outside the State Library. Took thongs from his backpack and swapped them for his cycling shoes.

He'd come here to preserve a memory. His mother was like mist in his mind, a shifting shape that he couldn't pin down or grasp. But this place had always been the site of a fixed fragment of her – a flashpoint that was his, not borrowed – so he came here from time to time to colour it in – keep it bright – as a child would a drawing.

This memory took place in the dinosaur garden at the Queensland Museum. A place Billie said he'd been brought to often with his parents as an infant. He could recall a small boy's wonder as he stood before the sculptures of a Tyrannosaurus Rex and the three-horned face of a Triceratops. These life-like replicas placed among tree ferns and cycads in an open-air space just outside the museum. Daniel still had the sense of awe as he placed his hand on the Triceratops's face, of turning, eyes and mouth wide, to who he instinctively knew was his mother. The second part of this memory was of this misty figure laughing. A sound that had resonated with him ever since, like a glass wind-chime, tinkling and playful.

Simple memories, but they were his.

Today, he sat on a bench in the shade under the replica dinosaurs and felt the same kind of awe for these creatures now that he had back then. He was still amazed by their scale, their peculiar shape and form, how they'd lived for millions of years till space and Earth suddenly conspired against them. Daniel could make peace with their loss. Made inevitable by a cataclysm.

He left the museum by way of the Whale Mall, a long space with a life-sized figure of a humpback and two calves suspended overhead. Beneath them was an exhibition of maps arranged across a number of display cabinets. Groups of school children stood around them; most of the kids looked bored. Daniel stopped to examine the display. Some maps dated back to 1895 – a McKellar's series – right through to recent ordnance survey maps. The early ones were about infrastructure and growth. They showed the gridded and boxed ambitions for what the city would eventually become.

Maps were like stories of what had occurred over time. Unlike the fragment of memory that told a brief but fixed story of him and his mother in the dinosaur garden, a map's story was ever-changing. Landscapes altered all the time. Rivers were re-routed or disappeared altogether. Dunes and cliff faces crumbled into the sea. Forests were cleared. Hilltops levelled. The story of those swamps, woodlands and rainforests he imagined earlier were not recorded on any of these maps. Nothing to show of the campsites or corroboree grounds of the Turrbal and Jagera people. Nothing of the network of paths that would have connected communities or led to places to fish and hunt. These were long overlaid by progress.

So while it wasn't a lie, neither was a map the truth.

The recent maps on display showed more topographical detail. He liked that about them, paused in front of one now in which he could see the street where he lived, the park where his mother's tree was, the bike trails he liked to ride in Mount Coot-tha Forest. It showed escarpments and spot elevations; rivers and creeks (one of the mistruths, as many were dry due to the drought); and reservoirs (another lie, as most would be smaller than shown). Vegetation – dense, medium and scattered – he assumed would have diminished in places. It showed train lines, highways and streets, recreation reserves and power transmission lines. Things added to what already existed. Features he figured changed more rapidly than the natural ones. The orange contour lines – some tightly packed, others broadly spaced – marked the land's elevation in twenty-metre intervals and was the most honest thing about it.

Ever since Daniel was a boy he'd been in awe of the forces that shaped – continued to shape – the earth, as much as he'd been in awe of dinosaurs. Billie had encouraged it. She was a woman of the land after all and had tried to make him a boy of it also. Some of it had stuck.

'You know what superpower I want?' he said to his grandmother once, a Hulk toy in one hand, Spiderman in the other.

She'd looked at him, trying to guess, then said, 'I can't imagine. You tell me.'

'A special eye … inside here,' and he tapped Hulk against his skull, 'that sees what the Earth used to look like.'

He imagined this superpower now as an accelerated version of deep time. Millennia reduced to seconds. All the collisions, crumples and collapses of the Earth's crust catalogued in his memory, to include those that wiped out the dinosaurs. This was the kind of knowledge he liked best.

'Oh, that sounds like fun,' his grandmother said, clapping her hands. 'And what would you especially like to see?'

'Volcanoes!'

All the changes they'd wrought: Mount Vesuvius, Ilopango, Krakatoa. He wanted to glimpse their violent histories, speculate on their violent futures, and the ongoing insecurity for those who lived at their feet. A boy's morbid fascination with life changed in a heartbeat.

Now, if Daniel had this superpower, he'd like to see his position in relation to the changes that had occurred on *this* piece of ground: a finger of land held in the pinch of a wide brown river. Was it once a mountaintop? Beneath a glacier? Covered in a lush and tangled jungle? And who had sat here previously – not just last year or last century, but last millennia? Last epoch? Who, what, had witnessed the changes in this land, *really* witnessed it? These were the kinds of things Daniel would like to see if he possessed this superpower, to be able to read the stories on this other kind of map.

He was still imagining these geological disruptions when a familiar face strode towards him, two girls in tow.

'You lost, mate? Not heard of Google Maps?' The guy's laugh was just as Daniel remembered.

One of the girls – neither from the school Daniel went to with this guy – put her hand over her wide, oh-my-god-that's-so-funny mouth before laughing loudly, too. The other girl looked on, nonplussed.

Why didn't the teachers who decided which kids got captain of this or that at school, see how they often chose an A-plus loser?

When Daniel didn't reply, Bryce said, 'Just playin' with you, pal,' and mock-punched his arm. 'This here's Dan,' he said to the girls. 'The brains of our year group. Expect you're studying astrophysics at UQ now, are you?'

'No. Working in a bar.'

Bryce laughed again, then realised Daniel wasn't joking.

'Expect you're doing something in sport?' Daniel asked.

'Yep. Personal trainer at a gym. Lovin' it.'

'Which bar?' asked the girl who was yet to laugh.

'Paradise Bar. In the Valley.'

'Not heard of it,' Bryce said.

Daniel turned to Bryce and shrugged. 'Not surprised. You never struck me as the kind of guy keen to press a backpack.'

Now the girl laughed and Daniel liked the sound of it.

Bryce didn't get it.

Daniel explained. 'It's mostly a backpackers' bar. And press ...' He mimed lifting a weight.

'You're funny, Dan,' the girl said.

Daniel liked her voice as much as he liked her laugh. *Funny Dan.* He liked that, too. It wasn't one of the labels he was given at school. *Dull Dan* was. *Sad Dan, Dan-nerd, Dan the Cold Man* as well. Mostly he ignored these names. But *Angry Dan* thumped it out of those who hoped to make any of them stick.

Once, in senior school, a girl had tried to get close to *Dan the Cold Man*. Her name was Megan, but she told everyone to call her Megs. Being liked was important to her. She tracked him down at break times. Sat beside him in the classes they shared. Walked partway home from school with him. People assumed they were going out. Daniel struggled with what to talk about, which didn't matter because she did most of the talking anyway. Took as many liberties with their conversation as his counsellor had.

'You know you can talk to me about anything, Dan. *Anything* at all.' He saw a saviour's face each time Megs spoke to him. 'Think of me as a friend who listens.'

Other sixteen-year-old boys would probably think about the boners they'd get if pretty Megs gave them as much attention as she gave him. But all he could think about was how tired she made him feel. So, he'd change the subject, ask her about an exam or an assignment they had coming up, what movies she'd seen, what she'd done on the weekend. But missionary types like her never doubted their mission. She would break him. Civilise him. Make him spill his guts to her just so she could claim some higher status.

'It can't be easy for your stepmum?'

But Carla was a circuit-breaker. She let the past sit between them as calm and transparent and necessary as the air in a room.

Cleared the way to a better future. Not back to the places Megs wanted to take him.

'I read somewhere that people who've suffered a trauma should keep a notebook by their bed. Write down their dreams as soon as they wake up. Have you tried that, Dan?'

Dream therapy. Listening therapy. Hypnotherapy. Journalling. Where did it end?

'What are you trying to save me from, Megan?' he finally asked her.

'Yourself.'

This was the most stupid of all the clichés he'd been dealt.

Saved from yourself. What did that even mean? That feelings and flesh were separable? He'd laughed at her. She'd looked at him, hurt.

'I'm not the enemy, Daniel.'

No, the enemy was still walking the streets. Still driving a car. Getting drunk. Laughing. Fucking. Eating. Shitting. And Dan the cold, angry, sad man, knew he'd remain a combination of all of these things until he got to look this man in the face. She had no idea what it was like to imagine the worst in every stranger he met.

Soon after, Megs took on a new project. Someone whose wounds were more visible. At least she had something to lay her hands on.

Daniel felt his fists ball with these thoughts. He straightened his fingers, eased the tension from his shoulders, put *Angry Dan* back in his box.

Bryce moved to usher the girls on. 'We better get going. I'll see you around, Dan.'

The quieter one didn't immediately follow. 'I've been to that bar,' she said. 'It's cool. Great music. Might see you there sometime.' She turned and waved before catching up with the other two. Daniel noticed a brown birthmark the size of a golf ball on the inside of her forearm, its edges as irregularly shaped as one of the reservoirs marked on the map. It suited everything about her: short bleached hair, cargo shorts, unbranded t-shirt and canvas shoes.

As he watched them walk away, he thought about how the captain of just about everything hadn't even had the manners to tell Daniel her name.

13

How many inspectors assigned to a murder case would stay in touch with the victim's family this long? Sixteen years since Jess's death, and Mark Quinn still dropped in for afternoon tea.

In the early days, Billie spoke with him several times a week, either on the phone or in person. As the months and then years passed those communications, and his visits, became less frequent, but this biannual pilgrimage to Billie's door now seemed a given. She was grateful for his visits because while they continued, even though infrequently, Jess remained relevant, and not just to those who had known and loved her.

Each of them had aged, Quinn a little better than Billie, despite the fact he'd have confronted many other murders and disappearances over the years. She reckoned he was in his late fifties now. Kept himself trim. He was of the size and shape that could take a forty-two regular suit off the rack and be safe in the knowledge it would fit. Those suits were always deepest navy, the shirt white. The only indication he paid any mind to fashion over the past sixteen years was in the changing colour, pattern and width of his tie. He was a family man. Kids grown up now. None of them had followed him into the Force. Billie wondered if she could expect his visits once he retired. Probably. She'd always felt he took the audaciousness of Jess's murder personally.

He was meticulous with the strawberry jam. Spread it evenly to the outer margins of his scone. Billie appreciated his attention to this task, to all tasks. Made her think how much it must torment him to not be able to find a killer.

Jess's killer was someone Billie often profiled in her mind. He was never ordinary. His cunning and cruelty showed in uncaring eyes and a cocksure gait. A brash, vainglorious man certain of his infallibility. Hardened possibly, full of his own kind of trauma. She imagined him agile, fast and strong – strong enough to overpower a mother protecting her toddler; the fiercest of women. Billie always assumed this man would carry some imprint of what he'd done and which she'd immediately recognise; Daniel would recognise. Now, she realised that they could pass him in the street – possibly had – and have no sense for who he was or what he'd done.

'She'd be forty-two in June,' Billie said. An anniversary she'd mark with a long walk, each step a memory, a thought, till she was too tired to think any more and would concentrate instead on what was around her, pay homage to that.

Quinn looked to do the maths in his head and nodded. 'Forty-two. I sometimes think our forties are our best years. Kids usually on their way to adulthood. Work more secure. A bit more money in the bank, but not yet feeling old.'

He knew he could talk like this with Billie, knew she appreciated the truth about what Jess had missed.

'I agree. My early forties were great. Fifties, obviously not.'

'Your sixties?'

Billie shrugged. There was a greater distance now at least from the rawness of the actual events, as if the reality of it was viewed through a cataract eye. 'Not what they could or should be,' she said. 'But, here I am. And unemployed now, too.'

Quinn frowned. 'By choice?'

'By conscience. Couldn't work for a criminal.'

'Someone I need to visit?' He winked at Billie and she smiled despite herself.

'He *should* be locked up.'

'What did he do?'

'Sold protected plants illegally. I called him on it. The environment department said there wasn't much they could do without evidence. He'd got rid of me before I thought to take photographs.'

'I'm sorry to hear that, Billie.'

They sat quietly for a time. Quinn spread jam on the second half of his scone. Billie sipped her tea. Meanwhile, the ceiling fan cut circuits through the hot air but did nothing more than shift pockets of heat from one part of the room to another. And still, he didn't appear to sweat.

'They're wanting to sell.'

Quinn looked at Billie, confused.

'Angus. Carla.' She gestured around her with open hands. 'This. All of it.'

'What's prompted them?'

'A lack of care.'

Billie said this bitterly and Quinn looked to weigh up what to say in reply. When he did, he sounded cautious.

'Maybe they think it's time for a fresh start.'

Some events didn't allow for fresh starts. 'Angus says he needs more space. That the neighbours will start complaining about the noise. There haven't been any complaints at the station, have there?'

'It's not really a police matter, Billie. Complaints of that kind usually go through Council.'

'Of course.' Billie felt stupid. Murder. Noise complaints. Not remotely close. Would he think she was trying to curry favour?

What a terrible thought.

'You're not so keen on moving then?' he asked.

'Jess is here.'

He nodded, and in the gesture Billie allowed herself to believe he understood her where Angus and Carla didn't.

The front screen door creaked on its hinges and soon after Daniel arrived in her small lounge room, hot air pushing in behind him.

The inspector stood and reached out a hand to her grandson. 'Hey, Dan.'

Daniel gripped the other man's hand – too firmly Billie saw, as Quinn eased off his own. A kind of submission, she supposed. Or surrender, perhaps, to the fact that there was no progress in his mother's case. Billie worried about the anxiety these visits caused Daniel, but she also respected his demand that he tell her when they were scheduled.

Daniel sat on the arm of her lounge chair, fiddled with the plaited leather strap he wore round his wrist. 'Sorry I'm late. Got a puncture. Have I missed anything?' He looked from Billie to Quinn.

'Nothing especially,' Billie said.

'Nothing new then?' Daniel looked Inspector Quinn in the eye, something he did with all men.

'No, son. I'm afraid not.'

'Just another courtesy call then?'

'Daniel,' Billie said gently, resting her hand on his arm. His need to blame pained her, because she knew where it came from: an inability to stop blaming himself. If Quinn were honest, he'd probably say it pained him, too. Reminded him that he'd failed as well.

'I've been with you from the start with this, Dan, so I'm not likely to stop dropping by anytime soon.'

And that was the truth. He had been in it from the start. Over those years, Quinn had taken seriously and followed up on all of Daniel's sightings of strange men in the park or neighbourhood. He'd re-explain as often as Daniel asked, patiently and respectfully, details of the investigation. And as Daniel matured, he demanded Quinn stop sanitising what he told him. Quinn had witnessed Daniel's various moods over those years, whether frustration, anger, rudeness or tears, and Billie had never once seen or heard him trivialise, judge or rebuke her grandson for any of it. And in turn, Billie had witnessed how those outbursts had affected the inspector; how she believed they massaged his own sense of powerlessness. All because he'd not been able to put the killer before Daniel and tell him this was the face he saw that day.

'There's never anything new though, is there?' Daniel replied. 'Hasn't been since day one, from what I can tell.'

While her grandson sounded angry, Billie knew it was disappointment more than anything.

There was silence for a time. The ceiling fan rocked slightly on its shaft as a hot breeze came in through an open window, then settled again.

'I never lose hope,' Quinn said eventually, looking from Daniel to Billie. 'Someone out there knows something and they might yet come forward. Or we might get lucky one day with a DNA match to the man from an unrelated incident … or a part-match if crime runs in his family.'

He said it every visit. Billie held no grudge for the inspector's repetition. Success for many things was due in part to the good conscience of individuals. But more often than not, she knew it was down to sheer bloody luck.

The air that night remained hot. Billie found it impossible to sleep. Everything stuck to her – nightdress, sheet, hair, skin to skin.

She'd come outside, which wasn't much cooler, but at least the air shifted a little. Even the night sounds were lethargic, lacked energy. She could hear a solitary cricket as it kept up its unanswered, solo vibration somewhere in the earth. She stretched out, the grass dry beneath her and watched the full and creamy moon, suspended above her like a sacrament. Billie imagined plucking it from the night sky and resting it on her tongue where it would dissolve, no more substantial than the body of Christ. The reality of her own body pressed against the hard earth, was that she wasn't about to dissolve, not even if it suddenly started to rain.

But one day she supposed she would. When Daniel cast her ashes about at some place of his choosing. Where might that be? she wondered. She didn't mind where. Maybe, like she'd done with Jess's, he'd seed her in many places. She liked the idea of how, with the first downpour, her remains would be taken into the soil. How she'd add to its already extensive catalogue. Archived and housed in everything that depended on it to live. Except it seemed a part of this archive was to be taken from her. No doubt dug up, turned over, by those great instruments that mauled the Earth.

A satellite blinked across an otherwise seemingly stationary sky. Billie tracked it till she lost it somewhere in the Milky Way. She tried to imagine the view from one of these hurtling insect-like crafts. Would love to see Earth from its perspective, get a better sense of this great blue orb she lived upon. Viewed at ground level it was too easy to believe that the planet was defined by its structures – homes, offices, shopping centres, cars, fences, roads, bridges – when in truth these were superficial. Scars.

'We tell ourselves lies,' Billie muttered. Humans weren't important to this place, only to themselves.

The back screen door of the main house flapped shut and soon after she heard the faint slap of rubber thongs along the concrete path that led past her home to the gate in the back fence. She knew without being able to see that it was Daniel.

'Too hot for you to sleep as well?' she called.

The footfalls changed tone, softened as they moved from concrete to dry earth. Daniel soon pulled up beside her.

'What're you doing out here?' he asked, lowering himself to the ground.

'Talking to the stars.'

'Are they talking back?'

Billie laughed. 'Nope. Not a murmur.'

In the moon's luminescence, Daniel and the surrounding structures were cast as monochromatic silhouettes, defining detail dulled.

She looked skyward again. 'Southern Cross still your favourite?'

'Nah. Too many guys have it tattooed on their chests.'

'Got a new one?'

'No. Don't really spend much time looking at the stars anymore.'

Billie was sorry to hear it. When he was little, the pair of them would lie on the grass, much as they were now, and stargaze. He'd point at various bright astral bodies and draw a line with his finger to link them to others and form crudely defined images – angels, cars, dogs, bridges – like a giant game of join-the-dots. He'd always start with the Southern Cross, called it his kite, and then he'd cast his eye outward from there. Sometimes Billie would have to sweep her gaze from one side of the galaxy to the other in order to follow his finger and connect the stars he pointed to. Oftentimes she failed to recognise what he'd described.

'Can't you *see* it?' he'd ask, annoyed, as though she was either blind or lacked imagination. Jess would have loved it.

'How was everyone in the big house tonight?'

'Meh.'

'That's not an answer,' Billie said, but honoured the silence that followed.

After a while Daniel asked, 'Do you think you can protect a person too much?'

'Depends what from.'

Billie suspected what was coming but she wanted him to say it. Did that mean she wasn't protecting him enough?

'I told Dad Inspector Quinn had visited. He wasn't happy about that. Told me if I needed reminding of the details then I was on my way to forgetting them, so why not let it go.'

Billie had never agreed with Angus on this. How could he be done with a crime that had no conviction? Only she was prepared to repeat the details to Daniel over and over, and as often as he asked. No matter how much the re-telling hurt any one of them, she considered it imperative they did. Because Daniel needed to own the story, too. And owning it might prompt memories. Deliver justice.

'What do you want to know?' she asked him.

'Everything you do.'

'I know it happened around seven-thirty in the morning,' Billie started. 'It was a Tuesday.' Billie had stood at the front gate and watched them leave for the park that day, just as she did most mornings that Jess and Daniel walked there. She could still picture them; both dressed in vibrant colours, not monochrome. Their true selves. Daniel's hand pressed into Jess's and him talking excitedly. Each new day rich with possibilities back then that he was eager to explore. And Jess endlessly willing to provide the opportunity. No gate in the back fence in those days. Had Jess's killer learnt their pattern? Watched them and planned? Or was it a case of wrong place, wrong time, luck run out?

'The day was mild being May, not hot like now.'

Billie often fantasised that had it been cold, if Jess had needed to rug up against it, then the knife might not have found its target. Could a zipped-up jacket or a scarf protect those vulnerable areas beneath them?

She left out details about the knife. That it was never found, only the place he'd washed it in a stormwater drain. Most likely washed his hands there, too. That the killer had used it against Daniel's mother five times. Fortunately, the media hadn't found this out either, saved them using the word *frenzied*. But maybe that number didn't equate to frenzied. Maybe it was just your regular stabbing.

'It was about an hour before someone came along and found you.'

'An hour,' Daniel mused. 'That's a long time.'

Afterwards, Billie would spend equally long periods of time doing unbearable things – gardening in biting winter rain in shorts and a thin top or digging barefoot with a shovel – just to try to experience a similarly endless pain, a flagellator, of sorts. Angus had asked her to stop, said Daniel found it upsetting. Now, she felt stupid for having thought she could even engineer a comparison to her grandson's anguish.

'Then an older couple found us, right?'

'Yes. They were out walking, too.'

Why couldn't it have been one of them?

The first thing Billie had done when she met these people afterwards was to thank them for their care of her grandson when they'd found him. The propriety of simple gratitude obviously so entrenched in her that even a murder couldn't bury the habit. She'd visited them from time to time for a while afterwards. Took Daniel with her sometimes, hoped they'd spark some memory in him. Believed, falsely as it turned out, that they would want to talk about it as well. But then she started to sense their dread at her visits. In the end, Angus encouraged her to stop. She expected they'd asked him to. She often thought of them though – they would be quite elderly now. How their lives must have been altered by what they'd witnessed. She can't see how they couldn't have been damaged in some way – making sense of what they came across, making the 000 call, remaining at the scene, comforting a child, the police questioning them afterwards. Worse: the impossibility of erasing the picture of what had been done to Jess from their memories. These people would always be one of the many ripples cast upon the pond of this violent act.

'I barely remember them now,' Daniel said.

Angus would say that was how it should be.

'And the DNA?'

'There was a little.' He'd been careful. 'And as Inspector Quinn keeps telling us, having the DNA is only part of it. They also need a suspect to match it against.'

Billie imagined the hairs and fibres they'd found on Jess sealed in something no more substantial than a ziplock plastic bag like those in her own kitchen drawer, waiting for serendipity to release them.

'No one saw him enter the park,' Billie continued. 'The police said it's even possible he went in there after nightfall and waited.'

'What about leaving the park?'

The park was large; much of it heavily treed, with narrow, often hidden trails weaving in and out between them. Billie had entered and exited the park from all of its points over the years since, tested her invisibility. Jess's killer had also known how to test his.

'No. There were no witnesses to that either.'

'He just vanished?'

'Yes. Vanished.' Filtered back into humanity, free to live however he chose.

14

It was only two-thirty but Carla opened a bottle of rosé anyway. She took two glasses from the kitchen cupboard and poured wine into each. Pushed one across the breakfast bar to Fran.

'Technically, I'm still working,' Fran said, bringing the glass to her lips.

'Well, after a morning in the sorting room at Vinnies, I need to get rid of the taste of old from the back of my throat.'

Fran laughed. 'You could be less philanthropic with your time. You wouldn't smell like old clothes then.'

'Ugh, do I smell of old clothes?' Carla lifted the hem of her blouse to her nose.

'Eau de moth balls and Youth-Dew circa 1974.' Fran made a show of sniffing the air. 'Undercut by subtle aromas of Winnie Blues and sweat.'

Carla dipped her finger in her wine and dabbed it behind one ear. She leant over the counter top towards Fran. 'Better?' The two women laughed.

Fran pulled out a chair from the breakfast bar, took a newspaper from it before sitting. 'I can't bear looking at that little face anymore.' She folded the newspaper in half, Marco's image now out of sight, and tossed it further along the kitchen bench. 'How does a kid just disappear like that?'

'Because somebody willed it,' Carla said.

'To lose your child would be cruel enough. But to not even have a body? Can't imagine.'

Neither could Carla.

Apparently Billie had though. Had conjured an alternative body in lieu of not having an actual one. Carla shared this fact with Fran now. 'Daniel said Billie told him that she sees the boy.' She spoke quietly. Imagined the walls listening, betraying secrets.

'Really?' Fran dropped her voice too. Leant in.

'In the bush supposedly, when she's out walking.'

Fran looked at her, half smiling, one eyebrow cocked. 'She should speak to the police then. I'm sure they'd like to know.'

'She'd be one of many from what Angus has said. He reckoned there'd be all sorts of crazies contacting the police about him ... people claiming they'd had visitations ... or conspiracy theorists. People dobbing in someone they had a grudge against.'

'Speaking from experience?' Fran hedged.

Reluctantly Carla agreed. 'Uh-huh.'

'He still talks about it then?'

Carla shook her head, regretted starting the conversation now. 'No. Just bits and pieces early on. More because I asked, trying to get my head round what I'd stumbled into.'

'You were brave taking on that kind of damage. Turning it round.'

'He wasn't damaged, Fran, just sad sometimes. And I didn't turn anything round. Angus did that by himself.'

'Still.' Her friend shrugged, not convinced.

'Marrying Angus wasn't a rescue mission, Fran. It was good old-fashioned love.'

Fran held both hands up, deferring. 'Okay. I believe you.

Sounds like Billie's still a work in progress. Do you think she's damaged … like … mentally?'

Carla sighed. 'Billie's just Billie.'

'Being so determined you not sell, though … despite having such a small financial interest in the place, just seems so … I don't know … selfish. Plus, you'd think enough time had passed by now for her to at least put the worst of it behind her.'

Carla didn't answer. Topped up their glasses instead. Each took a sip.

Fran wasn't done. 'I get why women are attacked at night when they're doing the walk of shame thing … you know, getting home after a big night out. But what happened to her was just so … *brazen*. Like the killer was daring someone to catch him. Or maybe she *knew* him.' Fran leant in again, eyes bright. 'A tryst gone wrong.'

This was pure Fran, crossing a moral line for a rise, entertainment, to shock. Carla rose to the latter. 'That's ridiculous!' she loud whispered. 'They loved each other!'

Saying this felt like she was abetting her own betrayal though. She loved the man she'd married but sometimes, inexplicably, she hated the triangle she'd unwittingly completed. The fact that there would always be another woman. Carla washed this bitter thought down now with more wine. 'Besides,' she said, 'who takes their toddler to a secret hook-up? Kids have big mouths.'

Fran looked at her, all innocence. 'Just speculating. Expect the cops did, too.'

Of course they had. Even interrogated Angus. No possibility left unexamined, despite the emotional damage. But Carla said nothing of this and was glad when Fran, big voice back, shifted the conversation from murder to deals.

Her friend opened her satchel, took a document from inside and handed it to Carla. 'Your ticket to double bathroom basins and soft-close kitchen drawers.'

'Drawers that even close would be an improvement,' Carla said, taking the listing agreement.

'I'll make sure what you get for this old place gives you that and more.'

Carla raised her glass. 'Cheers to that.'

'You and Angus look that over, get it back to me signed in the next day or so, then I'll take it from there. Have a *For Sale* sign out the front by the end of next week. First open house the week after. I'm aiming to take it to auction towards the end of April.'

The document was thin but heavy with hope. Carla stared at the A4 pages for a while, contemplating the possibilities they offered. Escape. New beginnings. But a Billie-sized worry, too.

'Sounds great. Just need to get Billie onside.'

Fran shrugged. 'Sign it anyway. At least I can get on with my part. Meanwhile, you and Angus keep working on her.'

'Don't worry, we will.'

'What about Daniel? Can he help?'

'He's not fully on board yet either. We've explained everything to him. He didn't question our logic, only our compassion.'

She didn't tell Fran that Daniel had reminded them that Billie was hurting, like they didn't already know. That Angus had stared at the floor for a time after he'd left the room. How she'd felt his courage slipping. Had told him to hold the course, that they were doing the right thing. That Billie would come round. He wasn't convinced though. 'Once it's sold, it's sold,' he said. 'There's no going back. We risk taking the consequences of that with us.' Which was a risk Carla was prepared to take. Because the consequences of staying were worse. They'd be trapped here, the past eternally trickling down into the present, when getting away from the place offered all of them a chance to navigate a way out of it.

'I think Dan's loyalties are conflicted,' Carla said to her friend. 'Last night Scout was in raptures about the move. And he was great. Played along with her.'

Scout had listed all the things she wouldn't miss about the house – its spooky windows that rattled in the wind, her small bedroom that didn't allow for the bunk beds she coveted, the lack of air-conditioning – and speculated on what she might gain – a swimming pool, two levels, a special TV room, her own bathroom. Daniel teased her. Said as the littlest, she'd still get the smallest room and that he'd use her bathroom anyway because he liked using her Ariel hairbrush. Scout fell for it. Mock-punched her half-brother. Daniel dramatised being hurt while Scout looked on triumphant.

Through their banter, Carla had dared hope her stepson was as excited as Scout about the change. That it was out of respect for Billie that he didn't feel he could express it.

A knock at the back door startled Carla. Soon after, Billie entered the kitchen.

Carla slid the document under the newspaper, tried to assemble a relaxed face. 'Billie. You remember my friend Fran?'

Billie eyed Fran suspiciously. 'The real estate agent?'

Fran took the lead. Rose from her chair, hand extended. 'Yes, for my sins, that's me.'

When Billie refused to take her friend's hand, Carla sought to shift the awkwardness of the snubbing. 'How's the baking going?'

'I came in to see if you had any muffin cases.'

Feeling like an adolescent busted doing something illicit, Carla sprang from her seat, went to the pantry where she could only find cupcake cases. 'Are these okay? It's all I've got.'

Billie took them. 'They'll do. I'll make mini muffins.'

'They'll last longer … having more of them.' But Fran's joke fell flat.

At the door, Billie turned back to look at Fran. 'You know you're implicated in ruining a person's life, don't you?'

For the years Carla had known Fran, this was the first time she'd seen her friend so utterly silenced.

★

Later that afternoon, as she was preparing dinner, a movement beyond the kitchen window caught Carla's eye. She looked out to see Billie and Namita leaving Billie's home together. Seeing her out, Carla figured. There was a narrow passageway that ran between the side fence and the workshop – the tradesman's entrance. Billie often used this route, or she came and went through the gate in the back fence. The alternative was for her to come through the main house. She had a key to the front door but Carla had never known her to use it.

They walked slowly together, Billie talking, Namita nodding. Carla imagined Billie lamenting the sale. Namita, as composed as ever, would be responding empathically to this new separation in Billie's life, without taking sides. *Hopefully* not taking sides.

Namita glanced in the direction of the main house. Looking, perhaps, for Carla, knowing she should come and say hello, but mindful too of Billie, and how she would perceive this. Traitorous? Disloyal? She felt for Daniel's godmother in that moment, because what a sticky bind it was to have one foot so firmly kept in the past with one friend while trying to help another navigate the future.

The pair disappeared into the workshop. Angus was in there. There would be an exchange of greetings. Carla pictured this. Billie might slip in some snipe about him selling, hoping for Namita's support. Namita would intercept this remark, put some optimistic spin on it for Angus's sake, or divert it altogether to something else, perhaps what Angus was working on, a remark about the wood's grain, its colour. Namita liked Angus, respected him. Carla knew that, so she would find it awkward having to split herself between the two.

Carla hoped all these imagined conversations and events were true. Hoped Namita wasn't here as a go-between for Billie. Someone her dead friend's mother had asked to negotiate on her behalf, testing the sincerity of that long-ago friendship.

The possibility of this suddenly made the kitchen feel

oppressive. She looked out the window, thinking, *Rain, please, just rain*. Anything to shift the hot, sticky air, tip the high humidity into something she could cup in her hands instead of it collecting as sweat in the folds of her skin. But the sky was a blank blue canvas. The back door was open and the shrill whistle of cicadas scraped at the still air. Scraped at her nerves and patience, too. It was like living with a drone overhead. She hated these insects as much as she hated snakes; intruders they'd had in the backyard often enough now for her to make a habit of surveying the path for one whenever she went to the clothesline. Why snakes would bother finding gaps under the fence to enter their yard when they had a great expanse of wild ground on the other side of it was beyond her.

If she had her way she'd see a deep swathe cut through the bush behind them, see it ripped well back from their boundary. Anything to create a dividing line between here and there. As it was, she felt this untamed place encroaching on her, trying to take possession. Sometimes she imagined the trees loosening their roots, slipping under the fence like the snakes, edging their way towards the house till they'd grown over it entirely. Then slowly, stealthily, they'd haul the structure back out and under the soil. Such was her mistrust of the bush. This feeling that it was out to get her.

When the two women emerged from the workshop again, Angus raised his hand to bid Namita farewell. Carla watched as Billie said her goodbyes but, before she could walk away, Angus gently put his hand on her shoulder. They exchanged words, about what she couldn't know. Angus tried to get Billie to look at him, dipped his knees a little so they were at eye level as he spoke. Billie wouldn't engage with him initially. But then she turned to face him. Her expression beseeching as she spoke. Angus wouldn't or couldn't look at her then, but seemed to squeeze her shoulder. Billie turned away, headed towards her house. Angus watched her go, his eyes scrunched against the sun's glare, so Carla couldn't tell what he might be feeling. Soon after, he walked towards the main house.

'I see Namita visited?'

'Yeah. Popped in to see Billie.' Angus filled a glass with cold water from the fridge. 'She said we should get together for another meal soon.'

'What did you and Billie talk about just now?' The question was meant to sound casual but there was a shrill edge to it, the cicada within.

'Just asked how she was.'

'And how is she?'

'She's okay.'

'Happy okay? Sad okay? *Coming round* okay?'

'Coming round?' Angus snorted. 'You're optimistic.'

Carla pinched the bridge of her nose. 'Why does it have to be so hard? We're moving house, not country! To one we won't boil in during summer or freeze in during winter. A place that won't even *have* laminated benches, let alone ones I can pick off with my fingernail.' She flicked at an edge of the breakfast bar's grey laminate to demonstrate, felt it give a little more.

'Carla, there's more at stake here than a better kitchen and air-conditioning. We're talking about moving someone's life.'

'Yeah. Ours. To a better one. She'll adjust.'

'I wouldn't be so sure of that.'

'She's being manipulative, Angus.'

'You don't get it, do you?'

She used to try and *get it*, think like Billie. Imagine something was owed the ground where her daughter had lived – respect, guardianship, whatever. But she'd decided the earth couldn't know, *care*, about who lived on it, so why should she.

Angus rinsed the glass, took up a tea towel and tentatively dried it, his smashed finger on the mend but still tender. Any other time she'd have told him to leave it, have done it for him.

'I'm going to pick up Scout.' She didn't care that she'd get there early. Need to wait in the worst of the hot February sun. Didn't care that she'd leave the house full of resentment. She just wanted out.

She took her bag from the bench. Spotted the contract sitting there and dropped it on the bench in front of him. 'Rip it up if that's what you and Billie want. I'm sure I'll get over it.'

As Carla strode out of the house she wondered if there was a skerrick of goodness left in her for Angus to even notice.

15

THE VOICES IN BILLIE'S HEAD were unhelpful and being jobless gave them the opportunity to vent. But grief was a wittering pest and difficult to silence, so she allowed it to mumble, sometimes out loud. Especially after a visit from Inspector Quinn.

He'd seen Jess at her most degraded, probably kept a snapshot of her body somewhere in his mind, not just on file in his office. It was this intimacy he had with her daughter that made the voices more insistent after Billie had spoken with him.

Every news headline shouted at her like an insult. Five-year-olds said to have 'had sex' not raped, football stars 'hit' with domestic assault charges as though they were the victims, 'good blokes' doing the most heinous things. Blame displaced without recompense.

And the missing boy. He was never far from her mind. It was reported that his parents had not yet left the country. Using her own template of loss, Billie could imagine what it would feel like to return home with one less child in their arms. The thread connecting them with their son would need to be cast a long way, across continents and oceans. His body not just lost to them now, but lost also in a strange land. But now there was mention of a person of interest. One man among several seen lingering around the search party. What made this man catch the attention of police over others? Was he too eager to help? Too curious? Not curious enough? There must have been some clue. Regardless, the boy's parents might yet get to see the face of their son's killer. Have justice, too. Cold comfort, but better than nothing at all.

Today, the voices were telling Billie to recheck details in the case of her own loss, look for similar clues. Maybe there was a man in the background of the newspaper cuttings she'd kept whose curiosity was overlooked? She would study them all again.

The morning was once again hot and the sky cruelly blue after the storm that had threatened the previous afternoon. Dark clouds had built in the west, distant thunder vibrated the air like war drums, but nothing had come of it. The small, spiteful cell struck like a king hit in the south – Springwood. Terrible hail damage to cars and homes apparently. Now, the air was humid once more, a thing Billie could touch.

Certain their blended family was out blending into their separate activities for the day, Billie hauled two archive boxes to the table outside the main house where she could better catch the breeze. One box contained newspaper articles and police reports. Another held hundreds of personal messages of condolence, sadness, regret and crack pottery. Many of the notes were signed simply: *Our thoughts and prayers are with you.* She wasn't sure if these people were religious, or if thoughts and prayers had become a clichéd couplet, even for atheists. Politicians used it all the time. It never felt sincere. Others provided just a name beneath the card's verse, many of whom Billie didn't recognise. She didn't mind; she could talk about Jess all day long but she knew it was difficult for others to know what to say, or to listen, if she did.

She pushed the box of cards and personal notes aside for now.

They offered no clues, only a reminder of the discomfort people felt when their own mortality was brought to mind. 'Too many white doves,' she muttered, removing the lid from the other box. 'Insipid flowers.' Jess loved rainbow lorikeets and bold-coloured gerberas. And if she were alive, Jess would have been a willing sleuth. She'd have gone on missions to the garden centre. Checked for illegal plants. Taken photos. Reported back. She'd have championed the cause. They'd been like that, the two of them. Always on the side of justice.

Which is why the newspaper clippings in front of Billie now were so important, headlines and key words jumping out at her as she removed each from the box. They demanded justice, too.

Mother fatally stabbed while walking with toddler.

Heinous crime.

Death sparks widespread outrage.

National outpouring of grief.

So many graceless details of her daughter's death had been shared with strangers through these reports: *defenceless, left to die, a terrible discovery.* Readers knew she hadn't been raped, which perhaps brought relief for some, allowed them to think: *At least not that, too.* But for Billie, this somehow made the crime worse, if that were possible. The pleasure came from the killing. It wasn't some bungled or panicked sexual assault. Jess was doomed no matter what.

Several articles mentioned the park vigil held a few days later. Up near a thousand had attended by all accounts. In one photograph, candle-illuminated faces extended so far back from the fig tree that it was as though the photographer had captured the very curve of the Earth. Billie looked closely at this picture now, wished she had a magnifying glass to better examine the faces. Could it be this man, here, she wondered, pressing her finger to a pale face in the foreground? He looked neither sad nor angry. Was passivity a marker, something that raised suspicion? Two faces either side of his looked the same, confirming the futility of what she was doing. She put the cutting down.

At least there was no blame directed at Jess in these reports. Not the way it was for some murdered girls, for the young sex worker, Susannah, whose life had been reduced to an occupation. Her daughter might have been killed in a park, but it was in broad daylight, a mother and her child – sacrosanct. Wearing a too-big pink t-shirt over floral yoga pants. Not asking for anything. Billie wondered if this contributed to the *national outpouring of grief*? That there were certain standards, a kind of hierarchy, to take into consideration for the murdered. If so, Jess was at the top of it. The blameless victim.

The back screen door pushed open and Carla came out, a basket of washing on her hip.

Not at work today then. Billie felt a quiver of guilt.

'Hey, Billie. How are—'

Carla paused, probably registering the archive boxes.

Billie didn't respond. She started to gather together her papers and clippings.

'At least the others aren't here this time.' Carla sounded tired. Her daughter-in-law or friend or woman-of-the-house – which was it today? – came over to where Billie had laid out the newspaper clippings and rested the washing basket on top of them. Carla pulled out a chair and sighed into it. 'When, Billie? Please, tell me *when?*'

Billie wouldn't look at her as she strained to lift one end of the basket of wet washing to retrieve the clippings from beneath it. She kept up her careful stacking then, as determined in this as the ocean was in pursuit of the shore.

This was no mother–daughter campaign; this was woman-to-woman, a whole different beast. And still, after all this time, neither one of them knew how to wage it. Carla was just like all those people who turned up at the vigil: co-opted into another's grief without ever really knowing – *showing* – the truest, most raw pain of it.

'Billie?'

But Billie kept her eyes on the papers as she stacked them back inside the archive box. Carla looked on, waiting.

Eventually Billie spoke. 'If you really understood you wouldn't need to ask me that.'

'But what about Dan? Angus?'

'Maybe they'd do this sort of thing too if you'd let them.' This hit its mark and Billie didn't feel good about it.

Standing, Carla picked up her basket of washing again. 'I'd let them,' she said, not unkindly. 'But they don't *want* to. And neither do they want *you* to.'

Billie watched Carla walk down the length of yard they planned to sell from under her. A woman unwilling or unable to sense the girl who had walked the path before her.

The unhelpful voices whispered on in Billie's head. *Jess wants me to.*

16

Daniel was usually glad of the impersonal barrier of the bar top. It meant he didn't really exist. He was just the guy dressed in black behind it pulling pints and pouring spirits. The Megans of the world didn't engage with him, reminding him of his awkwardness. And tonight there were no girls pinned against walls by drunken men to remind him of his lack of a conscience.

The bar was slower than usual and filled with happy, fun-seeking people. All the creepy, judgy, drunk-punchy arseholes were elsewhere, spoiling other people's nights, leaving just a good-time crowd here. Nights like these made Daniel feel hopeful.

Tonight, that barrier was lowered. The two British girls on the other side of the bar had been chatting with Daniel for the past half an hour. They weren't big drinkers, each nursing a bottle of Batlow Cloudy Cider for all of that time. His visibility felt good.

'We give hostels cockroach ratings instead of stars,' the chatty one said. 'Five being the worst.'

She was tall, soft-framed. Her friend was tiny, like Polly. Almost looked like a child sitting on the other side of the tall counter. Daniel guessed they were a similar age to him. A year or two older, tops.

'How many fives have you stayed in?' he asked.

Both girls looked at each other and laughed. 'Too many,' they chorused.

'I gave the one near here four cockroaches. On account of how many I've seen there so far.'

The shorter girl leant in. 'Gina's a harsh critic.'

Gina turned to Daniel, hand to the side of her mouth as though about to whisper, then said loudly, 'Sam finds the good in *every*thing and *every*one. Even said nice things about the guy who stole her pizza from the communal fridge in the place up at Airlie Beach.'

'But I bet he *was* broke and hungry!'

'We're *all* broke and hungry, Sam!'

'I'm not hungry.'

'Well, you should be, then you might grow taller.'

Daniel enjoyed the girls' banter. The ease of it. This was what normal looked like. What *free* looked like. What it was to have a blank history card, all the boxes empty and ready to be filled with what you curated for yourself. What he'd give for that kind of freedom.

He harboured a dream. In this dream he lived somewhere else. This other place could be anywhere, even England where these girls were from. Just so long as it was away from here. A place with different trees – no figs. Different air, too. Lighter. Air you could breathe without your throat drying out.

'Tell me about England,' he said.

'What do you want to know?' Gina asked.

'I don't know. What's it smell like? What trees grow there?'

The two girls looked at each other for a moment then burst out laughing.

'What's it *smell* like?' Gina leant in to read his name badge.

'You're funny, Daniel. Most people ask us about the royal family or football.'

There it was again: *Funny Dan*. How he wanted to believe it.

'In Millwall where I come from,' Gina said, 'it smells like the Thames, which at low tide isn't so good. What about you, Sam? What's Devon smell like?'

'Cow shit.'

'Wait … you two didn't know each other before you left?'

Both girls shook their head. 'We met in Ho Chi Minh City. Been travelling together ever since.' Gina put her arm round Sam and squeezed.

'Reckon you'll keep in touch when you get home?'

'Yeah!'

'Absolutely!'

The two girls chinked cider bottles.

So this was what travel could do. Allowed a girl from the country and a girl from the city to find each other and become friends. Futures changed, just like that. All it took was a flight.

A preppy, athletic guy wearing tight brown chinos and a white buttoned-up polo shirt sidled up to the bar. He rested one tanned arm next to the girls and leant into their space. Daniel shook his head, smiling. He'd seen the move dozens of times.

'Bundy and Coke, thanks,' he said, glancing at Daniel.

Daniel mixed the drink. When the guy paid, he tapped his phone on the EFTPOS machine without even looking at the screen.

'Receipt?'

Ignoring Daniel, the guy directed his brightest smile at the British girls. 'Say something and I'll tell you where you're from.'

The guy was lazy. Lacked originality. Daniel had heard that lame pick-up line more times than he could count.

The girls rolled their eyes. 'Uh … hello?' Gina offered.

'Scottish! You're Scottish.' The guy slapped the bar. 'I love Guinness.'

Ignorant as well. Reminded him of Bryce.

More annoying than the cliché standing on the other side of the bar was that Daniel had been enjoying talking to the girls. Didn't want it to stop. He tried on *Funny Dan*. Flexed his bicep, patted a hand over his mouth feigning a yawn. The girls laughed.

'What's so funny?' The guy turned to look at Daniel, who by then was rolling a lime on a small chopping board with the flat of his hand, ready for slicing.

'We're English,' Sam said. 'And Guinness is from Ireland.'

'Nah. I had Guinness in Scotland.'

Well, yeah … it's *sold* there. But it's an Irish drink. Like your Bundaberg rum is Australian.'

It was Daniel's turn to laugh.

'How about you just serve, mate.' The guy pushed his empty glass towards Daniel. 'Another Bundy and Coke.'

Daniel turned instead to another customer who'd pulled up at the bar beside him. 'What can I get you?'

He made the entitled prick invisible three more times, till he eventually sulked off and found someone else to serve him. He shouted the two girls a fresh bottle of cider. Wanted their company to last a bit longer.

Polly, who never missed a beat, leant in to Daniel. 'Nice work,' she said.

The air temperature had dropped by the time Daniel left work around two that morning. Mid-twenties. Less humid. Bearable. He took a rideshare home, but felt buoyed after work and too wired to sleep, so he asked to be dropped off near the park instead.

His visits to his mother's tree were infrequent now. And the times he did go it was mostly seeking answers. Today he wanted to go there without any expectations other than to see the sunrise. To see the good in the place.

He used the torch on his mobile phone to find his way along the trail. By the time he got to the tree he could just make out the shape of it. Seeing it tall and dark against a city-lit sky made him think of string and lessons and another time. This memory, like the one at the dinosaur garden, was special. It was all his.

His mother had brought the ball of string with her to the park that day so she could show him that the tree's girth was almost as great as its height. He vaguely recalled how she'd traced the string in and out and over the many pleat-like folds of the fig's trunk. Over time, Daniel had inserted her conversation to go with this memory, being too young to remember the detail of it.

'It's like drawing the lines on a map,' he had her say. 'A contour map.' He attributed this act by his mother, and the imagined conversation that went with it, in part for his love of maps.

It took her a while, but eventually the string traced right round the tree. She marked the length, shook it free, and laid it on the ground in one straight line. He remembered how he'd looked along the length of it – his mother standing quite far away at one end, and him at the other – then up to the tree's top. Up, down, up, down, he looked, until he could see what she meant.

Memories of his mother were mostly handed down from others. Translated from their experiences not his. He felt a fraud in trying to own them. But not this one. Not the dinosaur one.

He settled on the ground between two buttress roots, his mother's memorial plaque above his head, the roots rising up beside him like walls. Once, he'd imagined these great stanchions closing around him in a wooden embrace. How if he'd stayed there long enough they'd seal him inside the tree's trunk like an embryo, one never destined to grow or be born. And yet this tree had already birthed him once, sent a new version of a boy into the world. He was still trying to reckon with the shape of him.

Daniel nestled back into the comfortable alcove, earth and tree pleasantly cool through his clothing, and waited. The morning was in that twilight time: night creatures were settling down, quietening, the day shift beginning to stir. Daniel was in that twilight zone, too: feeling lazy but not yet sleepy, alert enough but winding down. Time suspended for man and Earth. His favourite time. Expectations – his own, those of others – about how he should act, think or live weren't pressing their demands. He could imagine himself as anyone, anywhere.

Was it a betrayal to leave? Not just his home, but if he were to leave the country too, travel like those two girls?

He was reminded of what Carla had said a few weeks ago, about honouring his mother. Everything about his life had been geared to maintaining his memory of her. But was he honouring her by doing that? Would she, as Carla suggested, hate to see him sitting here, beneath the tree where she was murdered, questioning his right to live a full life? Would she be angry with Billie – her own mother – for being the catalyst of that?

His grandmother had always asked him to imagine the pulse of his mother in the soil and in the rocks. In the eyes of birds and in the skin of trees. Revivifying her in the most improbable ways. Never teaching him to imagine the flesh and blood of her. The thinking, breathing, feeling, sometimes angry mess of a mother that she probably would have been. Sometimes he hated the manipulation. Was fed up with the lie.

The sky began to blush coral and things around him came into sharper focus. Daniel looked over to the barbecue shelter and saw the shape of a guy stretched out on the bench seat under it. He kept half an eye on him, not wary so much as curious. Expected he'd been on his way home from a big night out and decided to sleep it off in the park.

As the sun nudged at the horizon the man stirred, then before long, sat up. He leant back against the picnic table, adjusted his balls, farted. Stretched his thin legs out in front of him, crossed them at the ankles. He seemed familiar to Daniel. Came from always looking for certain features, he supposed. The man's build – an unhealthy kind of lean – was one thing, his thin, greasy hair another. And of course there was the stereotype of the lone, unkempt man thought to be dangerous. It was difficult to pinpoint his age. He could be an old forty or a young sixty. Either way, Daniel reckoned life had rubbed him up the wrong way, etched him with hungry angles and joyless lines.

The man looked about, spotted Daniel. 'Where'd you spring from?' He stood abruptly, stared at the ground for a time. After a moment, he turned back and headed straight towards Daniel. His thongs were longer than his feet and with each step they slapped loudly. Black jeans sat low on slim hips, pushed down by a small round belly, and navy jocks sat high. Daniel imagined his t-shirt was probably once white.

The man pulled up not far from where Daniel sat but wouldn't look at him. Spoke to some spot off to Daniel's right. 'I seen you here before.'

Daniel couldn't think when. But maybe he had and that was why he seemed familiar – he had seen him, too. He stared hard at the man. History gave him the right and need made it a habit.

With hands pushed deep into the front pockets of his jeans, the man shrugged, made his shoulders bunch up towards his ears, shortened his neck. He looked like a man used to playing invisible.

The man's head was in clear view, his right ear small and pressed flat against his skull. The ear lobe wasn't so much a lobule as a slim crescent of flesh. Room enough for a piercing? It was hard to judge. He tried to imagine a cross hanging from this man's ear, but stopped himself. There was a danger in doing this. Because how, if he made a career of trying to fix a familiar memory to the unfamiliar, could he ever hope to hold on to that one true fragment? What stopped the honesty of it being completely lost to doubt?

'You must be here often enough yourself to notice,' Daniel said.

The man still wouldn't look at him. 'Now and then.'

Or then, and again now?

The man turned to face Daniel and he recalled his nine-year-old self, out on a bike too big for him in their street, and a man back then asking the location of a hardware store in a suburb nearby. How he'd had to stand on the tips of his toes that day, the bike's bar pressed up hard against his balls as he struggled to turn his too-big bike around. How he only trusted himself to look back at the man once he'd steadied his wobbly escape. How when he did, the man's gaze was still fixed on him over the roof of his old beat-up car and Daniel had wondered if it was his mother's killer come back to test his memory. Because surely that man must live with the fear that one day the small boy who witnessed his crime would call from a crowd: *There! That's him!*

Could this be the same man now, ten years later, sixteen years later? How to factor in time and age to his memories of that man with this one, while always factoring it in for so many others?

This man. That man. Any man. Why was he even thinking about it? This wasn't living a larger life. This was following the same narrow tracks he always had. What a shit of a way to live, thinking every man could be the one.

Daniel adjusted his shoulders against the hardness of the tree and returned the man's gaze. His eyes were brown, that much he could tell from where he sat. Bloodshot, like he'd had a big night on the grog. As the light improved, Daniel could see his hands were small and his fingers slim, like a girl's. Not that he expected this would make them any less dangerous.

Daniel waited, for what he wasn't sure. The tree to speak to him, for a stone to be lifted on a trapped memory so that he was finally handed something useful?

The man seemed to be waiting, too. He glanced at the plaque screwed into the tree trunk above Daniel's head. A slight smile played at the edges of his otherwise uncharitable mouth. Was this the kind of confidence Daniel could expect from a killer who'd just realised he was unrecognisable? A man who carried a huge secret around with him while at the same time wishing he could let someone – anyone – know just how clever he'd been in getting away with a violent crime, his bragging rights till now denied. Or was he just some sadistic bastard who'd put two and two together and liked the miserable fit of them?

He looked away from Daniel again so that his right ear came into view once more. There was no scar there to indicate an old piercing.

'Stop acting like you're him.'

The man looked at Daniel again and he smiled. 'Torment ya, does it?'

Daniel dug out his phone from the front pocket of his trousers, aimed it at the man and clicked off several photos.

The man's slimy smile slipped from his face. 'Hey! What d'you think ya doin'?' he said, putting an arm up, too late, to cover his face.

'Tormenting *you*,' Daniel said, returning his phone to his pocket.

The man took a step closer and bent in towards Daniel, till he could smell his old-booze breath. 'I'm not your man, kid.'

Daniel didn't flinch.

The man straightened again. 'I done some things I ain't proud of, but I ain't done that.' He indicated to the plaque.

Fleetingly, Daniel cursed his grandmother for contributing to his mother being defined by the worst thing that had happened to her and not anything of the best.

'Stop acting like you did then.'

The man smiled and shook his head. 'Ballsy little bugger, aren't ya?'

But Daniel thought the man was wrong. He wasn't ballsy so much as had nothing to lose, which allowed for its own kind of sarcasm and risk. 'Trying to flatter me now?'

'Nup. Not one to flatter.'

'So why'd you come over?'

The man's smile widened. 'Wanted to see for myself what tortured looked like. But all I see is an angry little boy.' He swaggered away. A small, weedy man suddenly feeling big.

Everything came alive after that: birds, lizards, cicadas, heat.

The twilight time had passed. Expectations and the day pressed in. Daniel longed for that moment again when he could be anyone, anywhere. The simplicity of being a boy joking and chatting with two girls across a bar. No past, just a new and glorious future stretched before him. One his mother would be proud of.

17

THE PRACTICE PHYSIO STUDIED THE appointment screen over Carla's shoulder. 'Your next client rang to say he's running late,' Carla told her.

Linda rolled her eyes. 'He runs late every second appointment. Don't know why he bothers coming in at all. Not much I can do with chronic back pain in fifteen minutes.'

'Maybe he thinks you're a miracle worker.'

'Be nice if I was. Hey, how's Angus anyway? On the mend?'

'Pretty much. The fingernails still need to grow out. Not sure what they'll end up looking like.'

'And future plans?'

Carla looked at her, confused.

Linda shrugged. 'From what you've said his workshop isn't fit for purpose, so I figure it's only a matter of time before he injures something else.' Linda had a long career in occupational health before starting at the practice, so had a crystal ball gaze for hazards. 'So what's the plan to prevent it?'

Carla liked her colleague's straight talk. Liked how sure of herself she was. Linda could tell if her clients hadn't done their exercises between appointments. Called them out for it, told them they were wasting their time and hers. Something she'll probably tell the guy who's running late today. More than one person had come out of her treatment room looking upbraided. They almost always came back though. Knew she was right. Knew also that she was good at what she did. Carla wished she could stand as firmly behind her own convictions of what was in another person's best interests. Linda would've set Billie straight a long time ago.

'We're toying with the idea of selling,' Carla said. It felt like a one-person game at present, but she wouldn't give up on it. Not yet. 'Thinking to separate where we live from where he works. Find space in an industrial area somewhere for his business.'

'Sounds logical. So why only toying?'

Carla frowned. Tried to think of how to explain the complex family she'd married into without sharing all the facts. When she'd done that in the past it had brought out the morbid fascination people have with crime and violence more than it had empathy for her situation.

'It's complicated. Angus's mother-in-law lives with us ... she doesn't want to move.'

'Is she the one trying to build furniture in a garage?'

No, and neither did she see a man – or a grandson for that matter – struggling in other aspects of their lives. She saw only what she wanted to see, her vision blinkered by the fool notion that their block of land was a graveyard of sorts, one without a headstone. But if it did have one, its epitaph would read: *This land is mine. Hands off.*

'Unfortunately, where we see real estate she sees something else ... something more ... personal.'

'What? Like she's given the plants pet names or had the same neighbours for years?'

How to tell practical, straight-talking Linda that Billie believed the earth bore her daughter's energy, her spirit. That she believed this ensured her daughter's immortality. Even mentioning it, Linda would think Carla had lost her mind, not just Billie.

Instead, she edged round the reasons. 'Living there reminds her of her dead daughter because she lived there once, too. I think in staying, she believes she'll be able to keep the memory of her for longer.'

'When did the daughter die?'

'Sixteen years ago.'

'*Sixteen*? I'd have thought her memories would have moved on a bit in that time.'

Carla shrugged, had thought much the same. 'I guess she thinks staying will delay that as much as possible.'

'Meanwhile,' Linda said, looking at her watch, 'your husband risks ending up with an injury like Late Mate.'

As if on cue, Late Mate pushed through the doors frothing with apologies and walking like he had a rod up his back.

'These two hands can only do so much in the time given to them, Jim.'

Jim, admonished, skulked after Linda to the treatment room. Carla watched them go. What she'd give to have Billie make an appointment with her colleague and hear logic from someone else.

Another Monday. Another dinner with Billie. Carla placed the shopping bags containing ingredients for the meal on the kitchen table, unprepared for what was already there.

Neither her nor Angus had mentioned the sale document again. It had remained on the bench unsigned for a week. But there it was now, back on the kitchen table, Angus's signature flourished across the pages marked with *Sign here* tabs.

Soon after, Angus came in from the workshop. A film of red-tinged dust coated the pale hair on his forearms. Rested on his eyebrows and in the tufts of grey hair not contained under his cap. Carla knew if she brushed up against him that it would also sprinkle from his clothes. It dulled the usual sweat shine of his skin. Gave his body an ochre aura.

'You signed it,' she said.

'Yep. Your get-out-of-jail-free card.'

The joy left her. 'Don't put it on me like that, Angus.'

He looked at her confounded. 'Sorry. It was meant to be a joke.' He put his arms round her, pulled her in and kissed her.

There was a medicinal scent to him. Sometimes pine, at others cedar. Today it was eucalyptus. These aromas would linger in his hair, in the folds of his skin, under his nails. Even after he'd showered she could still detect traces of it. She'd come to associate it with the honest, natural smell of his labour, but also of his passion for a craft. Sometimes she'd press her nose to the space just behind his ear for the sheer pleasure of breathing him in, which she did now.

'So this is it,' she said. 'No regrets?'

'Some apprehension,' he said, 'but no regrets.'

She didn't care that her white blouse would be soiled, she pressed into him, held him tight. Felt some of that apprehension too, but mostly gratitude.

There was a knock at the back door and soon after Billie pushed it open.

Why did she still knock after all this time?

She greeted Carla with a Pyrex dish that looked to hold crumble. Her contribution to the weekly meal was always a dessert.

'Peach and pear.' Billie placed it on the stovetop. 'Still warm.'

'Thanks. It looks delicious.'

Next, she took a box of custard and a bottle of thickened cream from a string bag she had over her shoulder. 'Trimmings. Fridge?'

Permission always sought, like she was a guest. How did they never take that final step, see one another as family?

'Hey, Nan!' Scout called from the sofa in front of the television at the far end of the kitchen. 'Come sit with me!' Scout patted the seat beside her.

'Can I help with anything?'

'No, you go,' Carla said. 'There's not much left to do.'

Carla glanced at the television just as an impala's hindquarters collapsed under the claws and weight of a lion. David Attenborough made it sound like a celebration.

'You mightn't like what I'm watching, Nan,' Scout said to Billie as she settled in beside her. 'It's pretty scary. I love lions but they're not very nice to those deer.'

'I think I'll cope,' Billie said, and laughed.

Scout went back to absentmindedly picking at the scab on her knee while the two of them watched the cycle of life play out before them on the television screen.

Unusually for a Monday, Carla opened a bottle of wine, didn't explain why. Kept the sense of celebration to herself. She rested her hand on Angus's shoulder and squeezed it if she got up to collect something, stroked his shin with her bare toes under the table.

Billie fiddled with her paper napkin after they'd eaten. Folded it in half, then half again until she no longer could, at which point she undid it and started all over again.

'I read somewhere that you can only fold a piece of paper seven times.' Daniel indicated to the paper napkin.

'Wouldn't it depend on the size of the paper?' Billie asked.

'Apparently not. Even if it's the size of a table.' Daniel sat at the narrower end of theirs, reached with his hands now to its edges. 'Still seven.'

'What if it was the size of a block of land?' Billie asked.

All at the table fell silent, looked to their empty dessert bowls, except for Scout who was up on her knees on her chair, leaning over the Pyrex dish, picking at its caramelised fruit edges with her fingernail. 'Don't be silly, Nan. You can't fold up a piece of *land*.'

'I wish you could, Scout. Fold it up tight,' Billie demonstrated with the napkin again, 'and keep it in your pocket … forever.'

'You'd need a very, *very* big pocket.'

'And a lot of goodwill from others to help put it there.'

Till then, Billie had blessedly kept her bitterness out of the conversation. But there she was now, playing the martyr card.

Carla rolled her eyes. 'Here we go again,' she mumbled.

'You make it sound like you're getting on and off a merry-go-round, Carla. Is that what it is to you? A joyride? Do you get a thrill out of hurting me?'

'There's little joy in this for anyone, Billie.' Carla screwed up her own napkin, dropped it in her empty bowl.

'Billie, please …' Angus stalled, stymied perhaps by the constraints of a shared history as much as uncertainty about how to mitigate Billie's remark.

Even Scout sensed the venom in it. She looked from Billie to her mother, not understanding what was passing between them but clearly sensing it was wrong. A sensitive child, quick to tears, they sprang from her silently now, brought on, Carla imagined, by not knowing what to do with her confused loyalties.

'I apologise,' Billie said. 'That was rude of me.' She pushed her chair back from the table. Got up to leave.

Carla pushed back her chair, too. Rose to follow Billie out.

Another person wouldn't have noticed the split second indecision as Billie headed for the back door, how she momentarily turned left before quickly correcting herself and turning right. When they'd extended the patio at the back of the house four years ago – a concession by Angus to give them more outdoor space – the back door had to be shifted. There was a muscle memory to many of Billie's actions, navigating this changed exit was one of them. Recognising the misfiring of Billie's memory now made Carla's heart suddenly ache for this woman who was not her mother-in-law or her aunt, not her work colleague or her neighbour. But her heart mostly ached because she didn't even know if they were friends.

'Billie,' Carla said gently and rested her hand on Billie's arm. It was bold of her, though tentative. She wished her hands could work miracles like Linda's, just by touch and gentle pressure. But it wasn't to be. Billie wouldn't look at her, turned right and walked out of the house, leaving Carla's hand empty and useless at her side.

As Carla expected, Daniel was next up from the table. He went out the back door after his grandmother.

Later, Carla would wonder if she'd invited the confrontation. That she should have apologised, too, because she'd made a gesture, then a remark, that couldn't be dismissed, therefore putting in motion what followed. Maybe this was how the subconscious worked. It allowed things to push through the conscious mind unvetted, just to be rid of the burden of holding them. Carla would like to blame something, because the alternative was that she'd been intentionally unkind.

In bed that night, Angus pulled her in to him. She felt conviction in his arms: there was no going back, his embrace indicated. They were in this together.

Carla always thought it a miracle of good fortune that Angus, a man used to working with something ungiving like wood, could gentle them so readily to lay them on skin. Initially, she expected their pressure and movements would be too forceful, too firm. But she was wrong. Just as he took his time to examine a new piece of timber first for its beauty then its utility, the hidden in the piece, extracting it carefully knowing there was reward for both creator and benefactor, so it was that he divined the hidden in Carla now. Brought out what she hoped were her qualities, too. Although after what had happened tonight, she wasn't sure if kindness and grace were among them.

18

Daniel wasn't sure if it was the heat making everything feel as mean as iron filings under bare feet or if it was his family doing that. After the finality of Angus telling Billie that the sale would go ahead, Daniel's world felt like it would combust: house, land, family. And maybe that was what was needed. Everything reduced to ash so they could start again.

The only respite from Billie's sadness and Carla's mania, as she tried to make their old house look like an Art Union prize home, was his work. And that had just taken a turn for the better.

He'd worried if the girl did come to the Para, that he wouldn't recognise her. They'd spoken so briefly at the museum. He was pretty sure the girl with the short bleached-blonde hair waving at him now was her. When he spotted the brown birthmark on the inside of her forearm, he was certain.

'Hey, Dan!'

'Hey!'

'This place is seriously wild tonight!' she said.

It was. A new band was playing. They were getting a lot of

love out in the back courtyard, where it was a crush of sound and movement.

Daniel looked around her. 'Did you drag Bryce along?'

'God, no. Barely know the guy. He's a friend of Emily's … that other girl.'

He must have looked pleased, because she smiled. 'Not my type,' she said. 'Not enough happening up here.' She tapped her head. 'I'm Alex, by the way.' She held out her hand to Daniel with mock seriousness. He noticed that her fingers were remarkably long. They both laughed at the formality as they shook.

The music paused and the thirsty arrived with requests for bottled beer, Cruisers, Bundy and Cokes. Alex moved out of the way to let people in. Daniel and Polly served.

Once the rush was over, Polly nudged him. 'Someone's waiting to finish that conversation.' She indicated to Alex still down one end of the bar. She had her back to it, elbows resting on the timber top behind her, bottle of Kirin in one hand, looking out across the crowd.

'You don't miss much,' he said to Polly.

'I expect I miss a lot. But not so much when it comes to you.' She winked at him.

Alex turned to face Daniel when he came down to her end of the bar. 'You here on your own?' he asked.

'No. Came with my housemates. They're out there somewhere.' She gestured behind her with one arm.

Did they neglect her or did she neglect them? No, he didn't think it was either. She looked too at ease.

'How long have you worked here anyway?'

'Just over a year. First job out of school.'

'And you've stayed? Must be better tips here than any hospo jobs I've ever had.'

'Nah. Tips are shit,' Daniel said. 'Habit.'

She tilted her triangle chin, studied him. 'You like museums.

Old maps. Have the brain of an astrophysicist … *apparently.*'

Daniel liked the way she listed what little she knew of him. Made him into something.

'Doesn't sound like the kind of person who'd work in a budget bar for long *or* have habits.'

'I've disproved the brain part then,' Daniel said.

She ignored this. Instead, face suddenly animated, she said: 'I know. You're planning to couch surf your way round Europe and you use this place to get contacts?' She peered over the bar, looked at his trouser pockets. 'Where's your little black book?'

Daniel laughed. 'Great idea!'

'It's what I'd do.' She saluted him with her bottle of beer before taking a sip.

Somehow, he didn't doubt she would.

'Here she is.' A girl came up and put her arm round Alex's shoulders. 'Chatting up the staff.'

Daniel hadn't thought of it like that, but when Alex said, 'Sprung,' he reckoned he grinned like an idiot.

'We're heading off,' the girl said to Alex. 'You coming?'

'Guess so.' Alex put her almost finished beer on the bar top. 'Might see you here again.' She held out her hand to Daniel, regimentally, just as she had when she first introduced herself. Ending the encounter as they began, both laughing.

She raised her arm to him as she left and Daniel thought the imperfection on it was one of the most honest and attractive features he'd ever seen on a girl.

Daniel was glad he rode his bike to work that night. He was vigilant riding out of the Valley and away from the busy inner-city streets. Set a solid pace till he got onto the bikeway that ran alongside the Western Freeway, before he relaxed into a slower rhythm, took his hands off the grips, hung them loose at his sides. Enjoyed the cooler air. The solitude. Being the only cyclist about.

Luck wasn't a word, or a feeling, Daniel normally associated with himself. But lucky was how he felt at that moment. He felt lucky to have met a girl called Alex. Someone he thought he could really like. Maybe even trust not to pity or mother him with sympathy if she knew his story.

It made him think about how his father had managed it when he met Carla. It must have been hard, that story more real for him; the baggage heavier for Carla than it would be for anyone Daniel might meet. He realised how lucky he was in having her, Carla, someone who strived to give Daniel a life that resembled normal.

He breathed deep of the clean, night air. Caught the scent of eucalyptus. Felt lucky, too, to live in a city with a place like Mount Coot-tha Forest only a few kilometres from its heart. The scent came from that dark wall of bush on the other side of the freeway now. Coot-tha, *Ku-ta*: place of honey. Even called Honey Mountain for a time, then One Tree Hill after all the trees were cut down to build Brisbane, except for one left at the top as a trig station. The native bees and the people who collected their honey, forced to move on. It was a baldness Daniel struggled to imagine. Thankfully treed once more, it was a place of recreation and escape with its hundreds of kilometres of trails for riders and walkers. He knew it was a place of sabotage, too, but forced that thought aside. Stuck to those about sweetness and luck.

Because he reckoned life *was* about luck. So much of it depended on chance: encounters, opportunities, where a person was in any given moment in time in relation to another. And right now he'd only let himself think about the benefits that came from those chance encounters: Dinosaurs–Whale Mall–Alex.

When Daniel got home he saw Billie's kitchen light was on. He leant his bike up against her wall, peered in through her window to check if she'd just forgotten to turn it off. But there she was, sitting at the kitchen table, head bent over in concentration.

Not wanting to alarm his grandmother, he called out as he opened the front door. 'Not like you to wait up for me,' he joked, as he entered her kitchen. But hopes of making light of her being awake at this hour evaporated when he saw that the items of clothing on the table had belonged to his mother. Alongside them was a sewing box and scissors.

'Look what I've made.' Billie held up a square of fabric a bit smaller than his phone. 'Pouches. From your mum's clothes.'

He counted three on the table, plus the one in her hand.

It was no secret that his mother's clothes hung in a pine wardrobe in Billie's bedroom. As a small boy he'd run his fingers across them. He'd come to think of them as soft exoskeletons, dead and empty vessels in the shape of his mother.

The fabric of the pouches varied. He recognised the item of clothing each had been cut from: two from a floral dress, one from a chambray shirt, another from a navy skirt.

It unnerved him now to see Billie rub the square of floral fabric between thumb and fingers, the scratchy sound it made, and how her lips moved like she was in conversation with it.

'What are you going to do with them?'

'Bury them.'

Fatigue settled over him. He sunk into a chair opposite his grandmother. Reluctantly, he took hold of one of the cloth pouches. He could see that it had been sewn carefully, the seams were neat, barely a stitch in sight. 'Where?' he asked.

Billie leant in, eyes too bright for the hour. 'Here. There. Anywhere.'

'But why?'

She spoke like Scout did when she was sharing one of her facts: with unwavering conviction. 'They're a gift. To the earth.'

He rubbed the fabric between his fingers as his grandmother

had, felt something hard like a hairclip inside, something gritty, something fibrous. Was he holding his mother's ashes? His father told him that Billie had guarded them closely. Claimed she'd dispersed them, alone, when he was still a small boy. 'What's inside them?' he asked, not sure he wanted to know.

'Small treasures. Things of her.'

'Things *of* her?'

School history lessons about World War One came to him. How construction workers, Belgian and French farmers who lived or worked on what was the Western Front – Somme, Ypres, Fromelles, Verdun – continued to dig up bones and artefacts from the war. Was his mother to have a similar fate? Items of hers – pieces *of* her – harvested years from now by an indifferent worker? The thought gave him the creeps.

'Hair,' Billie said, without missing a beat. 'Other keepsakes.'

Items he hadn't seen. Had no desire to. He imagined how this hair from his mother would feel coarse now, lifeless, just as it looked on exhumed corpses in horror movies. Nothing like the beautiful long brown hair that framed her face in the photographs he kept in his bedroom. He dropped the pouch, suddenly repulsed by it.

His grandmother looked at him, confused. 'What's wrong?'

'It's creepy.'

'No, it's not. It's a tribute to her.' Billie gathered the pouches and clothing together. 'I thought you'd understand. That you'd be pleased.' She rose from her chair, treasures pressed to her chest, and left the room. He heard the click of her bedroom door close behind her.

To think that less than an hour ago he'd considered himself lucky.

19

The words hit Billie with the force of their betrayal.

Development opportunity or land bank for the future.

The *future*? What was theirs – Billie's and Jess's – to look like now?

The real estate sign had been erected on the nature strip in front of the house while she'd been out that day. It was large, taller than her when she stood in front of it. The *for sale* lettering all in lower case. A stupid display of try-hard modernity.

An aerial photograph of the property took up more than half of the advertisement. She recalled hearing the insect noise of a drone last week. It must have taken the image. She thought nothing of it at the time. Had she known, she'd have tried to strike the thing out of the sky with rocks.

The flat iron roof of the main house was prominent at the front of the block. Angus's workshop alongside it. The flat roof of her smaller home was tucked into a back corner. The image was overlaid with thick white lines marking the subdivision boundaries. It drew an imaginary wall between the two homes. A manipulation of proportions and lives.

Billie set about removing the sign. Used her weight to push the board backwards and forwards, tried to loosen the timber uprights from the earth. But it was a pointless exercise that ultimately strained her right shoulder. The board no longer stood vertical though, and she left it tilted towards the kerb like it was ashamed.

She waited in the shade on the back patio of the main house so she could hear when Angus came home. She had to talk to him again. Try to change his mind. But she was restless, couldn't settle in her chair. She walked across the backyard, stepped over the imaginary white line into the other block, *her* block, and set to work in the herb garden, the only bed she'd bothered to keep alive in the drought.

The air smelt brown, tasted impure, lacking succulence. Air so close and hot that Billie felt as though she could disrobe it from her body. Drought air. Cold was about activity – keeping warm – and drought was about inactivity, the sense that there was nothing to do but wait and wait and wait. Billie wasn't a person to wait. Inactivity caged her. To her, stasis was a kind of death. Daniel had always held the key to this cage of inactivity, kept its door open for her. He had been her reason to get up after Jess, her reason to keep moving.

The back door opened. Billie looked up to see her grandson walk out.

'You've seen it?' she called.

'Yeah. I've seen it. Looks like someone's backed their car into it though.'

That's what she should have done. Flattened the thing. 'I can't believe they're going ahead with it.'

She'd thought her pleas on behalf of Jess would have been enough to change at least Angus's mind. Because if not that, then what? Apparently nothing.

'What about Jess, Dan?' she said when he came up to her. 'What about your mother?'

Daniel eased her down to sit on the raised timber edge of the herb garden.

'If this goes, she goes.' Billie lifted her arms to encompass everything around her. 'She's everywhere, Daniel. Here.' She indicated to the plants at her back. 'And here.' She held out her hands for Daniel to see the earth under her nails, embedded in the broken skin around them. How could something so precious be taken from her?

Daniel sat beside her. Bent forward and snapped off a spike of dried grass, began splitting it with his thumbnail. Did he realise just how much of a gift was all around him?

She gripped his forearm. When he lifted his gaze to look at her, she saw a boy wanting to flee. She firmed her grip, forced him to stay.

'I don't know what you want me to do, Nan.'

'Tell him he can't sell. Tell him this ground is precious. Tell him whatever it takes to make him change his mind. He'll listen to you.'

Daniel gently released Billie's fingers from around his forearm and rested her hand back on the top of her thigh. He smoothed her fingers flat with his palm as though he were stroking a cat. Pacifying her. Billie bunched her hands into fists. Undaunted, Daniel spread his fingers wide so that his hand encased hers.

'Maybe it'd be good for us in the long run,' Daniel said.

Billie shook her head fiercely. 'I thought you were on *my* side. Now you sound just like them.'

'I'm not taking sides, Nan. I'm just trying to work out what's the right thing to do … for everybody.'

'You two must be baking out there in this heat,' Angus called from the back door.

'There's no other place I'd rather be,' Billie snapped. She knew she sounded churlish, but didn't care. Maybe that's what it would take, a grown-up tantrum, fists, hair-pulling, swearing and all.

Angus walked down the concrete path towards them. 'I saw what you did to the sign.' He looked right at Billie when he said this.

Billie stared back at him and she felt Daniel's hand tighten over hers.

'It doesn't change anything, Billie,' Angus said. 'I've straightened it again and I'll keep straightening it.'

'Dad. Go easy.'

'I've gone easy for years, son. I know you don't see it now, Billie, but I'm doing this for all of us.'

'Give me *my* block. Sell yours. I can stay here then.' Her compromise. Part of her daughter's land would be better than none.

Angus sighed, ran his hands down his face, eyes looking skyward now. His high-vis shirt was stuck to his front. Sweat pearled across his forehead, fringe plastered to it. Billie imagined he'd like to go back inside, rid himself of the heat. Rid himself of her.

And yet while his voice was weary, it was calm still, and gentle, and Billie was reminded again of why Jess had settled on him. 'It's only worth our while to sell if it's a double block, Billie. Plus, if we carved yours off it'll only draw attention to the council that your house doesn't meet planning requirements. That it's there illegally … full of asbestos. To make it comply or to get rid of that stuff would cost more than its worth. You know that.'

'So it's all or nothing.'

'Yes. All or nothing. I'm sorry.'

'Nothing then.'

'Billie—'

'You're selling Jess, Angus!'

Angus looked at Daniel like he wanted him to leave, be spared this scene. But Daniel didn't move, kept his eyes fixed on the ground, his hand still over his grandmother's.

'Jess is, and always will be, much more than this block of land to me. It's *you* that's made her this place. For me she lives *here.*' Angus rested his hand on his chest and by the quiver in his voice Billie thought he might cry.

Still, she flared up. 'Of course she lives there in me, too. But she's in the land as well. If only you'd let yourself *feel* her, Angus ...' She picked up a handful of dirt and threw it at his chest. 'But you won't even try!'

Angus barely flinched. 'I'm sorry. That's not *my* Jess. That's a Jess you've made up. And I don't think it's been helpful.'

He walked away then, leaving Billie breathing in big angry gulps, while the weight of Daniel's hand remained heavy on hers.

Anger accompanied Billie to bed that night. It crept under the covers, laid itself over her body, rested its head alongside hers. It poked and prodded and tormented her subconscious. Forced her awake every few minutes, heart pounding, ready for a fight. She wrestled with the sheets for a time, wrestled with herself, with Angus, until she'd eventually drift back off to sleep, only to start the whole cycle again a short while later.

By 3 am she'd had enough of her bedfellow. Was desperate to shake it off. Bury it beneath another, more dominant feeling. The only emotion she thought more dominant was fear. A pure distillation compared to the irrational state of anger. Anger sought retribution. Fear sought preservation. And if Billie was to fight for Jess, then she needed to be a crusader.

She swapped nightdress for shorts and a t-shirt, laced up her walking shoes and left the house. She didn't bother with her pack. Took only a small hand-held torch. Left the house quickly before her resolve faltered.

The gate opened soundlessly and she entered the bush. The moon was a weak sliver. She had to rely on the narrow, dull beam of her torch to find her way. She placed one foot in front of the other within the torch's creamy luminescence, it was impossible to see much of what lay outside of it. But this was what she'd come for. A place where fear played host, in the unseen. Her anger, as she hoped, rested quietly now in the background, while the rest of her – heart, senses – were on high alert.

To hear is to wonder. To see is to believe. Take vision away and what were your ears left with? Only the imagination. Billie's was running wild. Rustles, scrapes, cracks and thumps were now the work of large creatures. Some could be human. And the trees alongside the track introduced themselves differently to her now. Those she knew because she'd given them her own names to reflect the pattern or scars on their trunks – deer, cormorant, kettle, vulva, Buddha, glove – were markers she could no longer rely on. Instead, trunks and branches were cast with new names by their silhouettes: pitchfork, scythe, knife, man. Billie forced herself to walk on past these new entities, while at her back the night settled like a closing door.

She pushed over rises she'd not previously considered steep. Braced herself for a fall as her feet twisted and slid down gravelly gullies. Although the night wasn't as hot as it was during the day, sweat beaded freely on her forehead with the effort of concentration and caution. Every now and then she saw paired glows hovering like fireflies. They were quickly extinguished by either blink or retreat. Night calls of varying pitch, tone and urgency – guttural vibrations, clicks, screeches, hisses and growls – disturbed the otherwise still air. She imagined animals softening their breaths and holding up their noses as she approached, detecting her fear or perhaps assessing the depth of their own.

Then, with shocking suddenness, something large erupted from the scrub to her right. It cut so close to her on the path that they nearly collided. She felt the heat of its body. Heard its hurried breath. Smelt its animal excretions. The vibration of its feet and the straining of its muscles pulsed in hers as it pounded across the trail. She startled badly. Staggered backwards. Fell heavily. The torch flew from her hand. Pain seared in her left ankle. A sudden wetness at her crotch. The creature bounded off into the bush on the other side of the trail, a dark and obscure blur, quickly lost in the low beam of the dropped torch. It could have been anything: feral pig, wild dog, deer, kangaroo.

She pulled herself up to sitting. Tried to calm her breathing. Began to register pain in other places: left buttock, right thumb. But the other thing she'd registered was something altogether new to Billie, something she'd never truly experienced before. Terror. Her mind screamed *Run!* but it was as though her muscles were denied all the things they needed to make her get up and do it: blood, oxygen, will. She lay back in the dirt, a flaccid, powerless thing now, till her heart and breathing steadied and her mind stopped screaming for action. What washed through her then was a feeling inexplicably the opposite of terror. Was it rapture? Euphoria? Gratitude? Was this what survivors felt?

And in that moment of sudden quietude, Billie felt closer to her daughter than she had since she'd lost her. While only fleeting – a mere trace – Billie had just experienced something of what Jess must have felt in her last moments. Except Jess had no reprieve from her terror as Billie was allowed now. It would have screamed on and on and on till she was finally released from it.

Slowly, shakily, Billie got to her feet. Didn't even bother retrieving the torch from the side of the trail. Jess guided her along. She was right there before her, upright and strong, full of courage now that nothing more could hurt her. Billie limped along behind her on the dark path. The ground was tender beneath her shoes. Held them. A magnetic connection, and she felt safe.

20

'I FEEL LIKE IT's MY fault, her wandering off like that. And at night, too. Anything could have happened.'

'Stop blaming yourself, Angus.' But Carla might as well not be there. His conversation wasn't with her. It was a reckoning with himself, delivered to the piece of raw timber in front of him.

He shook his head. 'Daniel's right, I should have gone easier on her.'

'We *have* been easy on her! She's an adult. Responsible for her own actions.'

'Is she responsible, though?' And now he did look at her.

'Of course she is. She's got too much time on her hands is all.' Carla wished she had as much free time. Could go wandering off at a whim as Billie so often did. She wouldn't be stupid enough to take herself off at night though.

'I'm not so sure anymore,' Angus said.

Carla, incredulous when Daniel told her why his grandmother was suddenly limping, thought a good part of Billie's behaviour was calculated attention seeking. A childlike subterfuge. Acting all mad-minded with the hope of keeping her – Carla – in this rundown dump. God, she was tired of it. 'She's playing us, Angus. Don't fall for it.'

When Angus glanced at her, she saw disapproval. But she wouldn't be shamed. It was tough enough working and keeping an old house presentable for inspections. Knowing people would snoop through cupboards and drawers, as though anything inside them were also up for sale. Always nagging Scout to put her things away. Daniel and Angus, too, like they were children. Meanwhile, Angus's shed could remain as dusty as he liked and Billie refused to let anyone inside her place, kept her door locked. The job of finding them a suitable rental till they bought land and built new had also fallen to her. A rental she had to assume needed to be big enough for the five of them – Billie still wouldn't say either way. Viewing them on her own mostly, during her lunch breaks and days off.

'This isn't easy on any of us, Angus. But selling *is* the right thing to do.'

'So you keep telling me.'

'What's that supposed to mean?'

He shrugged, infuriating her more.

'You're acting like the decision was all mine!'

'Wasn't it?'

'That's not fair.'

The house could collapse around him and he'd still be happy to stay in it if it meant not having to confront Billie. Let her keep them all trapped here by events from all those years ago. Even Daniel must have started to see that leaving here was the only way to leap from the past into the present. How else to explain his sudden interest in leaving the country?

'I was wrong, you *are* to blame,' Carla said, 'for letting Billie emotionally blackmail you.' She didn't wait to hear what he had to say to that, not even when he called her name as she left the workshop.

Arguing wasn't their way. Never had been. Selling a home under any circumstance was stressful. Fran said she witnessed it all the time. Was counsellor as much as negotiator for some of her clients. Add in the ancillary problem of a woman who, literally, believed she had roots in the soil and it took that stress to a whole new level. And now, a bunch of bruises and a sprained ankle paraded around like a rebuke.

Carla stopped on the cracked concrete path and took in the shape of her home. Noted the subsidence in the right-hand corner of the house, the crack this had caused in the red brickwork from the ventilation blocks at ground level all the way up to the eaves; a crack that showed on the inside as one through the tiles of the children's bathroom. She looked to the corrugated-iron roof with its patches of rust, the guttering too, and the rotting timber fascia. The land would be worth more without the house than with it. Would take away the demolition costs Fran said potential buyers kept factoring in to what they'd bid.

She looked to Billie's small fibro house, set in the back corner of the block. The *asbestos* house. The dangerous illegality of it. Something Angus had been willing to overlook for years. A squat, invisible killer, the agent of that danger made friable and breathable if disturbed by something as unremarkable as a drill bit or a wayward cricket ball tossed too hard by a child and puncturing a wall. Carla was tired of living with dereliction, in home and in conscience. The whole lot needed to be razed. The sooner they got rid of the place, the better.

When Carla arrived at work late again, Linda wasn't happy.

'The phone's been ringing off the hook.'

'Sorry,' Carla replied, tossing her bag in the bottom drawer of her desk and opening the appointments page on her computer. Fran had flipped seamlessly from friend to businesswoman after

175

they'd signed and selling had taken on a force of its own. Carla had become hostage to it. Become the hand that fed this insatiable thing that she had come to call the Master, with all the energy and commitment of a loyal servant.

'I know it's short notice, Carla, but they're cash buyers.'

The mere suggestion of which somehow endowed these people with privilege; an inspection on their terms and time.

Were these people cashed up or was it a ruse by Fran to get her compliance?

'Half the art of being wealthy,' Angus said when she complained to him about it, 'is in acting like you are.'

Carla agreed to these short-notice inspections because she was a slave to her own ambitions. So with little energy or time to spare, she'd clear any evidence of their daily lives from the house, hang the plush new towels they'd not used in the bathrooms, leaving those inspecting her home free to imagine the litter of their own lives scattered across it.

'Getting lots of interest, Carla,' Fran kept saying. 'Just need to balance letting each one of them feel they're in the race.'

And it was a race. People's dreams and ambitions on the line. Carla's, too. And for her, those ambitions included a place that was as shiny and new as a freshly minted coin.

Linda passed her a slip of paper. 'Mr Gibbs rang earlier. I told him to come in at eleven. Hope that's okay.'

It wasn't but she'd make it so it was.

'I told everyone else who rang to call back.'

'Thanks. And I'm really sorry. The agent rang as I was about to leave this morning wanting to bring someone through and I had to do a quick whip around.'

'If they can't see through a bit of clutter then they're not serious buyers.'

'I know. But it's hard not to get caught up in it … wanting it to look as good as I can make it.'

'Tough order from what you've told me.'

Not helped by Billie sitting on her veranda like some old-time matriarch, minus the shotgun across her lap, glowering at people from her small eyrie. Refusing to let anyone enter the granny flat. Locking her front door if she went out, having requested Angus return to her the spare key to make sure it stayed that way. The only saving grace was that both houses would likely be knocked down for redevelopment once sold, so not being able to see inside Billie's was probably inconsequential. Still, she cut an intimidating figure to those people wanting to inspect the land.

'Any idea what your mother-in-law plans to do yet?'

'She's not my mother-in-law. She's Angus's.'

'Sorry. *Angus's* mother-in-law.'

'Still won't say.' Despite Carla having stressed the point with Angus that a decision needed to be made. How was she to know what to rent until they knew what Billie wanted to do? Angus had told her to stop worrying. *It'll all work out*, he said. Carla wasn't so confident. 'And we go to auction in less than four weeks.' The weight of that thought made the day feel long already.

'What do *you* want to happen?'

All Carla wanted was a normal family. She didn't want a husband who hid away from the tough calls in his workshop, crafting his pieces of wood with a lover's touch as if to demonstrate that men could be gentle. She didn't want a stepson who only went out at night to go to work. And neither did she want to tiptoe round a deluded woman making her daughter believe that the bush could tell her a bedtime story if she listened hard enough. What a weird, mad, sad bunch they were, every last one of them.

'We're her only family.'

'Have you told her that?'

'Well, not directly.' Neither had Billie ever called Carla family. 'But she lives with us so that makes her family.'

Linda shrugged. 'Maybe she feels excluded.'

Carla felt excluded. She had no experience of the real Jess. Hadn't been in the orbit of the event that took her life, felt repelled by it mostly, like a wrongly charged atom. But every day she lived with the enigma of this other woman, this silent partner who continued to exert an influence over everything they did.

21

It lacerated Billie's heart to see strangers walking over her land. Jess's land. These people who'd never care about what was in the soil, only what they could put on top of it.

The others had gone out whenever the house was open for inspection. But not Billie. She sat on the front veranda of her small home refusing entry to anyone. She liked that her guarding presence made people drop their conversations to whispers, how it prevented most from lingering too long in the backyard.

'Don't touch that!' she barked at one woman who had bent down to take a sprig of rosemary from her herb garden.

'I'll see you don't get it,' she'd said to the man who paced out the distance from the workshop to the back fence and then extolled loudly to the man she assumed was his business partner: 'Hey Bob, if we knock the lot down I reckon we'll easy fit a six pack on this one.' As though she had some control over the decision.

The man had picked up a clod of earth and smiled as he crumbled it in his hands. 'For the right price, love, I reckon you'll sell it to anyone.' He dusted off his hands, one against the other, like finished business.

The principal from the real estate agency – not Fran, Billie didn't reckon she'd dare – had words.

'She's not doing us any favours, Angus.' He indicated towards Billie, not three feet away, like she was just another item for sale.

Angus glanced from the agent to Billie, compromised by familial loyalty perhaps – if any still existed – and the need for a sale, but said nothing, neither acknowledgement nor rebuke. This was left for Billie to do.

'I don't owe either of you any favours.'

Afterwards, Angus had tried to reason with her. 'I'm doing this for *us*, Billie. *All* of us.'

Billie saw a man caught juggling the balls of history and progress, the latter of which seemed destined to be upheld.

'This land runs through me like a current, Angus.' Billie felt it through the skinprint of her hands, her feet. 'It's like you're unplugging me.'

'The current you feel is grief, Billie. It runs through all of us.'

Billie placed the trowel on the ground beside her. She sat back on her heels cautiously, her ankle still tender, and used the hem of her shirt to wipe the sweat from her face. Her arms were done in for the day. The cat's claw creeper had beaten her for now. She wasn't likely to dig out all of its tubers anyway; the crampon-like vine would be back at the foot of the tree before long, clawing its way skyward once more.

Knees drawn up to her chest, she rested back against the tree. It was easy to believe the murder of her daughter was the worst thing the tree had witnessed. But in truth, it could have witnessed the ambush of any number of people. Grown tall on the blood and bones of violence. But there would be good stories, too: all of those who'd rested, sheltered, loved, danced or celebrated under its spreading limbs over time. The comfort and protection it must have provided people, solace even, as it offered Billie now.

She tilted her head up to its thick canopy, absentmindedly raked her fingers through the dry earth. It was all leafy angles and shifting light up there. The leaves' upper surfaces were dark green and glossy. Their undersides matte brown and dulled. She closed one eye and it was like looking through a kaleidoscope. The angles shifted, reminding her that perspective was never fixed.

Trees spoke to one another – she believed that – and across great distances. Messages sent through a living soil. An enormous underground community in constant conversation, sharing information and stories about pestilence and threats, water and weather. The message of the death of one conveyed not as grief but as a need to fill a gap. She believed, also, that if she looked at a tree long enough, then she would feel it looking back at her; that something would pass between them. She waited. After a few minutes, the crick in her neck forced her to look down again. Today, there was no being seen. None that she was aware of anyway.

Not for the first time, Billie speculated on the age of the tree. Was it a hundred years old? Two hundred? More? She imagined how people would have told stories about it over the years. A grandparent to a grandchild: *I remember that tree when it wasn't any taller than you sitting on my shoulders.* That grandchild to its own: *See that aerial root, the one as thick as your arm? I remember when it barely touched the ground.*

A woman and a toddler came into view over the rise. This pair blonde, and blue-eyed, Billie imagined. The mother – if that's who she was – wore a coral sundress with thin shoulder straps and a big floppy-brimmed hat. The boy was shirtless, his small round belly protruding above his denim shorts. She remembered when Daniel was the same shape. How his hips weren't developed enough either, so all the bits inside his tummy could only press out. The shape of her grandson had changed in this and many other ways since.

As they drew nearer the boy's denim shorts became pale blue, whale-patterned shorts. His hair darkened. His skin became swarthy. She didn't try and blink the image away. The boy's visits made her feel chosen. For what she still wasn't sure. Assumed the purpose of them would eventually show itself. She waved. The pair waved back.

The person of interest was now in custody. Murder charges laid. It was all over the news. The man they had arrested was striking for his ordinariness: clean-shaven, barber-cut hair, trousers with a zipper, a shirt that buttoned, leather shoes that laced. He could be anybody's brother, husband, uncle, friend. Billie imagined people sharing a meal with this man and never suspecting that beneath his amiable conversation, behind his easy laugh or joke, was a man capable of an unthinkably cruel act. And their disbelief on learning of his double life, someone they thought they knew, perhaps intimately. Their *shame* at having such poor judgement. This was the thought that chilled her. That evil could sit right beside you at any time and you were completely unaware. Surely it left some kind of brand on a person?

At least the boy's family would have a resolution now, justice. To not have that was the cruellest thing. Billie knew this pain. Knew how it seeded inside you with the invasiveness of the cat's claw she endlessly tried to remove. How it took your legs from beneath you, robbed the breath from your lungs, forced you to stare at a wall, sometimes for hours. The way it left you naked and vulnerable to the smallest slights and setbacks. The way it made you retch and howl.

She watched the woman and child till they were out of sight then rested back against the tree again. Closed her eyes, as a soft, hot breeze yawned across the canopy. The earth was warm under her buttocks, the trunk surprisingly cool at her back. Somewhere in the distance she heard a mob of noisy miners haranguing something – probably a goanna – and, alongside this, the occasional exchange between currawongs. And in the distance, likely in the shade of the dry creek bed, a symphony of bellbirds. Beneath it all, cicadas relentlessly delivered their shrill-throated chorus; a sound Billie had learnt to reduce to white noise.

But behind closed eyes all sounds eventually faded as she drifted off.

'Come on! Let's swing on it, yeah?'

The shout coming from the other side of the tree startled her awake. She sat forward, unsure of how long she'd been asleep. Maybe only seconds. Perhaps many minutes.

'Awesome. I'm the strongest so I'll hold it down. You two climb on.'

'Whoa! It's like getting on one of them mechanical bulls.'

'Let's try and break it.'

The boys' laughter flipped between high-pitched and deep so it was difficult to tell how many of them there were. Billie craned round and saw a shadow on the ground: three figures straddling a low branch.

Loaded with the weight of the three boys, the long limb began to creak. Her spine tingled against the fig's trunk. Was the sensation a plea by the tree for her to act, or her own anxious anticipation that she knew she would anyway?

The groan of the limb grew louder, the shadow of the boys dipped lower; cries of *Yee-hah* in triplicate rang out. The tingling at her back became more urgent. No more encouragement was needed.

Stepping over buttress roots, she made her way round to the other side of the tree. Saw the three boys, barely teenagers, on the branch. 'Get off!'

They ignored her.

'Get off that branch now, do you hear me! This tree's precious.'

'Shit. Me balls are gettin' squashed,' yelled the one in the middle.

Their knees dipped deeply as their feet touched the ground and they pushed off again, going higher and higher each time. Billie could hear fibres shearing in the limb close to the trunk. Feared it would snap off.

'I said get off!' With no mind for her ankle, she rushed for the limb, timed it for when it next came down, and threw her weight against it, hoping to unseat them. A short, broken branch grazed her forehead as the limb catapulted up again.

'Hey, what d'you think you're doin'?'

'Piss off, ya old bag!'

Billie ignored the pain over her eye and the wet trickle down her cheek and charged again. The boys' hold on the limb started to waver, their landing no longer perfectly timed. She charged for a third time with a roar that surprised even her, and like Humpty Dumpty they fell. The boy seated at the back slid off sideways at the dip, the other two were flung from the summit. Billie breathed hard and watched the last two writhe on the ground where they'd landed. One winded, unable to catch his breath. The other screaming and gripping his right forearm, which rested at a peculiar angle against his chest.

Billie wiped the back of her hand across her eye and it came away red.

'That's assault!' screeched the one who fell off first, the smallest of the trio. 'I'm reporting you to the police.' He fumbled round in the back pocket of his shorts, pulled out his mobile phone with shaking hands and aimed it at Billie.

Photographic evidence. The young were so savvy.

'You've smashed it,' the boy whined, looking down at the screen, and she thought how this seemed to bother him more than his wailing mate.

She didn't acknowledge the boy as she moved past him to where the branch they'd swung on joined the trunk. She ran her hand across the area where she heard it shearing. Was relieved that it hadn't broken right through to the bark. The damage restricted to the inside. She turned to look at the tough boy who was on his backside on the ground. She walked towards him, tracing her hand along the branch. Not so brave now, he scuttled backwards on hands and heels like a beetle, till he came up against the wall of a buttress root.

Hand still on the limb, she leant in towards him and said calmly and quietly, 'If I ever see any one of you damaging this tree again I'll poke your eyes out with a stick. Do you understand?'

The boy didn't take his eyes from her as he hauled himself up. In his rush to get away he tripped over a root, had to get to his feet again. They left then, the boy still gripping his arm to his chest, snivelling. The winded one – the one who liked to swear, had called her an *old bag* – trained his eyes on the ground, appetite for name-calling gone.

'I've got photographs of you now,' the mouthy one taunted shrilly as he backed away, his friend's mobile phone aimed at Billie. 'His dad's a lawyer.'

'And he's gonna bust your arse,' the injured one snivelled.

Once they were out of sight, Billie slumped onto the ground, her back to the trunk again. She knew every aspect and angle of the tree's lower branches, could see now how the injured limb rested closer to the ground. She sensed the tree had already begun to repair itself though. Imagined the mobilisation of nutrients to the damaged area, gaps between fibres already reuniting, much like the broken bone in the boy's arm would eventually. How other trees in the area would be cheering it on.

The tree continued to hum against her spine, a gentle current of thanks. Now she felt seen.

22

DANIEL WAS SLOWER THAN CARLA to react. His stepmother had already taken Billie's arm, was guiding her from the back door to a kitchen chair. He couldn't quite believe it was his grandmother under all that blood.

'It's just a scratch, Carla. I came in to see if you had a bandaid.'

Daniel pulled out a chair. He and Carla helped Billie into it. When Carla took away the wad of bloodied tissues Billie had pressed to her forehead, he could see it was more than a scratch. There was a three-centimetre gash above her right eyebrow, the edges ragged and turned inward on dark purple flesh. Blood was smeared down the side of her face to her neck, soaked into the collar of her pale blue shirt.

'Stay with her Dan while I get the first-aid kit.'

'No need to fuss,' Billie called after her.

'I think you're going to need more than a bandaid, Nan.' From what Daniel could see the wound needed stitches. 'What happened?'

'I was protecting your mother's tree.'

'From what?'

'Three boys. They were attacking it. I told them to stop. But they wouldn't listen.'

Carla came back into the room with the first-aid kit. Placed it on the table. 'Told who to stop?'

'Three boys.'

'Did they do this to you?'

'They were going to break it. I had to stop them. Then this happened.' Billie gestured helplessly with her hands.

'What were they trying to break?'

'Jess's tree.'

'That damn tree,' Carla mumbled. Her hands shook as she opened a packet of gauze squares and wet them with something clear from a small plastic tube.

Was her tremor from fear or anger? Either way, Daniel admired his stepmother's forbearance in tending to this latest family drama.

His own anger flared as he watched Carla clean his grandmother's face. It reared up inside him like a solid column, steadied him. Was something he imagined gripping in his hand like a club. Made him want to act. 'I'm going to see if they're still there.' He headed for the back door.

'No you're not!' Her hands might be shaking, but Carla's voice was steady and firm.

'They can't get away with doing this!' He indicated to Billie, to the kitchen table covered in bloodied tissues and gauze.

'So you're going to teach them a lesson, are you? Beat them up?'

Daniel wouldn't answer Carla, knowing that was exactly what he'd do if he found them still there.

Carla shook her head. 'Makes you no better than them, Daniel.'

'They won't be there,' Billie said. 'They left before I did.'

'So they did this then just took off?'

'I think one had a broken arm, Dan. They were probably in a hurry on account of that.'

'You broke one's arm?'

'*I* didn't break it, Carla. It happened when they fell off the branch they were trying to break. Must have landed badly.'

Daniel looked to the ground so Carla wouldn't notice his smile.

His stepmother pressed the fingers of one hand to her forehead. 'Jesus. This just goes from bad to worse.'

Despite her brusque manor, Carla was gentle as she cleaned Billie's wound. His grandmother didn't flinch, only mumbled about it being nothing, that she didn't want any fuss. Each time Carla lifted the gauze, though, it flushed with fresh red. Which only confirmed the finite nature of the stuff. That you could lose too much.

'It's going to need stitches, Billie.'

'I'll be fine. Just stick something over it and I'll go and put my feet up at my place. It'll stop bleeding soon enough.'

'Nan, Carla's right. You need stitches.'

'But I hardly felt it when it happened.'

'I'll bandage it then take you to the hospital.'

'Will you drive me there, Dan?'

Carla stepped back. It was difficult to read her face. It wasn't relief he saw, or acceptance. If he were honest, he'd say she looked hurt.

Billie edged forwards in her seat, rested both hands on the table to push herself up – left thumb still yellow with bruises – but her arms, usually robust and reliable, seemed to lack strength. 'Help me up will you, Daniel.'

Daniel pressed his grandmother gently back into her seat. 'Not so fast, Nan. Carla still needs to bandage your head.'

The hurt his stepmother had shown was packed away and her practical side took over. Daniel watched this Carla carefully wrap a bandage round his grandmother's head, being sure not to cover her eyes or uncomfortably crimp her ears. It was hard to tell if there was love in this act or if it was something else, a sense of duty perhaps. Her voice was soothing when she said, 'Nearly done,

Billie.' But then the sigh that followed as she fixed the last piece of tape to the bandage, could just as easily have been a declaration of it being another problem plastered over.

Five hours and as many stitches later, Daniel finally helped his grandmother up her front steps and into her home. Some of her fight had returned.

'It was worth it,' she said, settling onto the sofa.

He looked at her, unsure what she meant.

'This.' She pointed to the newly dressed wound over her right eyebrow. 'They'll think twice about messing with our tree again.'

He didn't argue. Didn't remind her there were plenty of other shitty kids out there all too happy to do something similar. Didn't want her to think about the boys anymore. Wanted her to put what happened behind her. Get the bruises that would inevitably come from this latest event yellowed and faded like the ones on her hand, her ankle. Wanted to bring some calm to her life amid all the turmoil of selling.

Which was surely the catalyst for everything that had happened this past week. Her obsession with this place, the park, had become self-destructive in its magnitude. It frightened him sometimes, the violent potential in her. He needed to talk her down. Make her see that good could also come of selling.

'What's happening, Nan?'

Billie glanced at him, her turn to seem unsure.

'Look at you.' Daniel opened his hands to encompass his grandmother, pale and frail on the sofa. The bright white dressing across her forehead in stark contrast to her dirty collar, stiff with dried blood. 'You look like you've fallen off a roof. And people reckon I'm the reckless one.'

She waved him away. 'Rubbish. Neither one of us is any more reckless than the next person.'

He didn't believe her.

'I think it's about Dad and Carla selling. You've let it upset you too much.' He didn't add that it had also made her irrational. Dangerous even.

Billie side-eyed him, then surprised him by saying, 'Maybe the night walk was about that. But not what happened today. That was about respect … or lack of it anyway.'

He shook his head. 'I think it's about more than that. I think it's about leaving here.'

'No crime in wanting to stay.'

No, the crime was in not knowing how to let go, leave the past back there.

'Thanks for taking me to the hospital today,' she said, changing the subject.

He'd sat with her the whole time. Held her hand for a good part of it. But he couldn't hold her gaze now. Was tired of being her touchstone to the past.

Billie fixed her watery eyes on him. 'You're the only one who understands me, Daniel.'

But his grandmother was wrong. Often he didn't understand her at all. Only knew she was sometimes fragile, like today. He wished he could tell her he felt burdened sometimes, in always trying to understand her. Aged by her expectations of him.

She reached over, put her hand over his. 'You're the best thing your mother ever gave me.'

Which only made him feel worse.

23

ELBOWS ON THE KITCHEN TABLE, Carla raked her fingers through her hair. Gripped clumps of it, just for the sensation of being in her skin. Sure, those kids were out of line, tormenting an old woman like that. But to break the arm of one and not really care? That took Billie's obsession with the fig tree to a whole new level. Carla could understand now why Angus had once said he'd happily poison the thing. It also made her wonder what Billie was capable of when they finally sold this place. What if she came back and torched whatever ended up on the block, determined nobody would live here if she couldn't?

She had a sudden, ridiculous urge to go to the park. She'd always avoided it. Hadn't been there more than half-a-dozen times. Had never taken Scout, no matter how often she'd asked. If her daughter wanted to go to a park, Carla would get in the car and take her to one further away. Daniel had probably taken her there. She'd heard Scout pester him often enough, but she'd stopped asking now, which could only mean he'd caved in.

What did she plan to do there? Attack the tree like those boys had? Punish it for all the ill it caused? Of this she couldn't be sure.

She threw the last of her coffee down the sink. Found her trainers in the hall cupboard and left via the front door. The main trail started at the end of a cul-de-sac that ran off their street. One minute her shoe was on a suburban footpath, the next it was in nature. Just like that: a line crossed between what the suburb was now – on the arrowhead of progress – and what it had once been: a borderless, open expanse. She preferred boundaries. Liked progress. She was a city girl.

The up and down of the path was a good workout, reminded her she needed to get fitter. No wonder Billie was all nuggety muscles and tendons, like a long-distance runner. By the time Carla reached the clearing in the park, the fig broad and imposing at its centre, there was a seam of sweat down the front and back of her shirt.

She didn't go straight up to the tree. Stood back from it. Wanted to take in its great mass. There was no denying it was a beautiful specimen. Had a glorious symmetry to it. Regardless of aspect, its branches virtually mirrored the shape and reach of those on the opposing side. The peak of its crown sat dead centre over its trunk. Perfection. But this didn't seem like a thing of chance so much as something that it had worked at. That such a balance was a condition of its living. It made the awkward, messy state of being human seem all the more apparent when in the presence of its opposite.

Easy to recognise the branch the boys had tried to break. It reached nearer to the ground than any of the other low branches; the only asymmetry.

As she drew nearer she saw the plaque. *In memory of Jess, Loved then taken* and dated for sixteen years ago. She sat on the ground before it, knees drawn into her chest. It was such a tiny thing, this emblem of loss. Its words sparse compared to the gravity of what it represented. Part of her wanted to prise the piece of metal off the tree, but she knew it would be like shitting on a grave, fucking in a church. This memorial, like all memorials, regardless of how she felt about it, was untouchable. Sacrosanct.

Who'd look after this rectangular slip of metal once Billie was gone? She expected it would be Daniel. A task handed down like an heirloom. A burden. Never allowed to decide the terms of how he memorialised his loss.

'Ah, Jess.' She breathed deeply, looked up at the plaque. 'What would you make of it all, eh?'

Complete strangers learning something of her short life through a Google search. In this, the plaque gave Jess a kind of notorious immortality, something Carla wouldn't want for herself, although for a moment, she thought she understood the comfort a person might find in thinking this place was like holding on to someone they loved.

Except she'd never felt love for Jess. She'd felt pity for her. Sadness, too. Anger sometimes, at the unfairness of what had happened, the injustice of it, the consequences on others. But on other days, like the one she'd just come through – cleaning up the wound on Billie's forehead – or when she had to listen to a young man question his right to live a different life, then she could also feel dislike, maybe even hatred, for Jess. For her enduring un-deadness. But was it fair, or even sane, to criticise the dead?

The circumstances of Jess's death meant she was above criticism. Could do no wrong in the eyes of those she'd left behind. Any arguments she might have caused, any harsh words she might have said, any act of unkindness no matter how large, were all forgiven or forgotten long ago. Meanwhile, Carla had to turn up every day and be as good as, if not better than, a dead woman. That was what she hated, not Jess: the sometimes fraudulent nature of her own existence. Because she wasn't always good or kind. Not in thought or action.

An argument she and Angus once had came to mind, still vivid in her memory because of the rareness of them. She knew then as now that she'd been cruel. But at the time, like all disagreements, the aggrieved knew only their own hurt, and then magnified it.

It was over Scout. Her snooping mostly. She'd found a shoebox on the top shelf of a cupboard in Angus's study. Inventively for a young child, she'd hauled a kitchen chair into the room to reach the box. The box then proved too heavy for her as she pulled it forward off the shelf and it had fallen to the floor, spreading its contents everywhere.

It held keepsakes. Ones that depicted the life Angus had lost. There was a pair of small porcelain figurines, one of which broke in the fall – the boy. Scout pocketed the girl. There were toddler drawings done by Daniel. The usual round heads and bodies, stick legs and stick arms. Some with Mummy written above them in a hand that looked as though it had been guided. But mostly the box held photographs. Many were of Angus and Jess, young and happy. In love. There were others of the three of them: Daniel as a tiny baby through to toddlerhood. Some were of a younger, more carefree looking Billie, with soft, easy limbs.

The argument arose not so much because Scout, just five at the time, had been snooping and found the box, but because she had taken a black Sharpie pen to one of the photographs and drawn what she said were antlers on the top of the heads of the three of them – Daniel, Angus and Jess. Her creative endeavours had ruined what Carla could tell was an especially lovely image of Jess.

Angus had snatched the photograph from her. 'Naughty girl!' He'd never shouted at her before. His anger shocked Carla. Red-faced, hands working, she'd been fearful he was going to strike their daughter.

'Angus! You're over-reacting!' She pressed Scout against her, arms round her hitching, sobbing little body. Sensed, through her mother perhaps, that Angus might do her harm, so she started wailing.

'To you maybe!'

But Angus calmed quickly, which, if Carla had taken the time to think, she would have known he would. He wouldn't – couldn't – hurt anything. But he had hurt Carla in another way, one she hadn't expected.

'There's better ways to mother the kid, Carla. And it's not *your* way. You wrap her in cottonwool when she needs to be told off.'

It had infuriated her, being told by a father how to be a better mother.

The argument had escalated from there, cruelly on Carla's part.

'I'm sorry I'm not Jess enough for you.'

She couldn't believe she'd said it. Hadn't known where such horrible words had come from. It was like they'd tumbled from some small pocket of bile. Made her wonder if she could ever trust herself again to speak in the heat of anger.

Now, she recognised that seeing those images of a deep and blissful love had unsettled her. Maybe even made her jealous. A past love captured in rapturous joy. Mythologised. Meanwhile, the intensity of their love – Carla's and Angus's – had to ride the waves of time and the dampening of intensity this inevitably allowed.

All she remembered thinking at the time was: *How do I compete with a saint?*

Angus looked at her for a moment like she'd struck him. 'You don't need to be like Jess,' he finally said. 'You just need to be a better you.' One blow for another.

He left the room then, and the house, spent the rest of the day in the workshop, even though it was a Sunday.

Later, Scout had returned the unbroken figurine to him, her little face full of contrition, knowing, Carla suspected, that she'd been the catalyst to something bad. Angus scooped her onto his lap, told her not to worry, the figurine was hers, and father and daughter had remained snuggled together on the sofa for the rest of the evening.

Carla had tried to show her own contrition later that night.

Pressed her body round the curve of his back in bed, knees angled into the bend of his, not wanting any more intimacy than that, only wanting to mirror the exact shape of him. When he reached his arm round and pulled her in even closer, his forgiveness had felt like a blanket. She'd threaded her arm round him then and they'd slept fused like that for most of the night.

She'd not seen the box since. Nor the remaining figurine. She imagined the appeal of owning it had soured for Scout after what happened, and she'd put it at the back of a cupboard or drawer. Carla didn't like the thought of finding it again when the house was packed up. The fresh shame it would deliver.

'Carla. What are you doing here?'

The voice was familiar, but still Carla jumped. 'Billie! You startled me.'

'I thought you didn't approve of this place.' Billie placed her backpack carefully on the picnic table. Looked at Carla in a way that left her in no doubt she expected an answer.

'It's not for me to approve or disapprove of it.'

Billie walked past Carla without responding. At the tree, she rested her hand on its trunk briefly, as if in greeting, before turning again to face her.

The dressing above her eye was grubby and had a small patch of old blood at its centre. Billie's face was bruised and swollen, the right eye closed, but she studied Carla now with her good eye, like she was trying to catch her out at something. Maybe she'd been standing behind her for a while. Had read her thoughts. Knew now that she sometimes criticised her dead daughter. This thought made Carla uneasy, so she made to leave.

'I'll get going. Leave you to—'

'Stay.'

Carla paused, uncertain what to do with this gentle request.

'Please.'

Reluctantly, she settled back on the ground but held herself tight, wishing she were on the path now and heading for home.

Billie returned to her backpack and took a square of white cloth from inside. Rummaged further and pulled out a small tub of metal cleaner. Dabbed the cloth in the pale goo and headed with it back to the tree. She started to work the cloth across the plaque.

Carla knew she should say something. 'I'd not realised till today what a beautiful tree it is.'

'Isn't it? And when you come up over that rise,' Billie indicated behind her, 'there it is, like a monument. But you're a broody old girl too, aren't you.' Billie spoke tenderly to the tree.

'How can you love it so much?'

If Billie hadn't sounded so genuine that she should stay, Carla might not have found the courage to ask the question. But she needed to know where it came from, this love for something emblematic of such a terrible loss.

Billie polished a while longer before answering. 'Because it's not the tree's fault.'

Of course not. The fault rested with the choices made by a heartless man.

'But doesn't it make you sad? Being here … being reminded?'

Billie fixed her good eye on Carla again and her uneasiness grew. 'It was a witness, Carla. And it has Jess's blood in its veins. There's a kinship in that. Something that's owed respect.'

How to argue against such a firmly held belief? To reason that it was just a tree, nothing more. That it perceived nothing of Billie. Nothing of the past, or of Jess. That it had no mind for the future either, not Billie's or any one of them.

Billie resumed her polishing. Muttered as she worked. Carla could make out a few words: *Dear girl* and *that's better.* It was an intimacy she had no right to share. Felt like an unwelcome guest, a trespasser. Someone praying at the wrong church.

She stood, dusted off the back of her shorts. 'I'll head back now.'

She had to get away from this creepy place and the tree's alluring power. It no longer seemed beautiful to her. It felt malevolent.

Billie didn't acknowledge her, kept up her soft conversation with the tree – *How's that? Nearly done* – as she slowly worked the cloth over the already shiny rectangle of steel.

Carla imagined it bright like an eye once Billie had finished. The sun glinting off it. The moon, too. A portal that witnessed and catalogued everything and everyone that passed before it.

She walked quickly down the trail towards home, wanted to get as much distance between her and the tree as possible. Escape the scrutiny of its all-seeing, all-knowing presence.

24

BILLIE HELD THE DOOR OPEN for Inspector Quinn. 'News travels fast,' she said.

'Bad news does.'

'Who's your friend?'

'Constable Stephens.' Quinn indicated to the younger policeman standing beside him. He was in uniform, not a suit like Quinn. Then he gestured towards Billie. 'Wilhelmina Porter.'

The younger man acknowledged Billie with a nod before entering her home ahead of the inspector.

'You just here for show?' she asked Quinn, left standing on the front mat.

'No. As a friend.'

Billie thought of all those good-cop, bad-cop television dramas she'd watched and nearly laughed. But then her humour quickly soured as she realised the younger officer was using Quinn's association with Jess's death to make his job easier.

'Couldn't do it on your own?' she asked the younger man.

'Inspector Quinn insisted on coming.' The two men exchanged a look. It wasn't friendly.

Billie didn't offer them refreshments. Such kindnesses were reserved for Quinn's visits about Jess, not this.

'So the father's come through on his brat's threat?' The wound above her right eyebrow, just five days closed, throbbed, and the swollen upper eyelid still twitched from time to time.

'The boy's arm was broken, Mrs Porter.'

'It's Ms. *Ms* Porter.' Billie studied the young constable. Her good eye missed none of the shape of him, which was mostly square: jaw, shoulders, fingernails, haircut. It was like he'd come out of a box, or he'd been shaped into one. 'You expect me to feel sorry for him?' she asked.

'Regret might help your case.'

'But I don't regret anything. Except maybe this.' She indicated to the dressing on her forehead.

'The boy's father wants to press assault charges against you.'

'Bullying must run in the family.'

'This is serious, Mrs Porter.'

'So is vandalism.'

'It was only a tree branch. Boys having a bit of fun.'

Billie ignored Stephens, looked at Quinn instead. She challenged him as best she could with her good eye to call out this other man, to say it wasn't just a branch but a part of something much greater. That the tree was something to be respected. Billie was disappointed when he said nothing and somehow she thought he knew it.

Perhaps as a sweetener, Quinn said, 'I've spoken to the boy's parents, Billie. Explained the site's significance to you. But they're understandably upset about what's happened to their son.'

'I understand the concern for their boy. But I also have the right to protect Jess's tree.'

'A tree doesn't have legal rights, Mrs Porter. But a young boy does.'

'Oh shut up,' Billie said to the younger policeman, tiring of him.

Stephens went to speak, but Quinn held up a hand to silence him.

'Unfortunately, Constable Stephens is right, Billie. In the eyes of the law, trees don't have rights.'

Stephens, every square line of him in sharp relief against her pale green sofa, took a bundle of photographs from a folder he'd brought with him and passed them to Billie. 'Can you verify these images are of you, please?'

Billie flicked through the photographs, though blurred and grainy, she was shocked by the sight of herself. She was a thin, grey pillar in each, while all around her the tree's broad canopy was a lush green mantle. She stood alongside the branch the boys had tried to break, her hand resting on it. In every photo the right side of her face and neck were bright with blood, along with her shirt, which she'd had to throw out in the end. She looked a fright. Unrecognisable. She hated to admit, even to herself, that she looked frail. It was as though she was using the branch to hold herself up, and not what she'd felt at the time: that she was trying to give the tree strength. When had she become so diminished?

'I don't exactly look like a dangerous criminal in these.' Billie tossed the photographs on the coffee table, where they scattered. She saw herself upside-down and right way up, from the left and the right, none of which showed her for the determined woman she'd felt herself to be that day.

'I told them it was precious. If they'd just got off it as I asked, none of this would have happened.'

'Billie, I don't know too many thirteen-year-olds who could spell precious, let alone appreciate its meaning in this regard.'

Billie didn't answer Quinn. She looked at Stephens. 'Do *you* appreciate its meaning, Constable?'

Stephens ignored her. Gathered up the photographs from the coffee table. Made sure their edges were perfectly aligned before tucking them back inside the folder.

★

After they'd left, Billie went in search of water. Which she supposed meant she was searching for hope. So far she'd found none. Not even a stagnant billabong remained in the creek anymore. She tried to remember when it had last flowed, but couldn't.

The frustration at weaving between urban walkers was long gone. Gone, too, was the endless thrum and rumble of vehicles, the smell of exhaust fumes and baked tar. The city – a bar graph of tall buildings on the horizon from Mount Coot-tha only an hour ago – was well out of sight now. She picked her way past sedges that grew alongside the creek. These grasses, once blades of green, were now brown papery tapers. They were resilient, though, would bounce back if the rains ever came. The sun was past high. The sky a great cloche of blue overhead. It was hot. Endlessly hot. A thing worn. Like a coat. It was suffocating, reminding her of the dust storm she'd seen on television the day before – the image of a roiling red mass of dirt descending on a small inland town. Looked every bit like Uluru had gathered up her skirts and was on the move. While not liquid, the dust storm had pushed forward as though it were. Its rolling shape like the slow arrival of an avalanche, its storm-stolen soil rich with the decay of lost livelihoods, embalming everything it encountered. Billie imagined it eventually reaching the ocean, where it would benefit nothing and no one. It was an unusual event. But nothing about this summer felt normal.

Billie licked her dry lips. Put her fingers to the dressing over her right eye. It was wet with perspiration, like her shirt beneath her pack. She took a sip from her water bottle before striding out along the parched creek bed.

It was a cobbled path of various-sized water-worn stones. Every now and again there was a crazy paved montage of dried silt where the last of the water had pooled then evaporated. The cracked pieces curled at the edges like old bread, and the silt crumbled, fragile as meringue, under her shoes. Gums, she-oak, wattle – drought-hardy up to a point – grew along the creek's bank. In places she stepped over their proud, preserved roots. They provided only partial protection from the heat, so when she finally found a nice flat-topped rock in full shade, she decided to rest.

The day mimicked the many that had come before it: dry, hollowing, unforgiving. Like grief. But grief was also a liquid thing, something that came in waves. She imagined a wall of water rushing towards her down the dry creek bed now, a paralysing and unstoppable force. That was grief. Something that knocked the wind from you. Bent you in two. Threw you off your feet. But at other times the liquidity of it was much more subtle. A mere ripple on the surface of your awareness, a feeling of being unsettled but not knowing why, then the truth washed in to remind you.

Drought and grief. Each susceptible to vagaries beyond anyone's control. Each unpredictable like the weather. As cruel as its extremes. She and the land had a good deal in common. She stretched out and lay flat on her stomach, fish-like, her left ear turned to where water once flowed. She pulled the hot, dusty air across the moist membranes of her mouth and nose. She felt the sense of suffocation a fish must feel as these dried out; its fear hot on her tongue, gritty in her eyes. What a helpless, hopelessly slow death for any animal to endure.

'Hey! You alright?'

Startled, Billie looked up but she couldn't see who'd called out.

'Are you hurt?' The voice sounded panicked.

A young man, lithe and agile, moved quickly into view from the direction Billie had just come. She drew herself up from the ground and sat back on her heels, watched him approach. His long brown hair flared like a cape from beneath his black peaked cap. He had a pirate beard pulled into one short plait with a purple bead at the end. The bead made Billie think of the bright fruit of a lilly-pilly.

'You're okay then?' He sounded breathless as he approached her.

'Yes. I'm fine.'

'You had me worried. Thought you'd fallen or something.'

'No, just imagining what it was like to be a fish.'

If this amused him, he didn't show it. Instead, he looked up and down the dry watercourse, purple bead twitching. 'I don't reckon the fish are having much fun at the moment.'

'I expect they're all dead.'

'There'll be pockets of water further upstream,' he assured her. 'They'll restock from those once the rain comes.'

She guessed him for about twenty-five. So, not that many seasons under his belt, how could he be so sure?

'But what if it *doesn't*?' she pushed. 'Or it comes too late for the fish?' She wanted to provoke him. Force him to think about the loss of irreplaceable things.

But he wouldn't be drawn. Simply shrugged. An inconceivable thought.

'What did it feel like anyway … being a fish?' he asked.

Billie scrutinised his face, looked for the smart-arse there, but didn't find it. 'Like having someone's hands round your throat.'

He grimaced. 'Poor fish.'

'Yes. Poor fish.'

'So you're right then? You don't need a hand?' He made to move off.

Billie nodded. 'What brings you here anyway?' She wanted to keep him there a little longer, learn what he cared about.

'I came along here earlier.' He indicated upstream. 'Lost my bandana from my rucksack somewhere along the way. It was a favourite. Thought I'd retrace my steps for a bit, see if I could find it. No luck so far. Think I'll give up on it now, though.'

She watched him as he moved back down the way he'd come, quick and sure-footed despite the rough terrain, till he disappeared round a bend. Billie headed upstream, eyes fixed mostly on the ground, not as certain of her feet.

Only a few hundred metres further on, she came across his lost bandana. Black and white in what looked like a Mexican design. A *Canteen* logo at its centre. She thought about going back, trying to find him. Figured she'd never catch up with him. Instead, she tied the soft, worn fabric to her pack. Understood why he favoured it. She'd tie it to a tree on the way back. Hope that he'd return and find it.

The terrain changed as she walked steadily uphill. The creek narrowed and the banks grew steeper. There was more shade. But thickets of lantana, too. Pebbles became rocks and she had to watch every footfall now, for fear of hurting her ankle again. She imagined the water, if it flowed, would be a torrent through here. The exertion felt good. Purposeful. It took her mind off dying fish, off box-shaped police officers and no-justice lawyers. And off the written apology that had been demanded of her.

If Mrs Porter could demonstrate contrition in a letter to our son, so that he might appreciate people are capable of such a thing, then we would consider withdrawing the charges.

Billie had ripped up the letter in front of Constable Stephens. Told him she'd go to prison before she wrote the man's bloody apology. His shoulders weren't so square when he left.

As she rounded a slight bend, Billie saw ahead what would be a waterfall if the creek were running. Then, as if by mirage, a pool of dark stagnant water at its base. The closer she got, the more jubilant she felt. Here was hope! Here was a future!

The pool was the size of a small car but she could tell it had once been much larger; there was a dark stain line on the rocks surrounding it, about a foot above the current water level. She made her way round to a suitable rock, being careful not to cast a shadow over the water, not wanting to frighten anything that might live in the pool. Once seated, she kept very still.

The pond was an airport terminal of insects. Water-skaters taxied across its surface. Hoverflies, gnats, damselflies moved above it in holding patterns of their own ambition. There were faint plops and sploshes and small discreet bubbles that erupted here and there from the still water. A small pale gaping mouth broke through the meniscus then just as quickly disappeared again, leaving only ripples. She thought of the young man who'd lost his bandana and felt chastened now for doubting his optimism.

Small birds – wrens, whistlers, shrikes – flitted across the pond in flashes of brown, grey, yellow and white, either in transit or feeding on the wing. This place had all the goings-on of another kind of city, pulsing with as much activity as the one she'd left behind a few hours ago. Like that city, there were winners and losers here, too.

Billie rummaged through her pack till she touched on soft cloth. Cotton. Once deepest navy; a good colour for the stagnant water. There was a long lineage to the contents of this pouch: Jess, Billie, Billie's mother, hers in turn, and on and on. Lives reanimated over and over and held now in this indestructible grit in a pocket of fabric. Those women had been in the shadows as she'd sewn it together, stitch after careful stitch. A wonderful disturbance of voices echoing throughout time: laughing, encouraging, sustaining. They'd kept Billie company into the night. Jess had been there, too, her voice younger than the others, which only reminded Billie of the prematurity of her loss.

What would her daughter's voice sound like now, at almost forty-two? Would it be wiser, like those of the other women, her forebears? Would the voice of wonderment Billie remembered so dearly have been eroded by now into wary scepticism? She'd never know.

Billie rested the square of fabric on her flattened palm and with a gentle underarm push, tossed it into the middle of the pool. Bugs lifted with the intrusion, then quickly settled again. She imagined the pouch tilting left and right as it sunk, and how the thing with the mouth might follow its path to the bottom. She thought also about how the water would have started to mix with its contents, how it would eventually form a slurry of cells – the life-death-life cycle – allowing her daughter to live with vigour again.

A kingfisher flew in and landed on a log at the top of the waterfall. The light was strange up there with the fat sun low in the sky. The bird's back was a glorious turquoise – Jess's favourite colour. Its belly the colour of clotted cream. The bird fixed its Zorro-banded eyes on Billie. She stared back.

The light, shimmering through the trees, cast bright stripes across the elevated rocks, so that the bird appeared large. Its broad shoulders radiant, beak and body unusually long. An opalescent silhouette suspended within an ethereal light. Billie wasn't much into holy visions – which is how it looked – so she squeezed her eyes shut for a moment to try to bring it back to scale. But when she opened them again the bird had gone and in its place stood the boy. He still wore his brown leather sandals, his pale blue whale-patterned shorts and red peaked cap. His slim, suntanned chest and round belly were bare. He looked about as though searching for something, arms flaccid at his sides.

'Hello, Marco,' Billie called softly.

She stood to see him better. But the light shifted and the boy faded from sight. All she saw then was sun-striped rocks. No bird. No boy. No hope.

25

Daniel wanted the old Carla back. The one without a dusting cloth or bleach bottle in her hand. The one with an easy smile. He wanted a father who didn't hesitate every time he reached out with a dusty arm to open the back door and enter the house. And Scout, nosy but normally sweet, was irritable. Alternated between sulky and whiny whenever she was asked to do anything, especially if it meant stopping whatever game she was playing. Having to vacate his bed by ten for house inspections on Saturdays, having crawled into it only a few hours before, was making Daniel irritable, too. But these were short-lived inconveniences. He knew that. What worried him most was his nan. How she was like a mouse permanently testing the air with its senses, assessing threats.

The stitches above her eyebrow had been removed several days ago, but the wound remained red. The ends of the cut were puckered, like they'd been pulled too tight, and the edges of it hadn't come together anywhere near perfect. He didn't think it was because the doctor had botched the job, more that Billie hadn't taken it easy and given the wound a chance to heal. And the bruising was slow to fade, with much of the right side of her face still mottled yellowy brown like the skin of an old lemon.

He sought out his father. Needed to know if he was worried about her, too, or if Daniel was overthinking it.

Angus was in his workshop bent over another of the slabs of blue gum. It was the narrowest of the five pieces, one cut furthest from the heartwood, but it was also Daniel's favourite. The colours of it varied more, honeyed through to russet, and the grain had more character. Made him think of an aerial view of Lake Eyre. In this piece, Daniel saw what had lured his father from carpenter to craftsman.

Angus looked up from the belt sander he was fiddling with and smiled. 'Hey, mate.'

They'd had some good times in this workshop, he and his father. So many that Daniel considered turning around now, walking out again, not wanting to spoil the memory of them.

'What time do you start this evening?' his father asked.

'Five-thirty.'

Daniel used his thumbnail to pick at a small chip of bark still stuck at the edge of the raw timber, then decided there was no courage in stalling. 'Do you think you should be selling the house right now?'

When his father's shoulders slumped in that *here-we-go-again* way, Daniel almost wavered. 'I mean, can't it wait? I think too much is happening to Nan at the moment. That missing boy. Losing her job. Now the police are asking her questions about that kid with the broken arm.'

Angus didn't answer straight away, put his attention to changing the belt on the sander.

'Dad?'

'I heard you, son.'

'Well?'

His father rested the power tool on the wood and finally looked at him. 'Do you think later would be any easier for her?'

In truth, he didn't. But she seemed especially fragile at the moment. He told his father as much.

'She's always going to be fragile, Dan. I should know, I've been trying to balance the tough decisions with her since you were little.'

Daniel thought about what some of those tough decisions might have been. Not allowing him to be held back from starting school, as Billie had wanted, was probably one of them. *Just one more year*, his grandmother had pleaded, but Angus refused and Daniel remembered being quietly jubilant. Then later, Angus telling her Daniel was old enough to walk to and from school on his own. He was at secondary school by then. His father remarrying would be another. A decision that forced Billie from the main house. Daniel wondered how much Angus had weighed Billie's shift in purpose against his own need for love and companionship when he met Carla. But another thought came in quick defence: who could blame his father for choosing happiness?

Had these been tough decisions, or necessary ones? Most would look like progress to a normal person. But none of it would have been easy on his grandmother.

'It was sprung on her though, selling. You should have spoken to her about it before you made a decision.'

'I agree. But I can't change that now. Quite aside from Scout shooting her mouth off, the decision was made for me, Dan. I can't run a business from here anymore. It's too small.' Angus lifted his arms to indicate the workshop. 'And while it's regrettable she didn't hear it from me first, her reaction would've been exactly the same if she had.'

'You don't know that.'

'I do though, Dan.'

'But look at her! It's like she thinks she's gotta fight everything!'

Angus rested his hands on the rough-sawn wood, dropped his head to look at the timber's desert grain. When he faced Daniel again it was with a sigh so deep it raised a plume of sawdust between them.

'What happened with those kids in the park had nothing to do with me putting this place on the market. That would have happened anyway. It's that bloody tree ... what happened there ... that's what makes her think she's gotta fight. But sometimes things just happen, Dan ... things we have no control over. Things like what happened to your mum.'

It was rare for his father to reference that day, so his remark felt honest. But his honesty wasn't done yet.

'Now, you can choose to fight against the unfairness of that day for the rest of your life too, like Billie, or you can choose to live a different way. What way do *you* choose, son?'

Neither spoke for a time. In the silence, Daniel thought about having unlimited choices over how to live this one life. But also how many of those choices had already been made for him: by a faceless man, his grandmother. But there was a cold truth about those things that had been decided for him, too: were it not for Billie, he wouldn't even know to grieve for his mother because he wouldn't remember her. Most of the things he remembered about her, or thought he remembered, or had imagined so many times now that they were as real as a memory, had been forged by someone else: Billie. And perhaps that was the real problem. He wasn't fighting against the unfairness of that day: he was fighting against the choices someone else had made for him because of it. But if he chose a life that didn't consider others then wasn't he choosing a selfish one?

'It seems no matter what I choose, someone gets hurt,' he said to his father.

'But there's also self-preservation, Dan. And there's no shame in choosing that.'

214

His father said no more. Returned to his task, left Daniel with that thought.

At the door of the workshop, Daniel glanced back at his father, watched as he wiped a sleeve across his eyes. He felt a sudden wrench of loyalty for this man, equal only to the loyalty he felt for his grandmother. He owed his life to both, but each seemed bent towards different purposes for how he should live it.

Angus wrapped his knuckles on the timber, a back-to-work gesture. He took the ear muffs from round his neck and placed them over his head, pulled the face mask up from under his chin and covered his mouth and nose. The belt sander came shrilly to life and his father fiddled with the tracking knob to make the new belt run true. Satisfied, he put the tool to work on the rough surface. Daniel knew he wouldn't stop in this task till it was as perfect as he could make it. It was a job that would take him hours. But cared for properly, treated with love and respect, what he created would be beautiful and could last a person a lifetime.

The broken fig branch was as thick as Daniel's calf and the length of two small cars. It had to be the one Billie tried to protect. There was a saw line partway through the broken end. The weight of the branch – or the bodyweight of a couple of boys – would have easily snapped the remainder from the trunk. This act of vandalism suddenly felt personal, like the wound had been inflicted upon him, and he understood something of how his grandmother had felt.

He rested his hand on the tree and surprised himself when he said, 'I'm sorry they did this to you.'

He had to get rid of the branch. Save his grandmother from the hurt of seeing it. She'd still notice its absence – reckoned she knew every branch of the tree – but for her to come across it as suddenly as Daniel had would be like finding your pet bludgeoned to death on your front lawn. Part of him wished now that he'd not cut through the park to get to work, stuck to the bikeway instead.

With some effort, he started hauling the branch towards the edge of the park. He'd take it deep into the scrub, out of sight, unsure if what he was doing was an act of kindness or, as his father suggested, an act of self-preservation. Or if it was just another mess he needed to clear away.

What would a girl like Alex say if she saw him doing this? he wondered. He imagined her tapping her head as she had at the bar that night, saying: *Too much going on up here.*

And none of it good or helpful or logical.

But his life wasn't logical. His perspective on it was directed by a grandmother who lived in the past and a father who mostly ignored it, leaving Daniel to zigzag between reality and its denial. Where was the middle ground? The space that allowed him to walk alongside his history without always feeling the dark pull of it? That place of choices his father spoke of. Maybe a girl like Alex could offer that space.

Daniel could picture himself with someone like her. Pictured them going out: boyfriend and girlfriend. It was an image he liked. She'd have the smarts to make sense of his stupid thoughts. He imagined her tilting her triangle chin, index finger tapping it as she pondered this big old tyrant, this tree. *It's just a tree, Dan,* she'd say, *where something awful happened.* And coming from her he'd believe it. *Let it go,* she'd add. That was the kind of friend he needed. One who undid Billie's work with words that made sense; be his release.

He'd come this far with the branch now, so persevered with his task. But it felt lighter, the scrub less challenging, as he hauled it well out of sight. Job done, and that's all it was – he must believe that – he stepped easily over the scrub on his way out again. Didn't look back as he rode away.

26

THE WEEKLY FAMILY MEAL HAD started to require a Hollywood performance of smiles and diversions as Carla attempted to keep the conversation light. She could barely be bothered trying anymore.

Every day she'd spend time cleaning. Dust found its way in through windows that didn't close properly and under doors. It trickled down from gaps in cornices, settled on ceiling fan blades and light fittings. Blew in whenever anyone came or went, back door or front, which had been a lot during Saturday's open house. She'd wipe down all the surfaces one day, and by the next could trace her finger through it again like the earlier work had never been done. If only it would rain. Suppress it. But the sky remained blue and cloudless.

And where was everybody else when this work needed to be done? Scout could look busy cleaning up her room but in truth was just shifting one toy or game to a different spot on the carpet. Daniel slept in late after work, which was fair enough, but meant the work was usually done by the time he got up. Angus was being pushed by the client to finish the table he was working on. And Billie? Carla couldn't expect her assistance with anything that might help sell the house. As it was, she'd had to placate Fran over the way Billie scowled at potential buyers; the way she followed them round the backyard as though they might steal something. Nothing she said to Billie would change anything anyway.

Carla was fed up. Tired. Irritable. And now Scout was acting up over some bloody dog.

The best she could do was focus on getting dessert on the table and hope everyone soon finished up. 'Look, Scout, Nan's made your favourite, chocolate mousse.'

Scout turned to Billie with wet eyes and sniffed back tears. 'Sorry, Nan, but I don't think I can eat any. I'm just too sad.'

Neither had she eaten her chicken schnitzel and salad.

Billie put her arm round Scout's shoulders and hugged her. 'It's okay to be sad, Scout. And it's even okay to enjoy dessert at the same time if you want.'

'Do you think so?'

'I *know* so.'

Carla tried not to roll her eyes when Scout accepted her bowl of gooey chocolatey goodness with a martyr's sigh and began eating it, feigning punishing swallows. Finally, for a time there was blissful quiet round the table. But as soon as Scout was finished, she brought the conversation back to her friend's missing dog.

'The vet told Becky's mum that it probably *chose* to leave them.'

The dog was old and sick apparently. Had wandered off two days ago and not been seen since. Scout's friend was beside herself. And in solidarity, so was Scout.

'That's probably enough about the dog, Scout,' Carla said, but Scout ignored her.

'Why would it *do* that, Nan? They'd had him for like a *hundred* years.'

Scout had directed most of her talk about the dog to Billie, obviously the best person to consult about things lost. Billie, to her credit, had been careful in her answers so far.

'Maybe it was trying to protect them.'

'From what?'

'From being sad.'

'But they *are* sad.'

'Yes, but if the dog was dying like Becky said, then maybe they'd be even sadder to see it die, and the dog knew this. So in a way it's a kind thing the dog's done, saving them from that.'

Angus added his optimistic angle. 'Nan's right, Scout. Animals are smart. And loyal.'

Billie nodded. 'I bet Becky's dog thought it through. Decided to take itself off somewhere ... somewhere really, really nice and just went to sleep.'

Billie and Scout held each other's gaze. In the older woman's face Carla saw absolute belief and in Scout's a desperate need to.

'Scout, dogs have an instin—'

Carla nudged Daniel's leg under the table to stop him from saying more. Up until now he hadn't said anything. That alone made Carla think he knew the likely truth just as she did. That the dog's pending death had probably elicited an old instinct, one that couldn't even be bred out of a domesticated dog. Knowing it was weak and vulnerable it had hidden somewhere to protect itself from predators, and had eventually died there. Alone.

Scout looked at her half-brother expectantly, trusting his opinion.

Daniel glanced at Carla before he spoke. 'Dogs have an instinct to protect the people they love, just like Dad and Nan said.'

'So what a wonderful thing, Scout,' Billie added. 'To choose the time and place to—'

'If everyone's done, I'll start clearing the table.' Carla didn't like the shift in Billie's language, sought to wrap it up.

Daniel, too eagerly, got up to help.

'So you think it *is* dead, Nan?'

Billie went to say something, but Angus cut her off. 'No more about the dog, Scout. C'mon, teeth. Bed.'

'You can't hide from death, Angus.'

'You can when you're seven.' Carla started clattering empty bowls on top of each other.

Scout started to cry again. Angus took her by the hand, ushered her out of the room.

'I'll come in when I'm done here,' Carla called after them.

'No compassion,' Billie muttered.

Carla turned to Billie. 'There's compassion in not letting a child realise the sadness of another creature dying alone.'

'It wouldn't have died alone though.'

'No. Of course not.' Carla couldn't keep the sarcasm from her voice. 'It would've had any number of other little beasties in the dirt just *waiting* to throw it a bloody party.'

'You're cruel. And faithless.'

Cruel? Possibly after that remark. But not faithless. 'I just have a different faith from yours, Billie.'

'The only thing I've seen you worship is the desire for a big, fancy house.'

How had it come to this, the pair of them acting like schoolyard bullies?

Carla ignored Billie. Took the bowls to the sink and waited for the water to run through hot, hating the waste, in time and resource.

Daniel, who'd remained quiet, began gathering the other plates still on the table. 'Nan and I can clear up, Carla. You go and say goodnight to Scout if you like.'

Carla felt dismissed, not helped. But with no energy to argue further, she flicked the water from her hands, dried them on a tea towel and left the room.

Scout was in bed, bedside fairy lamp still on. She budged over to make room for Carla to lie down beside her. Her crying had stopped but she looked worn out by her earlier tears. Carla eased the small frown from between her daughter's eyebrows with her thumb.

'The dog was very old, sweetheart.'

'I know.'

'And very old things eventually die.'

'People, too?'

'Yes, people, too.'

'Daniel's real mum wasn't very old.'

Carla tried to think of a suitable answer.

Scout saved her from having to. 'But Nan told me that's because she was too special to stay here, so got called back early.'

Called back. Such a Billie thing to say. But Carla felt guilty now for her earlier remark. Chastened, too. Because Billie had known what to say when Scout had undoubtedly asked about Daniel's mother. Carla hadn't. And if she was honest, what Billie had told her was beautiful. Personal experience – and yes, a certain kind of faith helped, she supposed – gave Billie the right words. Carla had only her imagination to rely on, which was sensationalised. Influenced by media and gossip. Fact-laden. One-dimensional. No more substance to it than a flat page of newsprint. While those who knew Jess, *really* knew her – Billie, Angus, friends like Namita – undoubtedly still held Jess in their minds and hearts fully formed, multidimensional, real. So how could Carla have had the right words for Scout? How could she describe what such a loss did to a person's soul? How it changed their worldview. What it made faith look like. So maybe Billie was right. Maybe she *was* faithless. Driven by nothing more than a desire for a better roof over her head.

This thinking unsettled Carla as she massaged her daughter's now seamless brow. And that feeling remained long after Scout's tight little body melted into the mattress and her breathing purred into sleep.

★

The kitchen, when Carla went back in, was spotless. The dishwasher hummed. Nobody was about. She could see the light on at Billie's. And Daniel's shone beneath his closed bedroom door. She knocked on it now and waited for him to invite her in.

When he did, he was at his desk, laptop open.

'Thanks for cleaning up.'

'No worries.'

'I'm sorry about that conversation earlier.'

'Nan was, too.'

So they'd talked. Carla expected they would. She imagined Billie would be happier if she had Daniel all to herself. He was the closest person to replacing the missing half that Namita spoke of her losing. But then she checked herself: Billie loved Scout like she was kin. So maybe it was children she cared for most. The ease with which they embraced alternative thinking.

'She said to say sorry.'

'Really?' Carla couldn't hide her surprise.

'She does care. Probably too much.'

Carla slumped onto the edge of Daniel's bed, elbows on her knees, chin cupped in her hands. The same could be said for Daniel, that he cared too much. His life in a holding pattern: not going to uni, working a bar job four nights a week, speaking of travelling but never acting on it. Never quite selfish enough to fulfil his own ambitions or desires. He'd emptied himself of those in order to make room for his grandmother's.

'I do believe in things other than a fancy house, you know,' Carla said. 'I believe in creating a home. A safe place where we can all come together without fear of judgement or criticism. That's what a home is. Not what's buried in the soil beneath one. That's the stuff of fairytales.'

'Are fairytales so bad if they make a person happy?'

'I think they are if they prevent others from moving on, living a fuller life.'

There they were, skirting reality as always. Speaking as though a third person was in the room, which maybe she was.

'Maybe this is as full as it gets,' Daniel said.

'It can be much fuller for you, Dan. Leave. Travel. Live big.'

'She relies on me. I'm the only one who understands her.'

This wasn't a criticism of her, Carla, or even Angus, for failing to. She knew that. It was an admission of his burden. Perhaps the first time he'd ever openly made it.

'Plus, I'm worried she'd see it as a betrayal if I left.'

'A betrayal of what?'

'Mum.'

And there it was. What everything was measured against.

A woman remembered only through photographs. Frozen in time, not subjected to the vicissitudes of it. In only a few more years Daniel would be the same age as Jess when she died. But still he called her *Mum*. Not *my mother*, someone who'd served a role he'd surely forgotten. *Mum*. A figure who still lived large and bright in his mind, all thanks to his grandmother. Carla didn't know whether to feel proud of Billie for ensuring Jess remained indelible in this way, or hurt at being prevented from completely filling the role herself because of it.

But Carla sought to make it work in her stepson's favour for a change. 'And what do you think your mum would see it as?'

Daniel looked stuck for an answer, only confirming Jess's chimeric quality.

He might not call Carla *Mum*, but she sure as hell was one. 'I know exactly what she'd see it as, Dan,' she said with more force than she'd intended. 'Her son living the life she'd always intended for him … eyes to the future.'

Carla dreamt Jess came to her that night, sat on the edge of her bed. Even sensed the gentle compression of the mattress, which she expected was just the weight of her own bent knees. She rolled away from her, pressed the jigsaw piece of her body against Angus's. The fit was perfect, no space for another.

27

Daniel and Polly sat together on the opposite side of the bar to where they usually worked. They'd found all the dirty glasses – stacked in corners, balanced on ledges, resting in pot plants and inside bathrooms – washed and put them back in place for the next session. The swill and smear of sticky alcohol and mixers was gone from all surfaces. Chairs were up on tables. Everything neatly realigned. The smell of alcohol lingered. Always would, Daniel reckoned, even if the place was blasted with a fire hose.

They were having a *morning cap* (Polly's phrase) – Daniel orange juice, Polly a double-shot of Cointreau.

She'd winked at him when she'd poured it. 'We each have our preferred sources of Vitamin C, Dan.'

Now, Polly was counting the notes Malcolm had handed her. Some were stuck together. She took a damp cloth from the bar top and used it to wipe each. 'Genius idea making plastic money.'

'And not likely to find its way into a sea turtle.'

'Dead right there, Earth Boy.'

She finished tallying her tips. 'Tight wads tonight.'

'It's a budget bar, Poll. They're tight wads every night.'

'They can afford to get turped though.'

'Saturday night's job description, isn't it?'

She pushed the notes into the front pocket of her jeans. 'And what's *your* job description, Sunbeam?'

'To clean up after them.' He wasn't stupid, knew exactly what Polly was asking. Chose to ignore it.

But she'd never let him off easily, so put her blue eyes on him now over her glass of Cointreau, took a sip, then said, 'You could choose to make the mess from time to time, you know.'

Why was everyone pressuring him about choices? His life was a landfill site of messy ones, so why would he add more to it like getting drunk, losing control?

Polly knocked back the last of her drink. 'C'mon,' she said. 'You can walk me home.' She collected her bag from a cupboard behind the bar, called goodnight to Mal.

Their boss looked up from the till and waved. 'See you two tonight. Have the same fun all over again.'

Polly rolled her eyes. 'Can't wait.'

Out on the street, desire moved people along in unsteady and raucous packs. One group would join another looking for connection then they'd separate, or not, as they were accepted or rebuffed. It was a kind of mating ritual, one Polly probably thought he should be a part of, but for which he had little desire. His experiences with Megan and other girls at school was that hooking up demanded honesty, intimacy necessitated the Big Conversation, and a guy's soul could be emptied for curiosity or gossip. He saw no future in starting anything evasively or as a liar.

At school, he and his past were a package. Inseparable. Those who didn't know about it were told by those who did. Passed on like a virus. Bryce had probably told Alex and her friend about it after seeing him at the museum that day. A juicy bit of ingratiating gossip to win big-man favour. Except Alex hadn't seemed won over by Bryce. *Not enough happening up here. Tap, tap.* Daniel smiled remembering the picture he'd had of them the other day at the tree: together, a couple. He could kick himself now. Wished he'd shown her that he was interested. Asked for her number. He'd looked out for her each night at work since, but she'd not been back to the bar. He could contact Bryce. Get her number from him. Probably have to put up with a Bryce-style putdown for being keen on her, but it'd be worth it.

He and Polly wove through the crowd and once free of it, he breathed deeply of the mild early morning air then released it as a long sigh.

Polly did the same. 'It's like being born, isn't it?'

He could hear the smile in her voice. 'The air feels cleaner out here than at work, if that's what you mean.'

'That's not what I mean, Sunbeam. It's a new day. Fresh start. Anything's possible.'

'Except we'll go home and sleep through half of it.'

'Jesus, you know how to bring a girl down.'

'Just being honest.'

'Which is why I wanted you to walk me home. So *I* can be honest.'

'You're not going to hit on me are you, Poll?'

'Ew! That'd be like sleeping with my brother.' She pushed him playfully and they both laughed. 'But as your honorary big sister, I'm gonna give you something better. *Advice.*'

He'd had something of the Big Conversation with Polly. She knew the hard facts: mother murdered. She was good at judging no-go zones, though, so never asked about the personal stuff, like how a three-year-old kid grew up with that kind of shit in his life. He expected she'd Googled his mother's name, filled in some of the gaps, as most people probably did when they found out about his past.

'So, here's me,' Polly started, 'thirty-three and still pulling beers, dishing out too much mostly, so I end up having to clean

227

up a good whack of it again at the end of the night. And I look at you … you're what, nineteen?'

He nodded.

Polly shook her head. 'Same age as me when I started in hospo.' She stopped walking and turned to face him. 'Dan, it's meant to be a stopgap job. The one you do during uni or to earn a bit of extra cash. Why risk making a career of it like me and Mal have?'

She might be small but her presence was huge. Daniel felt the five-foot nothing of her bearing up on him now. 'I don't know. Because it's a job I've already got and don't have to find? Because I like working with you.'

She was sharp, Polly, knew false flattery when she heard it. 'Bullshit. It's because you're afraid. Not of the dark like the rest of us. You're afraid of the *light*. Of being seen. But I watch you watching the people at the bar, and I see someone longing to cross a line into something else … *being* someone else.'

Was it that someone else who felt the rub of Polly's words now?

'Listen, I know you can't rewrite history. God knows, I'd give it a crack if we could, but you sure as hell can choose how you live with the one you're given.'

There it was: a lesson about choices again.

'Tragic as it is, Dan, violence can happen anytime, anywhere. Hate to think how much of it we've caused just by working where we do. But if you let those events hit the pause button on your life then the bastards who do those things screw you over twice.'

Daniel wondered if Polly had been screwed over. Whether they'd done it twice.

It also made him think of Billie. Because what if Polly was right and his future was to look like his grandmother's: a young man, then an old one, on his own, beating a deeper and deeper path over the years from one piece of ground to another to polish a rectangle of metal on a tree that held more memory than substance? The thought was an icy finger down his spine.

'All this *maybe, sometime, eventually* talk you do about travelling has to stop, Dan. Buy the fucking ticket. Pack your bag. Leave before you find any more excuses not to go. And when you get back, I wanna serve *you* a drink on the other side of that line you keep gazing over … even if it's a bloody lemonade.' Polly was breathing hard by the time she finished.

Daniel imagined this door she'd have him escape through. Wondered at the possibilities it offered. Then thought of Billie, small like Polly but fragile. 'I hear what you're saying, Poll, but … it's complicated.'

Complicated. A single word that suggested a thousand others, all of which Daniel had trouble articulating. Because they were words embedded with guilt and duty.

'*Life's* complicated, Daniel. Doesn't mean you hide from it.'

Was that what he was doing? He always thought he'd squared up to it. But maybe what he squared up to wasn't life so much as his mistrust of it.

Polly sighed. With fatigue, with frustration, he couldn't be sure.

'Look,' she said, 'you're a nice kid who was handed a shitty start. Doesn't mean you don't deserve a happy ending.'

They both suddenly laughed at the unintentional innuendo, and the energy in the air between them calmed. Satisfied perhaps that her advice had been delivered, Polly put her short, strong arms round his waist and hugged him. It felt like she was hanging on more than holding him, as though she really was his big sister and he was about to get on that plane and not come back for a very long time. Her head barely reached halfway up his chest but Daniel felt the force of her body, the strength of her concern, and something opened inside him and he thought it might be trust. He put his arms round her shoulders and for a time he felt lighter for her closeness. He held on to that feeling, made it last as long as he could. His throat remained tight, words held back, but when they did finally come the depth of his emotion surprised him. 'Thanks for caring, Poll.'

She patted his back, like any good sister. 'C'mon, Sunbeam. We better get going before the sun comes up. God knows what'll happen to us.'

They walked on; the city not entirely asleep but certainly subdued, while Polly, a talker, chatted away. 'You said you love volcanoes, geology, dirt … shit like that. Have you ever thought of finding a job in it?'

'What, like a gravedigger?'

Polly laughed. 'I was thinking more in mining.'

'Now that *would* hurt sea turtles.'

Daniel slowed his pace to match hers, liked the soft sound of their twin steps.

28

THE BOYS HAD WON IN the end. All that remained of the branch was a four-inch stump on the main trunk. Billie massaged the sawn half of it, coarse like sandpaper, with her thumb. The bottom half splintered from where the last of it had been ripped away. She looked around for the branch but couldn't find it. Was glad she didn't have to see the leaves browned and shrivelled. A skeleton of what it once was.

What went through their minds as they did it? Did they feel powerful? Justified? Smug in their revenge?

She wiped her eyes. Didn't want to think about those boys anymore, their impunity. Instead, she concentrated on the screws and why she was here. They were difficult to remove, the threads corroded by three, almost four years. But eventually she worked one loose, then the other. The plaque – *Loved then taken* – held its place in the trunk regardless. She used the flat edge of the screwdriver to prise it off, wondered as she did this if the tree felt her digging. Once removed, a perfect rectangular depression remained in the trunk. It looked like a small dark window into the tree. But she knew it as a window into her grief, too.

She took the new screws from her pocket, shiny like the plaque's face, and scanned the trunk for a suitable place to refix it. The only rule: it had to be positioned above where Jess and Daniel had been found. No looking away.

Imagining them there on the ground, Daniel sitting alongside his mother, holding her hand according to the couple who'd found them, and Billie could still picture his small, bewildered face. His bewilderment had lasted for months as he struggled to find words to make sense of the terrible thing he'd witnessed. He'd never found the right ones, got stuck instead on the same two: *Where's Mummy?* But was it any wonder? Billie was an adult and hadn't been able to find the words either.

'Nan?'

Despite Daniel's voice being the most familiar of all to her, Billie still jumped at the sound of it. Dropped both plaque and screws. She turned, screwdriver still between her teeth, to face him.

He was so tall now and filled out across shoulders and chest. A young man. She had no idea why she was only just noticing this. She'd watched the transition after all. But the days then weeks, months and years of a child's growth were drip-fed before those who raised them, till suddenly their cup was full and an adult stood before you.

She took the screwdriver from her mouth. 'I'm surprised to see you here.'

He came so rarely now after a childhood of coming often with her. Initially he found excuses – homework, mountain bike riding, school sport – till eventually he just said *No.*

'I was here the other day. Saw what they did. Wanted to check you were okay.'

'I guess they won.'

'No they didn't. They lost.'

'Can't see how. The branch has gone.'

Daniel shook his head. 'When any of them comes past here as a grown man, they'll look at the tree and be reminded of what they did and feel ashamed they were that kind of boy.'

This hadn't occurred to Billie, their meanness smarting them from time to time like an old splinter in the sole of a foot.

Daniel picked up the dropped plaque and screws, wiped the dust from the metal with his thumb but didn't hand it back to her. Billie resisted the urge to snatch it from him, thought of Gollum and his precious ring.

Studying it, probably for the first time not attached to the tree, he turned it dull side up then down again. *Loved then taken*, he read.

Some of the few *right* words she'd found.

'I've always wondered … what's it for … really?' Daniel still didn't look at her, bounced the metal in his hand, perhaps testing its weight. He made it look flimsy.

Billie rescued it from him. 'What's it *for?*'

It was a symbol of their loss. A way for Jess's name to touch more than just those who knew and loved her. That her loss be witnessed, perhaps even felt, by others. A reminder: beware, be careful. The wail Billie hadn't always felt able to release. A window through which she communicated with Jess; one she kept shiny and open. Surely he knew all of these things?

'It's so she's never forgotten,' Billie summarised. 'Not for as long as this tree's here for it to be attached to anyway.'

'Isn't that the same as staking a claim on the tree, though?'

'And what's wrong with that?'

'Because you tell me she's everywhere, so she can't just be that piece of metal on that tree. And this is gonna sound weird, Nan … but finally believing she *is* everywhere stopped me turning up here like I had a score to settle with the place.'

So this was why he'd stopped coming to the tree: it had stopped hurting him.

'It's also helped me realise that selling the house isn't such a bad thing if that's what Dad and Carla need to do, because where we live isn't Mum either.'

'But it is, Daniel. It *is* your mum.'

The ground took his attention for a while as he kicked at the earth with a grubby canvas shoe. 'Get rid of it,' he finally said, indicating to the plaque. 'Let go of some of the sadness.'

'Get rid of it?'

'Why not? Doing something like that is more symbolic than when it's stuck to the tree.'

Billie made a fist round the plaque, felt the sharp edges of the metal press into her skin. The plaque, the tree, her attendance here, gave Billie purpose.

She opened her hand so that the plaque rested in the flat of her palm. The size of a playing card, a fragment compared to the imposing canopy above her. But while small, it represented so much.

'Why the change, Daniel? What's happened?'

'Nothing's happened.'

But he wouldn't look at her. She followed his gaze as he looked up, down, left, right, taking in this place she'd visited several times a week for the past sixteen years. But now, it seemed, he would have her see it through different eyes.

'I've always seen this place as the enemy,' he said eventually. 'But that meant every time I came here I felt like I was here for a fight.' He shrugged then, like a letting go, before looking directly at Billie. 'I got tired of squaring up to the place, Nan. I just wanted to see a tree in a park and feel happy when I walked past it.'

Billie looked again to the piece of metal in her hand. The thought of giving it up was unbearable. 'I'm sorry, Daniel. I can't.'

Disappointment flashed across his face and his shoulders dropped. The cup of his adulthood no longer looked quite so full.

Facing the tree again, she held the plaque in place on the trunk and carefully began turning the first screw.

29

When Inspector Quinn left, Carla and Angus sat staring at one another. Carla broke the silence. 'Bastard!'

Angus agreed. 'Despite the jerk knowing the tree's history.'

Which proved certain histories were only important to others if they benefited from them.

'But a letter of apology, Angus? She's never going to write that.'

'I know.'

'Bastard!' Carla said again. She stood up, paced the kitchen, arms tight across her chest. She pictured the boy's lawyer father. Couldn't decide between the lean and tanned or the jowly jawed with milky, wine-sipping skin. But always he was a man of steepled fingers, crossed legs and a tick-tocking foot as he appraised those he considered less than himself. Appraised Billie. And her tragic past of no account either. His son's behaviour nothing more than a boys-will-be-boys game that someone had taken the fun from. A disappointment his father now sought punishment for. For all Carla hated Billie's obsession with that tree – for all she hated the tree itself – there was no fairness, no *decency*, in Billie being expected to virtually get down on her knees and beg forgiveness of a father for his brat's delinquency. God, how his sense of entitlement galled her.

Quinn had asked them to persuade Billie to write the letter. Billie had refused, of course. Wouldn't budge, Quinn said. Ripped the demand to pieces in front of the constable who'd delivered it, by all accounts. And who could blame her? In essence, she was being asked to renounce the sanctity of the tree, give those boys, and others like them, free rein to its vandalism, all without recourse or conscience. Something Billie would never accept. The request was dehumanising.

'Bastard!' Carla kept pacing, raging inside, none of which would change anything.

Angus came to her, pulled her to a halt and wrapped his work-hardened arms round her, stroked her hair.

'I'll write his bloody letter,' Carla said. 'Fudge Billie's signature. I expect that's what Quinn was hinting at by coming to see us anyway.'

'You don't have to. I will.'

'No, Angus. You shouldn't have to make this tacky apology any more than Billie should.'

Angus rocked her gently till her tension eased. But the surrender wasn't to him so much as the task she'd set herself.

Later that evening, once Scout was in bed, Carla sat at the kitchen table and stared at the blank page before her. She wanted to make the letter something other than a victory for this creep. Not a trophy for his son either, something to brag about as he passed it round his private school mates: *Look at what my dad made the old hag write.*

To make it more than an apology, she also needed to make it an explanation. But how to explain something she didn't understand? To do that she needed to think like Billie, to view the tree from her perspective so that she might better understand Billie's motives for protecting it. And she'd never tried to do that before.

Under the heading *What tree represents*, Carla jotted down a few key points.

Site of terrible loss.

Place to grieve.

Holds memories of daughter.

Should she include what Billie really believed: that the site *was* her daughter, so in harming it, those boys had harmed them both all over again?

Frustrated, Carla sat back in her chair.

An image of Billie holding a soft white cloth came to mind, polishing the plaque with such care that day. The way she spoke to the tree as she worked. There was a mutual bond there, Carla recognised now. A connection. Perhaps something spiritual. Was the tree Billie's church? Her god? Were her memories its scripture? Were these the things that defined *sacred*?

Carla laid the pen on the kitchen table. Who did she think she was, believing she could do this? What even gave her the right to try? She'd never once tried to walk the perimeter of that tree in Billie's shoes. Was it fear of where they might take her that had kept her safely in her own? But even that suggested an emotional investment she knew she'd never made. The reason she hadn't was because she hadn't *wanted* to feel that kind of pain, to have to imagine living it. But now she was literally being forced to. And god how it hurt.

But she felt something else, too. Ashamed. Not just in failing to try to understand Billie's loss. Ashamed of the betrayal she was about to commit in attempting to write such a letter. Because writing anything to this man was the equivalent of telling Billie her history was less important than his ego. Something Billie had already refused to admit.

Other sacred trees came to mind – so many disappeared

arborglyphs, centuries-old direction trees, the sly poisoning of the Tree of Knowledge, old-growth forests felled for woodchip – their significance – their *history* – threatened or erased with a hefty dose of Roundup or a bulldozer. This letter, once delivered, would be a similar poison. And no matter how much Carla hated it and the tragic history it allowed to shine bright in her family's minds, she couldn't – wouldn't – be the executioner of the tree's significance.

Angus came into the room as Carla closed the notepad.

'How'd you go?'

'I can't do it.'

'Don't worry about it. I'll write something later.'

'No. I mean I *can't* because I *shouldn't*. And neither should you.'

'But what about Billie?'

'It's because of Billie that we can't. To write it denies the importance of the tree to her. We have no right to do that.'

'Would she even find out if we did? Reckon she'd just assume the kid's father changed his mind.'

'*I'll* know.'

Angus leant back against the kitchen bench, palms resting on the edge of the countertop, fingers tapping the cupboard beneath. He studied her, puzzled. 'It's a letter, Carla. An apology none of us means but one that'll get this jerk off her back. I don't get the change of heart.'

Carla struggled to get it, too. All she knew was what her conscience was telling her: she had no right to assume Billie's words and make them into something Billie never would. And she had to listen to that voice or live with the regret of having ignored it.

'That's what I thought at first, but it's more than a letter, Angus. That's why Billie refuses to write it. It's like her connection to that tree is *holy*. Any letter – by her or us – is a betrayal of everything it represents. It's like asking a person to give up their religion.'

Angus looked to the ceiling and let out a long deep breath.

Morality was a heavy burden, especially in the face of an easy solution. Carla felt its weight.

'Okay. But where does that leave us?'

Carla thought about the alternatives. Billie charged for her actions. But surely they wouldn't jail a woman of her age? They'd probably fine her or give her a good-behaviour bond. Maybe force her to do community service. Humiliate her without a doubt. But none of these things felt as bad as betraying her.

'Supporting her through whatever happens next.'

'And yet we sell this place out from under her without a qualm?'

She didn't – wouldn't – answer Angus.

This was where the extent of her shame stopped. Because how many places of worship could Billie possibly need?

30

DANIEL HAD ONCE WATCHED THE sea rush in and over a distant coastal town, claiming hundreds, maybe even thousands of lives. His imagination had filled in what he couldn't see of the grainy mobile phone footage being broadcast on television. He'd imagined people running ahead of the surge, pictured them glancing over their shoulders. Some were never going to outrun the wave but still they ran, survival the imperative. He'd imagined small children being swept from a parent's arms, despite their determination to not lose their grip. How they'd tumble away in the turgid sea water alongside cats and cooking pots, chairs and hope. And he'd imagined how those on high ground prayed they were high enough. While those on the highest felt safe enough to let their phone cameras roll. He'd thought about this as he watched the tsunami sweep over the town. How luck found some, misfortune others, and no one had any control over which tracked them down. He knew something about this.

Authorities had been accused of turning off the tsunami warnings too soon. The earthquake that triggered it was so far offshore they didn't think there was any risk, while deep within Earth a seismic pulse was mobilising the ocean. His father had said the villagers shouldn't have relied on warnings. That they should have used their instincts: to run like hell the moment they felt the Earth shake. Despite the easy disconnect of his father's remark, it had made Daniel think: where did it come from, this instinct to run when the ground shook? Perhaps its origins grew from a single event that occurred millennia ago. How this first story of an engulfing sea was repeated over and over and with enough drama for it to become an echo, snagged permanently at the edge of memory of all those who came after.

Old knowledge abandoned now, just like the dead livestock and belongings washed up at the high-water mark of the tsunami. The bones of these legacy stories, like the bones of the dead animals, eventually bleached to a mere rumour of their original form before being forgotten altogether.

It made him think now of his own past, experiences from his childhood washed up somewhere in his mind. The bones of his legacy story lost, too. They must still exert their force though. How else to explain his instinct to run? To get as far away as possible from this place before it engulfed him entirely.

His father came out of the workshop, spotted Daniel on the swing under the jacaranda tree in the far corner of the block, the same tree that supported Scout's tree house. It was a place Daniel hadn't sat for years.

'Surprised it still holds your weight,' Angus said coming up to him.

They both looked to the branch the swing was tied to.

'I replaced the rope just before Christmas. Didn't want it breaking and Scout getting hurt.'

'You're a good brother.' His father sat on the ground, knees up and wide, plucked at dried tufts of grass between them. With all that had been going on, it was the most relaxed he'd seen his

242

father for weeks. He rarely took the opportunity to sit at the best of times, except for meals, and hardly ever on the ground.

'Tomorrow, eh?' Angus said.

Nearly all of April gone in a stressful blur, now here they were: the eve of the auction.

'You reckon it'll sell?'

'Fran says it will without a doubt.'

'How long after till we have to move?'

'Thirty days.'

Daniel nodded. These were the surest things he'd been told. Yes, it would sell. They'd leave it in thirty days. He was surprised by how much the certainty comforted him. Less comforting was the imminent change for his grandmother. He looked out across the site of that change now.

'Nan told me once that we learn who we are by how we treat the land.'

'I think we learn who we are by how we treat people.'

His grandmother would say the two were inseparable.

A pair of cockatoos landed in a tree in the bush behind them. Their chatter sounded like a child learning to talk: gargled, pitch varied, imperfect. Daniel imagined he and his father were the topic of their conversation. Imagined them surveying all the roofs, fences, roads and cars from up high and remarking on the foolishness of a life encumbered with so many *things*. The birds launched in a flash of white, screeching with what could be alarm, but for all Daniel knew was disgust or humour.

His father followed their passage across the sky. 'Noisy pests.'

'I don't know how to help her anymore, Dad.'

Or was it that he no longer wanted to?

'Why do you saddle yourself with the belief it's your responsibility to, son? We're in this together.'

'But she doesn't go to you for help.'

It sounded like a criticism, which he hadn't intended. And

243

neither had he intended to shame his father, but feared he'd done that, too.

'No. She doesn't … and I'm sorry for that. I'd have it any other way if I could, but you've always been her link back to your mother, not me. Maybe if I hadn't remarried …'

'No!' That his father would question this choice shocked Daniel. 'That was definitely the right thing to do. I still remember what that house was like before Carla.'

The spectre of his mother at the edge of every conversation. Back then he was a boy who lived with the sense that he was implicated in something big, something terrible, but never fully understood what or how. Carla had eased some of that.

'She saved us, Dad.'

His father released a quavering breath. 'I think so, too.'

They sat quietly for a time, Daniel with his legs stretched out, shifting the swing backwards and forward with his heels; his father preoccupied with the space between his feet.

'It's hard to believe three months ago she had a job.' Daniel said. 'Now we don't know where she is half the time.' He looked across to her small home, knew Billie wasn't there, that her front door was locked, that she'd left via the back gate hours ago.

'In her own head mostly,' his father said.

Daniel reckoned that was the worst possible place she could be.

'*Are* we abandoning Mum if we leave here?'

'That depends on what you believe. Where do *you* feel the memory of your mother the most?' his father pressed.

In the photographs on his desk. Through a manmade dinosaur. A length of string. But what of the imprint she'd left all the way to his bones? An imprint his father had left, too. Daniel's cells the product of theirs, washed up in his body with his creation, so that their legacy was also his. Neither tsunami nor time could wash that away, regardless of where he lived. He wished his grandmother recognised that.

31

BILLIE WATCHED THROUGH HER SMALL kitchen window. At least thirty people were milling around the backyard, waiting for the show to begin. Heavy-footed and impatient in the heat, she imagined the already compacted earth compressed further. Some people had brought their children with them. A family day out. Bored, two walked along the top edge of her raised herb bed, arms held out for balance. One slipped off, a foot landing in her garden, crushing a lavender bush. No one chided her.

The auctioneer stood in the shade of the back patio. Middle-aged and pithily dressed in a charcoal suit with a matching tie and a white shirt, he spoke quickly, loudly. A voice box designed for vocal calisthenics, equipped to elicit the best offer. He looked hot and uncomfortable in his suit, neck and face red above his buttoned-up collar, blood vessels at his temples engorged. Billie wouldn't care if they ruptured.

Carla and Angus stood together away from the crowd, along with Fran. They kept their faces neutral, not wanting to give anything away about expectations, Billie supposed, especially should they be exceeded. So much rode on them getting a good price. The appreciation of the property – not the appreciation felt in the heart, only the wallet – about to provide them, *Carla*, with a home and address she could boast about. But what had she brought to the value of the place, except the love for a man?

Some of the faces were familiar. People Billie had seen inspecting the property. The man who said everyone had a price was swatting at flies with his bidding paddle.

When the auctioneer started to call numbers in fifty-thousand-dollar lots, Carla leant in, looked to have started the race of her life.

The inevitability of this moment had leached the anger from Billie. An ache filled the space. It grew from imagining men and their machines with mechanical arms. The block razed of the familiar – houses, workshop, shrubs, trees, paths. Everything gone. Reduced to a square of dirt. And that dug up, too, turned over, unanchored, made loose for progress.

To see the ground stripped and laid bare like that would be like witnessing the skin peeled from a body – peeled from *her* body – leaving only the bones. Bones that could belong to anybody or anything. Except Billie knew those bones. Knew their bone memories. She felt the weight and angle of them, the way they'd always held her strong. That was the ache she felt now: a bone ache, like her marrow had been emptied. While outside, people were imagining a new skin for this piece of earth. No aching links for them. Only grand dreams. A quarter-acre of potential and profit.

She couldn't let it happen. Had to put a stop to it. Now! Before it was too late.

She thrust her front door open so forcefully she heard the screws on the hinges give. 'Stop! You can't do this. You have no right!' She stood with her hands on the veranda rail, like a minister at his pulpit.

The auctioneer barely hesitated in his race-like call. 'Do I have a quarter rise now?'

But he'd lost the attention of many in the crowd, who'd turned to look at Billie. All except the man who'd laughed as he'd crumbled the soil between his fingers. He merely glanced at her before turning back to the auctioneer, bidding paddle raised.

'At my right here! Bidder number twelve! Thank you, sir.'

Now that she had their attention, how to explain what it was she felt? How to make them understand that it wasn't her – Billie – who'd staked a claim on the land, but the land that had staked a claim on her. That it was the site of her most memorable moments with her daughter. Held traces of her still, like scripture. How it allowed Billie a route back to better times.

'This ground hurts,' she said. 'Buy it and you buy its pain.'

Some people looked to their feet. Not, Billie hoped, because they were embarrassed for her, but because they were wondering what might be under them, what force greater than themselves. Some people looked up again, shrugged at the person beside them, pulled a strange face that said, *Nup, can't feel a thing.*

The auctioneer forged on. 'A wonderful opportunity. Come with me now, folks. And up twenty to bidder eight! Thank you, sir!'

Carla, head in hands, looked like someone whose party had been spoilt. Angus glanced behind him, searching for Daniel in the crowd. Finding him, he indicated to Billie with a nod. Coward, Billie thought of her son-in-law, as her grandson pushed through the crowd towards her. It made her more determined.

'There's a story of loss here and whether you want it or not, what you do to this land will make you a part of it.'

Should she also tell them that the story was unfinished, that it would disturb their sleep, fill their dreams with an unfamiliar but strangely understandable language of regret and sadness that was felt more than heard? That they'd wake feeling as though they'd been visited by someone or something just beyond their reach but which they ached to touch?

But as she looked out across those uncurious faces, she knew she didn't stand a chance. There would be no light-bulb moment of understanding, not while they stood on the raw material of their ambitions. This spectacle she was creating was nothing more than a momentary obstacle to other people's progress.

The auctioneer doggedly continued, added to the already staggering amount in ten-thousand-dollar lots.

Daniel came up the steps. A journey he'd made so many times that Billie knew his feet had worn down the timber treads almost as much as her own. And soon those steps would be gone, all trace of those journeys erased.

'I can't let them take it away, Daniel.'

'Everything'll be okay, Nan. It'll be tough for a while, but it'll all work out. You'll see.' Daniel put his arm lightly round her shoulders, guided her back inside.

The strength and will to fight him or anyone else had left her. Her bones were sucked dry. There was nothing left to give. If Daniel were to pick her up now, it would be like carrying a bird.

And soon it was done.

'Sold!'

People had started to leave. Some glanced towards her home. Sought one final glimpse of the mad woman who'd called for something from them, but still unsure of what.

'How long?' she asked Daniel.

'A month.'

One month to archive almost twenty years of memories, just as she'd archived the details of the event that had made this ground so important to her. But how to box up what this land *meant* to her? It was a place she knew intimately, loved. Just thirty days, and her connection to all of this would be taken from her. How to cope with the added weight of such a loss while still unable to bear the weight of the other?

Daniel turned her away from the window and encircled her with his long arms. 'I don't want this place to own us anymore, Nan.'

'Places just *do*, Daniel. We don't have a say in it.'

She felt his frustration wrapped up in his tight muscles. But then he released her and she felt something infinitely worse: alone.

'It's hard to grow here,' he said.

This shocked Billie. Their roots were deep here, abiding. Surely that sustained him, allowed him to grow? 'You're just looking for an excuse to forget her.'

'Nan, I'm flat out remembering her,' he said quietly.

The pain of this admission was written on his face. It made him look older.

'I only remember what you've taught me. I've spent my whole life since she died trying to learn my own words for who she was. But the only ones I've got are yours. That's what I was trying to tell you the other day. This place ... the tree ... they aren't Mum. *We* are. You and me. And the *everywhere* you talk about? It's *our* everywhere. It's about knowing where ... who ... you come from. I can't know Mum, but she came from you. You're my everywhere and you go with me in here,' he tapped his chest. 'And you're with me wherever I go, not just this place.' He spread his arms wide. She presumed to encompass the room, the house, the block of land, maybe even the world.

So it had come to this: *I love you, but ...*

Billie's legs, normally robust and sure, still felt birdlike, hollowed out. Too thin, too fragile for her body, let alone this conversation. She reached for a chair. Daniel helped her into it then pulled another out for himself and sat facing her across the kitchen table, took her hands in his.

I love you, but ...

Was Daniel saying she was no better than the people bidding on this land today? That she had the same desperate need of possessing, of saying *mine*? Had she been anointing herself with the wrong ideology all these years? That she could and should care for it but it was never hers to own? But if that were the case, then why did the thought of letting this piece of ground go hurt so much?

I love you, but…

She'd had flashes today of the ground opening up and swallowing every single person standing on it. Wanted to hurt them. Imagined them forming a dark, fossilised seam in the earth's strata: a geological record of human greed. And she'd broken a boy's arm for the tree. Felled him. Felt no remorse for doing so. Believed it was her right. Expected she'd probably do it again if called upon.

But what did these thoughts and acts make her? Cruel? Heartless? A criminal as the boy's father claimed?

No, she didn't believe so. She was victim and survivor. The one left behind. Her trauma rippled out from the origins of that one event – that man, that knife, his intent – just as seismic waves rippled from deep within Earth, sometimes undetected but always exerting a force, realigning lives and making people do and say things they might not otherwise. Billie felt the tremor of her trauma most days. Sometimes so strongly that it nearly knocked her off her feet. At other times it was as subtle as a breath.

32

CARLA PUT HER MIND TO the question: What would she miss about this place?

She'd miss nothing of the house itself, only the memory of moments shared within its rooms. Being introduced to Daniel that first time. A shy, skinny eleven-year-old she'd immediately taken to. Not because he'd seemed broken, in need of a mother's love – he had that, from Billie, and in surplus. It was the unnatural ease with which he could be alone that she recognised and hoped to change. She'd spent the years since trying to build a bridge between the two of them, but also between him and the rest of the world. A bridge that felt solid and safe. One he could trust. Sometimes he'd meet her on it, at others not, leaving her and the world at a distance. And she'd learnt to accept that, respect it even.

Angus had told her that Daniel would say how much he liked her after she'd visited. Possibly all the encouragement Angus had needed: his damaged son's consent. What was it he'd liked though? Was it Carla the person, or the change she'd brought about in his father? The energy and presence of a mother-aged woman around all the time? Normal routines, conversations and stories that revolved around the everyday, and not those of sadness or the intangible? Maybe it was seeing for the first time that there could also be lightness in the world. Then a little sister he adored came along and she wondered if *family* became a word and a notion that he'd not previously been wholly aware of.

Her moments here with Billie were remembered less fondly. Initially, Carla had felt like a guest who'd outstayed her welcome. Tolerated, but an intruder nonetheless. The first time Angus introduced them, he'd seemed more anxious than when he'd introduced her to Daniel. She'd received a *Hello* with little warmth. At the time, she assumed Billie held a strong matriarchal presence in the home, was the one who'd stepped up. It was only later, once Carla got to know her better, that she realised then, as now, that Billie strived to keep not just the memory of her dead daughter alive in her grandson's mind, but also the physicality of her. Carla's presence was an obstruction to this ambition. A pollutant.

But again, along came Scout and Billie mellowed, perhaps in being reminded of the continuity of life, through real flesh and blood, and Carla finally felt, if not accepted, then at least tolerated in their home.

Home.

A recurring word in her thoughts. Where all these things had taken place, glowing like a lit window at the margins of her consciousness, reminding her of what this place meant to others. To Carla it had always been a place of transition. A place passed through on the way to establishing the real one. And maybe that was the difference between her and Billie: Billie's life was deeply rooted here, whereas Carla's existed on the surface only, easily packed up and moved on like a campsite. No foundations. No permanence. And no desire for either.

Angus disturbed Carla's thoughts. Came up behind her, reached his arms round her, and she felt it again.

Home.

He'd learnt the contours of her body in this house, these rooms. Traced them with fingers that she'd always imagined still held the memory of the contours of the one he'd lost but still loved. Sometimes she feared they'd even compared.

'Let's celebrate.' He eased her back against his chest, kissed the top of her head.

What were they celebrating though? A financial gain that exceeded anything they'd hoped for or imagined? The means now for a bigger, better house? Freedom from this one and its sad history?

Now that she'd finally been delivered a means of escape, Carla was no longer certain that she would in fact be free. She'd always thought things would be better with a fresh start. New rooms into which new memories could be built. Rooms that created their own shadow play and sounds. But what if she'd pushed them all into a pointless and hopeless direction in the pursuit of her own happiness? A state that was never likely to wholly materialise because the people she loved best *were* the history and wherever they went it would follow.

'Have I done the right thing?' The *I* in her question came as a shock. Was she solely responsible for this upheaval? The thought terrified her.

'What d'you mean?'

'Pushing to sell.'

'Bit late to think about that.'

Sold. Unconditionally. No backing out by buyer or vendor.

The finality of it suddenly hit her. Up till now it had been another task within many she'd struggled to keep up with. Got lost in the mania of it. A compliant servant to the demands of its master. But along the way she'd lost sight of the end point too, the goal.

Now they were to leave this tired old kitchen and its outlook. There would be no more trying to identify the wood Angus was working on by the smell of the sawdust coming from his workshop or off his clothes when he came in for a glass of water or lunch. These things would now occur elsewhere. He would come home in the evenings, traces of his day dusted off before he'd even got into his car. No Scout tipping to and fro on the swing that hung from the jacaranda or building her imaginary worlds in its tree house. No more Billie and Daniel sitting on Billie's front step, chatting about god only knew what, but creating an image of such tender intimacy that she'd often envied it.

She pictured the vacant land they'd inspected. Pictured the house they could build on it; the smaller one they'd build for Billie. The flat, fenced block, surrounded by other new and lovely homes, that represented the clean slate she'd always wanted. But would this new home she hoped to create be enough? Was it the history carried here that gave this one its character, blemished and scarred as it was but all the more real because of it? Would the new place just be concrete and bricks, plaster sheeting and paint, with nothing of them beyond their material possessions furnishing its rooms?

No, she wouldn't let that happen. She'd make sure they built a new history there, a happy one. The rental they were all to share was as good a place as any to start. There they could begin again, learn to live as a proper family, Carla and Billie no longer like forced acquaintances, endeavour to ameliorate some of the ill-feeling between them. Maybe she'd ask Billie about the daughter she'd lost – she'd never really done that – try to better understand who she was. Not eulogise her – that she wouldn't do – but let her in, just a little.

She turned in the circle of Angus's arms, pressed in firmly against him, feeling possessive still, and hoped she could find it in herself to leave space enough.

33

BILLIE HAD BEEN WALKING FOR hours. Was prepared to walk for several more. She hadn't set out with a destination in mind. Had given her feet free rein, let them decide whether to go left or right. They'd taken her deep into D'Aguilar National Park.

Home – for the brief remaining time that it would be – was many kilometres away now. Enoggera Reservoir was well behind her, too. She'd sat on the bank there for a while, watched a white crane wade knee-deep along the water's edge. When it eventually took flight its reflection across the still water created an infinity sign as its arched wings skimmed the glassy surface. It was a beautiful symmetry of the real touching the illusory. Which was how Billie felt now: half real, half not. Part of her already gone, the other part not bothered if it followed.

Now, she moved through unspoilt bushland. As unspoilt as her limited knowledge allowed her to believe it to be anyway. In truth it was probably decimated ground, used for so many different purposes over the past few centuries that little of its original vegetation remained. Still, she allowed herself to imagine that the various blue-green-grey hues of the eucalypts had always been there, growing without uniformity, not planted or shaped for efficiency or exploitation. That the canopy of these trees, a vast blanket that followed the contours of the land from crest to gully, was just as nature intended.

Ahead, a fallen tree at the side of the trail. A good spot to rest for a time. From there, Billie looked down into the gully. She knew there was a creek at its base. Dry, as all but the largest were. But she hoped that somewhere along its length there was still a billabong or two, a stagnant pocket of water waiting to release its concentrated cargo when the rains finally came.

She thought about how the kingfisher became Marco the last time she was out here, then how he too had disappeared. She couldn't forget how hopelessly lost the boy had looked. And still lost it seemed, the location of his body unknown, despite the killer being charged: a secret kept only by this man. Billie imagined him stubborn, smug in his refusal to say. A withholding that delivered a final chokehold, this time to torment the boy's parents. How ordinary he had seemed as the police led him to court in handcuffs. He could be someone she'd sold plants to, shared an escalator or bus seat with. He didn't look heinous or evil or mad. He looked weak, vapid, craven. More likely the one bullied than the bully. A man who'd apologise for bumping into you, say *Keep the change* or pick up something you'd dropped and smile when he handed it back. He didn't look like a man who could snatch a four-year-old boy and do god knows what to him.

The boy's family had returned to Italy now. A fresh wounding would have greeted them when they entered their home and saw the remnants of the last chaotic preparations before they departed for a holiday in Australia. Billie imagined the boy's socks turned inside-out on the sofa, his pyjamas strewn on an unmade bed and still carrying the scent of his body, his toothpaste spit dried and stuck so firmly to the side of the bathroom basin that they'd have to scratch it off with a fingernail. Every trace a reminder that they were once a family of four. And no matter how small or commonplace that trace might have seemed back then, it would be a torture now. And the return of their beloved son now dependent upon the generosity of a man's conscience. Billie couldn't bear it.

She slipped off her shoes and socks. Spread her toes, felt the air cool between each. Nuzzled them into the soil and imagined life shifting to make room for them, the microscopic realignment of whole communities. Their inhabitants just in this patch alone greater in number than all of the people on Earth. She tried to picture the vastness of this citizenry but her human mind struggled with the scale of it.

Pathetic, she thought, frustrated at her inadequacy. Reaching forward, she scooped soil over the tops of her feet, rooted them in like plants, her legs their spindly trunks. What a triumph, a gift, that the survival of all of humanity was dependent upon this stuff. This ancient, unwritten agreement that all things would come again through the soil, making all life possible. But what an undervalued relationship, too. If there were one door on Earth behind which the same thing was offered, it could never accommodate the thoroughfare of those who came and went through it, hoping to share in this great fortune. But here it was under the feet of all every day and few marvelled at the significance of it.

What would she feel at this new place where Carla and Angus proposed to plant her? Ground stripped of its past, just as her ground – Jess's ground – would soon be stripped, too.

Ants hurried across the earth around her feet, slater antennae tested the air from gaps in the rotting log where she sat and a Bess beetle, armoured like a mini tank, came out of one cavity and disappeared inside another. Billie imagined how these creatures lived without expectations or ambitions for a grand future. How they lived without pursuits beyond their immediate needs. She envied them their simplicity of purpose.

A rustle and shift in the scrub beside her caught Billie's

attention. The grass parted and a slim, brown-coloured snake, as long as she was tall, slithered onto the trail near her feet. Startled, it immediately sprang up in a series of s-shaped folds, its pale belly on show, mouth open like a roar, tensed and ready to strike. She knew it immediately for an eastern brown – a fast, nervy, aggressive snake, one of the most venomous on the planet.

They stared at one another. Billie admired the small glossy plates patterning its skin, solar panels, one and all. The strength of its spine to hold itself upright like it was. The courage of its stance, despite Billie being huge in comparison. Its forked, odour-sensing tongue, darting about collecting samples from the air, trying to identify what threat she posed.

Mostly though, she recognised that she felt no fear of it. Realised she had in fact been courting this moment for years. All her solo walks in the bush, never paying attention for dangers such as this. Never much more than a bottle of water and a small bag of trail mix in her daypack. No first-aid kit with snake bandages. No phone. And here she was now confronted with the perfect moment for this subconscious neglect to be played out. And she welcomed it.

She held her arm out to the tensed creature, invited its strike. Which it did. Once, twice, into the soft flesh of her inner forearm. Struck with such speed that she barely registered more than the pressure of it hitting her arm. Then a burning pain radiating from the puncture sites – a cluster of four, two more like scratches than holes, thinly seamed with blood. The snake, ambivalent now, eased itself flat to the ground and slithered away into the scrub on the other side of the trail.

Billie rose, left her shoes and socks where they were. Backpack, too. She had no need for any of that now. She walked slowly on, thinking about time. How she rejected the idea that the past moved linearly to the present with human achievements pegged along its length like washing on a line. She saw her life as a circle, the end brought back to its beginning. And hers would complete that circle now.

The landscape surrounding her receded and a different one manifested. Here, there was rain. It fell gently. She lifted her face to the cloudless sky, welcomed the moisture's cooling effect as it pattered softly against her skin. It collected in tiny droplets at the ends of her hair, bounced off the dust-covered tops of her feet. She heard the gentle splat and trickle of it on leaves and blades of grass. What a joy it was to catch the petrichor emanating from the earth as it accepted this gift. How right everything suddenly felt.

She wouldn't stop to savour it though. Not yet. She needed to make it down to the creek bed. There she could rest. Watch the water collect. First in small puddles, then maybe a torrent. She would allow her eyes to close then, allow the rain to rest on her eyelids, trace a path through the dust on her cheeks to her neck. Wash her clean.

At the creek she settled with her back against a rock. They came to her then, as she knew they would.

Jess's hair was as wild and curled as it ever was in the rain. She stood behind Marco, her hand resting on his shoulder. Billie held out her hands to them. They took one in each of theirs and tenderly led her home.

Epilogue

THE WOMAN SERVING BEHIND THE bar told Daniel which way to head, her Dorset accent rounding the vowels as they crossed her tongue.

'Turn right out of the pub and keep going up the lane. You'll come to a footpath sign on your left.'

He walked that footpath now, hands held above the nettles growing thick on either side. He was glad of his long trousers; at least he could push through without his legs being stung. Farmland stretched out in all directions, fenced by impenetrable blackthorn hedges. Living boundaries. Unlike anything he'd seen at home. At home trees were felled for this purpose, their trunks cut to length, split, placed upright in holes in the ground, wires strung. Manmade boundaries. The cost to the environment high.

Curious, long-faced ewes watched him from over the tops of these hedges as he passed, new-wool lambs at their withers. The air smelt sweet and savoury at the same time, a blend of bluebells, cow parsley and wild garlic. Just breathing the aromas made him salivate. This too was different from home. The creeks here flowed endlessly, a constant chortle of water moving across rippling weedy beds. And the paddocks were a shock of thick, often knee-deep grass. When Daniel left home four months ago the land was still hungry for rain, its livestock hungry for fodder, with no opportunity for either on the horizon.

His grandmother would like this trail, the lightness of it. She always favoured places where humans had left the least impression. Which is why he had known which trails to search along when she didn't come home that day. Why he was in the party that had found her.

He pictured her striding out that last time. In his mind her steps were sure and purposeful. Fearless, too. He refused to question why she kept walking after the snake bite. The coroner suggested she was disorientated due to the poison in her body, that it muddled her choices. He'd thought of Scout's friend's sick dog, its instinct to take itself off somewhere to die. Wondered if Billie had wanted to choose the right spot, sensing the inevitable. This powerful image of his grandmother writing her own ending settled him.

Carla had a second plaque made and fixed it to the tree, just below his mother's. *Returned* it said simply, with Billie's name and the date of her death beneath it. The rightness of this word made Daniel weep when he saw it.

Whenever he visited there, both plaques shone as brightly as his mother's always had when Billie was alive. He wasn't sure who did this. Carla? His father? Namita, his godmother? Or perhaps all of them took their turn at various times. A thought that pleased him.

Now, the path widened and sandstone walls gradually rose higher on either side. He had a sense of entering a tunnel and knew he'd come to the ancient sunken lane – the holloway – that the woman in the bar had suggested he find.

The further he walked, the deeper the path became, the walls reaching several metres high on both sides. It shifted his perspective so he wasn't sure if he was on the earth or entering it.

Underfoot the ground was soft with rotting leaves from the

large beech trees that gripped the thin topsoil along the cliff edge. Being spring, their new growth created a fluorescent emerald roof. Their roots, thick as his arm, thrust out of the sandstone face. Some had found pockets of soil and burrowed in, while others were exposed, blindly reaching, searching for anchor points. Creepers cascaded from up high and lush ferns unfurled from the banks to meet the speckled light.

At the deepest point of the sunken path, Daniel took off his heavy pack, rested it on the ground. The earth beneath his boots was ancient, laid down aeons before. Perhaps as far back as Palaeolithic times. Could he be walking on soil where this land's first man had walked? If he dug a little would he find flint spearheads? A hand axe, painstakingly knapped to perfectly fit its owner's palm? Like those he saw earlier in Beaminster Museum, which he'd stared at for long minutes through the glass-fronted cabinet wondering at the hands that had first held them. Things like this were turning up at home, too, as lakes and rivers dried up – grinding stones and stone tools, wood boomerangs, miraculously preserved.

History was cleaved open here, a deep gash in the earth that lay time bare, but not by drought. If he set his mind to it, he could imagine any number of stories of human occupation for tens, maybe even hundreds of thousands of years. But in truth such stories were well beyond the limits of his understanding; a time inconceivable to his modern mind. They were stories that now survived only in the fragments of bone and stone left behind by the owners of them. Left to be dug up – sometimes by chance, at others by intent – examined and interpreted as best they could and hopefully by people who respected them as a living heritage. This he'd learnt observing those prehistoric artefacts in the museum.

The thought of being one of those people sent a sudden and decisive thrill through his body. He pictured himself on his knees in the dirt, trowel and brush in hand, carefully, meticulously, unearthing a deep-time history, trying to bring it into the light.

Not just the detached gathering of information, but hearing through his hands the echoes of lives lived and lost. People who would have watched the same sun and moon rise and set as he did each day. He reckoned Billie would be pleased.

Daniel took his eye from the then to the now and could see that while the holloway was a majestic landform, it had been forged by the will of people over centuries, their livestock and carts, opening the way for water to erode the earth still further, sandstone soft enough to yield to all of those forces. It reminded him of how deeply people impressed themselves upon the earth. Periods of time measured by the laying down of grains of sand, only to be peeled back again by hoof, foot and wheel. Human history written determinedly into the land without lightness or cautious existence, only bold ambition. And no hope here of restoration.

This breach in the land would be the merchant of many stories. He felt them lodged in the silence between the opposing walls. He sensed not all of them were good. As well as offering free passage it had also been a place of ambush, just as the park near his old home had been a place of ambush for his mother. He saw that it was also home to new stories, those of *Poppy, Merlin, Luke, Kez*; names etched deeply into the soft sandstone walls. They were like plaques, but not of death: of existence.

He picked up a stick, reached his arm above his head and used it to scrape a shallow line in the cliff face. 'Pilgrim,' he said softly. Seven hundred years ago, he predicted. Journeying for penance or worship.

He moved the stick down to chest level, scratched another line.

'Farmer.' Five hundred years ago. To market, to market, to buy a fat pig. He laughed, thinking of Scout.

Hip level. 'Soldier.' Three hundred years ago. To war.

He knelt, scraped a line at the cliff's base, path level.

'Me.' Present day.

And his purpose? Certainly not for penance or prayer, nor to sell, buy or fight.

He stood back and looked at the four lines he'd made, these epochs of travel, and thought about how he – the most recent man – was standing now on the oldest deposited ground exposed so far. Maybe his purpose was to journey through the earth's strata like this, to witness the deep time Billie loved to speak of, and in doing so determine his own future.

Her flesh and bones were reduced to grit and ash now. It was a thought that didn't hurt him, because he imagined her having a good death. Unlike his mother's. One in which she chose the place, maybe even the time for all he knew. Had fulfilled what she had always told him happened: that they were all returned to the soil, that they became a part of something much bigger than themselves.

'The ground knows you,' Billie would say of the place where they used to live.

This ground didn't. They were only just becoming acquainted. He liked the newness of this relationship. Liked that they shared no history, other than the one they were making today.

His phone pinged with a text.

Two weeks to go! An emoji of a plane taking off and one of a heart in flames followed this. He laughed at that.

He texted back: *Can't wait!* Added an emoji of a plane landing, another of a fire extinguisher. *Funny Dan* was much better company than the old one. She'd taught him that.

Daniel put his phone back in his pocket, shouldered his pack and walked deeper into the holloway. Listened out for its stories. Continued with his ambition of adding to his own. This, and the one to begin in two weeks, might be temporary, a story in transition to another, but it was his. And one he wanted to own.

Acknowledgements

SPECIAL THANKS TO MY EVER-PATIENT publisher Aviva
Tuffield – your gentle guidance and faith in this story helped steer
it in directions that it is all the better for having taken. Gratitude
and thanks to my wonderful editor Jacqueline Blanchard – once
again you asked the best and right questions. Thanks to Yasmin
Smith for sharpening her editor's eye on this manuscript. Deep
gratitude to Madonna Duffy, Kate McCormack, Louise Cornegé,
Jean Smith and the entire team at UQP for your ongoing support
and care of your authors and their books, and for including mine.
And thanks to Sandy Cull for the stunning cover and Brisbane
artist Tiel Seivl-Keevers for allowing the use of her striking artwork
'Mt Coot-Tha Walk 2' in the design. I am also indebted to Jane
Gilmore for the important work she does in drawing attention
to and 'fixing' the prejudicial reporting and representation of
female victims of crime in the media. Her excellent book, *Fixed
It* (Penguin, 2019), guided some of Billie's thoughts and actions.

Thanks and gratitude to the Queensland Government who
generously supported the development of this novel with a grant
through Arts Queensland. Thanks to the very special Varuna,

The Writers' House for allowing me the space and uninterrupted time to work on this story. Thanks also to Arvon in the UK where I spent time at The Hurst learning new ways to think and write about human connections to place under the wise and generous guidance of Jay Griffiths and Paul Kingsnorth. I also thank the other writers with whom I shared time there – your generosity of spirit and words was inspiring. Thanks also to Brian Earl, Curator of Beaminster Museum, for sharing his time and knowledge when I visited there, and Will and Linda Bowditch for their warm hospitality and helpful conversation about Dorset's holloways.

A special shout-out to the rangers at the Queensland Department of Environment and Science for the work they do to protect our wild plants and animals and for answering my questions about those who seek to exploit them.

Thanks and gratitude to Ashley Hay, John Tague and the entire ace team at *Griffith Review* who published an early excerpt of this work. Your support helped me to believe this story had the bones it needed.

Special thanks to Brisbane's literary bright lights – Laura Elvery, Anita Heiss, Krissy Kneen, Cass Moriarty, Mirandi Riwoe. Also Fiona Stager and her tireless team at Avid Reader Bookshop – Brisbane (and indeed Australia) is all the better for your books, events and laughter.

To my dear friends in the UK – thank you for the beds, meals and wonderful company while I was there researching this novel. Those weeks were invaluable in helping me to work out what this story wasn't and finding the direction it needed to take, a task that would have been tougher without your nurturing care.

Kristina Olsson, you've walked and talked many of these words with me. Without the benefit of those hikes and conversations I'd be less fit and this story less formed. Thank you for your fine friendship, both on the bush trails and off them.

Thank you to my sister Kerri, whose love for books is as great as her generous spirit, and to Elise for giving me hope that the voices of women will continue to be heard long after I've gone, and for always being the first to answer my weird texts about popular culture.

Finally, with love and thanks to John, Aaron and Liam. You are my everywhere.

THE GEOGRAPHY OF FRIENDSHIP
Sally Piper

*We can't ever go back, but some journeys require walking
the same path again*

When three young women set off on a hike through the wilderness they are anticipating the adventure of a lifetime. Over the next five days, as they face up to the challenging terrain, it soon becomes clear they are not alone and the freedom they feel quickly turns to fear. Only when it is too late for them to turn back do they fully appreciate the danger they are in. As their friendship is tested, each girl makes an irrevocable choice; the legacy of which haunts them for years to come.

Now in their forties, Samantha, Lisa and Nicole are estranged, but decide to revisit their original hike in an attempt to salvage what they lost. As geography and history collide, they are forced to come to terms with the differences that have grown between them and the true value of friendship.

'There's a little bit of *Big Little Lies* about this deft and powerful study of female friendships under pressure.'—*Australian Women's Weekly*

'Piper does a fine job of exploring the nuances of her characters and their battles with themselves: strengths are weaknesses and life is perceived ambivalently as a consequence of this.'—*The Weekend Australian*

'This is a gripping, haunting, moving novel that made me want to call up my best friends from high school and talk about all the things that were too terrible to face back then.'—Emily Maguire

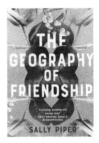

ISBN 9780 7022 5997 5

GRACE'S TABLE
Sally Piper

A wise and tender novel about food, friendship and marriage.

Grace has not had twelve people at her table for a long time. Hers isn't the kind of family who share regular Sunday meals. But it isn't every day you turn seventy.

As Grace prepares the feast, she reflects on her life, her marriage and her friendships. When the three generations come together, simmering tensions from the past threaten to boil over. The one thing that no one can talk about is the one thing that no one can forget.

Grace's Table is a moving and often funny novel about the power of memory and the family rituals that define us.

'A wonderful book reflecting on love, relationships, friendship … all of it centred around food.'—*The Big Book Club*

'The characters of elderly Grace and her girlfriends will draw readers to *Grace's Table* like bees to honey cake. These women don't heed the rules for ageing quietly, and they pull us into their past and present with their wisecracking talk, acerbic wit and quiet wisdom. But the younger characters in Grace's difficult family, street-smart, funny, nearly upstage them over a long lunch in which food is a character itself, filling this fine novel with the after-taste of roast garlicky lamb, sponge cake straight from a country fair, tomatoes fresh from the vine.'—Kristina Olsson

UQP

9780 7022 5004 0

Lightning Source UK Ltd.
Milton Keynes UK
UKHW020741190123
415610UK00014B/1553